# ALICE

## and the

# FLY

## JAMES RICE

**H**

**HODDER**

First published in Great Britain in 2015 by Hodder & Stoughton
An Hachette UK company

First published in paperback in 2015

1

A CIP catalogue record for this title is
available from the British Library

ISBN 978 1 444 79009 2

Typeset in Warnock Pro by Palimpsest Book Production Ltd, Falkirk, Stirlingshire
Printed and bound by Clays Ltd, St Ives plc

Hodder & Stoughton policy is to use papers that are natural, renewable
and recyclable products and made from wood grown in sustainable
forests. The logging and manufacturing processes are expected to
conform to the environmental regulations of the country of origin.

Hodder & Stoughton Ltd
Carmelite House
50 Victoria Embankment
London EC4Y 0DZ

www.hodder.co.uk

For my parents, who are not the parents in this book – you are amazing and you raised me well.

Also for Nat, who is my favourite human being.

I

The bus was late tonight. It was raining, that icy winter rain, the kind that stings. Even under the shelter on Green Avenue I got soaked because the wind kept lifting the rain onto me. By the time the bus arrived I was dripping, so numb I couldn't feel myself climbing on board.

It was the older driver again, the one with the moustache. He gave me that smile of his. A hint of a frown. An I-know-all-about-you nod. I dropped the fare into the bowl and he told me I'd be better off buying a weekly pass, cheaper that way. I just tore off my ticket, kept my head down.

The bus was full of the usual uniforms. Yellow visibility jackets, Waitrose name badges. A cleaner slept with her Marigolds on. No one who works in Skipdale actually lives here, they all get the bus back to the Pitt. I hurried up the aisle to my usual seat, a couple of rows from the back. For a few minutes we waited, listening to the click-clack of the indicator. I watched the wet blur of rain on the window – the reflection of the lights, flashing in the puddles on the pavement. Then the engine trembled back to life and the bus pulled off through Skipdale.

I got a little shivery today, between those first couple of stops. Thinking now about all those passengers on the bus, it makes me wonder how I do it every night. It's not people so much that bother me. It's **Them**. I heard once that a person is never more than three metres away from one of **Them** at any time, and since then I can't help feeling that the more people there are around, the more there's a chance that one of **Them**'ll be around too. I know that's stupid.

We soon reached the Prancing Horse. Even through the rain I could make out the small crowd huddled under the shelter. The doors hissed open and Man With Ear Hair stumbled through, shaking his umbrella, handing over his change. He took the disabled seat at the front and made full use of its legroom. Woman Who Sneezes was next, squeezing beside a Waitrose employee, her bulk spilling over into the aisle. A couple of old ladies showed their passes, riding back from their day out in the crime-free capital of England. 'It's such a nice town,' they told the driver. 'It's such a nice pub, it was such nice fish.' Their sagging faces were so expressionless I could have reached out and given them a wobble.

And then there was you, all red curls and smiles, stepping up to buy your ticket, and the warmth rose through me like helium to my brain.

You were wet today. Shivering. You smelt of disinfectant, stronger than any other work-smell on the bus. Is it legal for you to work there? The landlord probably doesn't realise how young you are. You look older. You're not the prettiest girl in school, conventionally speaking. There's a gap in your teeth and your hair's kind of a mess with your roots coming through, and you always wear those thick black sunglasses, which is kind of weird. You have an amazing smile, though. Once I walked right past you and you smiled, right at me, as if we knew each other. It was only a slight smile, your cheeks bunching at the corners just the right amount, but it made me want to reach out and stroke them, brush them with the backs of my knuckles, like Nan used to with mine. I know that's sad but it's true.

You took your seat, on the front row. Working after school must tire you out because you always drift off as soon as you sit, sunglasses clinking the window with each back-and-forth roll of your head. We pulled off through the square, past Hampton's Butcher's. I couldn't help thinking of your dad and the others, shivering with all that slippery meat while I was on the bus with you.

Then we turned onto the dual carriageway and sped out to the Pitt.

I wonder what it's like, living in the Pitt. Do you tell anyone? I can't think of a single kid who'd admit to living in the Pitt.

It's odd you have Skipdale friends, very few Pitt kids get into Skipdale High and even then they tend to stick to their own. Their families are always trying to set up in Skipdale but it does its best to keep them out. We have a Pitt neighbour: Artie Sampson. I've lost count of the number of times Mum's peered out of the dining-room window and complained about him. She tells Sarah and me to keep away. 'He's trying to climb too high in the property market. He'll fall and he'll break his neck.'

There's a physical descent into the Pitt, ear-popping and stomach-churning at the speeds the bus reaches, which might be why you choose to sleep through it. My father calls it the 'Social De-cline'. I remember when I was little I'd play a game along the Social De-cline where I'd try and count how many houses were boarded up, how many were burnt out. Sometimes I'd find a house that was boarded up and burnt out. It was hard because Mum always drove the Social De-cline so fast, even faster than the bus does. It was as if the very air could rust the BMW.

Of course, you slept right through. Every pothole, every bend, every sudden break at traffic lights that threw us from our seats. The bus jerked and rattled so much it felt as if it might come apart, but you just slumped there, face pressed to the window. We stopped by the retail park and Old Man BO got on and sat right beside you but even then you didn't wake up, didn't even squirm from the stink of him. You stayed slumped, lolling like a rag doll, completely at the mercy of the rhythm of the bus. I watched you in the mirror for as long as I could, only looking away when the driver caught my eye.

We turned at the lights, past Ahmed's Boutique. As always you woke the moment we passed the church, Nan's church, just in time to miss the large black letters spanned over its sign:

## LIFE: THE TIME GOD GIVES YOU
## TO DECIDE HOW TO SPEND ETERNITY

You rang the bell. The bus pulled up at the council houses behind the Rat and Dog. You stood and thanked the driver, hurried down the steps with your coat over your head. I wiped the mist from the window and watched you blur into the rain. I felt that pull in my stomach, like someone clutching my guts. I wished you had an umbrella.

The trip back was even harder. I got shivery again, goose-pimpled. There were a lot of gangs out tonight, mounting bikes on street corners, cigarettes curling smoke from under their hoods. I nearly fell out of my seat when one of them threw a bottle up at the window. I wasn't too bothered about people any more, though – all I could think about was **Them**. I lifted my feet up onto the seat. I knew they were everywhere I wasn't looking. I had to keep turning my head, brushing any tickles of web on my neck, checking the ceiling and floor. They're sneaky.

We ascended the Social In-cline. The houses grew and separated. Potted plants congregated in front gardens. The rain eased. Eventually we came back through the square and the bus hissed to a stop at Green Avenue. As I stepped down the driver gave me that smile again. The smile he always gives me when I get off at Green Avenue. The smile that knows it's the same stop I got on at just half an hour ago.

Miss Hayes has a new theory. She thinks my condition's caused by some traumatic incident from my past I keep deep-rooted in my mind. As soon as I come clean I'll flood out all these tears and it'll all be OK and I won't be scared of **Them** any more. I'll be able to do P.E. and won't have any more episodes. Maybe I'll even talk – and talk properly, with proper 'S's. The truth is I can't think of any single traumatic childhood incident to tell her about. I mean, there are plenty of bad memories – Herb's death, or the time I bit the hole in my tongue, or Finners Island, out on the boat with Sarah – but none of these caused the phobia. I've always had it. It's **Them**. I'm just scared of **Them**. It's that simple.

I thought I was in trouble the first time Miss Hayes told me to stay after class. She'd asked a question about *An Inspector Calls* and the representation of the lower classes and nobody had answered and so she'd asked me because she'd known I knew the answer because I'd just written an essay all about *An Inspector Calls* and the representation of the lower classes and I'd wanted to tell her the answer but the rest of the class had hung their heads over their shoulders and set their frowning eyes upon me so I'd had to just sit there with my head down, not saying anything.

Some of them started to giggle, which is a thing they like to do when I'm expected to speak and don't. Some of them whispered. Carly Meadows said the word 'psycho', which is a word they like to use. Then the bell rang and everyone grabbed their things and ran for the door and Miss Hayes asked me to stay behind and I just sat there, waiting for a telling-off.

Miss Hayes perched on the edge of my desk (which worried me at the time, it still being wobbly after Ian and Goose's wrestling). She crossed one leg over the other and then crossed one arm over the other and said she'd given me an A- for that *An Inspector Calls* essay. She said I was a natural at English. I wish I'd said something clever like, 'Well, I've lived in England all my life,' but I can never think of these things at the time so I just nodded. She said she'd spoken to the school nurse about me and about **Them** and about my condition and she wanted to know if I'd come with her to her office for a little chat. I didn't know what to say to that either. I just nodded again.

Since then I've been waiting behind every Tuesday for a little chat in Miss Hayes' office. We never chat, though. We tend to just sit in silence. I pick the dry skin from my hands while she twists that ring on her finger, like I'm an old-fashioned TV set and she's trying to turn up the volume knob. It doesn't bother me, silence. People talk too much. They make awkward talk every five minutes about school or my parents or how my sister's dancing's going. It's nice to sit in silence for an hour in the same room as Miss Hayes, just knowing we're both there experiencing that silence together. It gives me a bit of a warmth.

Miss Hayes doesn't think silence is very progressive. A couple of weeks ago she gave me this little leather book and said writing stuff down might help me express myself. I asked her what I should write. She said, 'This isn't an assignment, just write down your thoughts. Your feelings.'

Tonight she asked if I'd written down any of my thoughts or feelings and I said I'd written one thing, last week, but it wasn't much, only a few pages. I didn't know what to write so I ended up writing about a bus ride I took.

'It's OK to write about a bus ride,' she said. 'You can write about anything.'

I told her it's hard writing to myself because I already know everything I have to say. I said that last time I pretended to be writing to someone else and that helped. She said that's OK too. I don't have to write to myself. Her diary's called Deirdre and she finds Deirdre very easy to write to. I asked her who Deirdre was and she just swallowed and said, 'Nobody.'

Well, Miss Hayes may write to nobody, but I think writing to nobody's pretty stupid. That's why I've decided to keep writing to you. I hope you don't mind, you just seem like a good way of getting the words on the page. I know you don't know me, but nobody knows me, and by knowing that you now kind of know me better than anyone.

My name's Greg, by the way.

We live in one of the avenue's corner houses with a total of ten rooms and every couple of months my father gives Mum his credit card and she goes to work on one. New style, new theme, new colour scheme. Sometimes she gets walls knocked down or fireplaces installed. Last summer she had little lights set into the dining-room wall like stars, but they looked too tacky so she had them ripped out and the foundations gave and I spent weeks with my head under my pillow while hairy Pitt people hammered and plastered and swore in loud voices.

At the minute Mum's re-envisioning the lounge. Everything's hospital-white, from the carpet to the curtains to the candle-sticks. There are piles of catalogues under the coffee table and Mum spends most of the day flipping through them, making phone calls. She's still waiting for the Italian leather couch. She's designed the room around it. It's the most expensive item of furniture she's ever encountered. My father said it costs more than the rest of the room combined, including the decorators' wages. He's had to take on three new clients to afford the initial deposit. The last time we saw my father was Sunday. Mum told me not to tell anyone this. I don't know who she thinks I'm going to tell.

Today's decorators were a father-and-son plastering firm, smoothing over the cracks in the lounge ceiling. (My sister's room is above the lounge. My sister dances.) By the time I was dressed and packed up for school they'd stopped for a coffee break. They were sitting on the dining-room window seat, the cafetière steaming between them. Both plasterers wore grey vests and khaki camouflage trousers. The father's belly was slipping out of the bottom of his vest. He had a lot of moles.

I sat at the top of the stairs and waited for them to get back to work. I wanted to slip down for breakfast unnoticed. Decorators make me nervous. They scratch their armpits and sniff their fingers. They speak loudly as if they don't care who hears them. Sometimes they say stuff to me or try and joke with me and I don't know how to reply. I always feel bad for not giving them a hand.

They make Mum nervous too. If she saw one shopping in Waitrose she'd tut and give them her sour-face but when they're in her home she's all smiles and 'Can I get you some more coffee?' This morning she came to collect their empty coffee mugs and noticed the dustsheets they'd laid down were old bed sheets and joked, 'Are you going to have to wash these before bedtime tonight?' grinning like she was advertising toothpaste. They were pretty good-natured about it. They laughed along. Then they watched Mum's legs as she stepped back out into the hall. The son spotted me at the top of the stairs and winked. I left without eating breakfast.

The rest of the morning was pretty normal. I guess I don't lead a very crazy life. If Ian Connor was writing this then he'd have all kinds of stories to tell you but all I did this morning was go to my lessons. First lesson was P.E. This month they're doing football. I sat in the sports hall and watched them out on the field, breathing white and shivering. They still laughed, though. To be honest I'd be fine out on the field, but I don't think Mr McKenzie wants me to join in with P.E. any more. Not after last time. He doesn't even ask me for a note now, he just says, 'You sitting out again, Greg, yeah?' at the start of each class and I just nod and head for the sports hall.

Second lesson was Chemistry. We sterilised the desks. We covered them in alcohol and set them alight, watched a blue tide of flames spread over the wood. I guess that's exciting enough to write down.

Third lesson was History with Mr Finch. We did nothing in History exciting enough to write down.

Right now I'm sitting in the library. I come here every lunchtime. It's quiet. I can hear my pen scratching the paper. There's just the murmur of the crowds out on the playground, the tick of the clock, the steady waves of Miss Eleanor's ultra-loud breathing: in and out, in and out. Sometimes she stops on an in and I hold my own breath waiting for the out. It always comes, eventually.

I saw you a few minutes ago. You were sneaking across the field with Angela Hargrove. I stepped over to the window, as quietly as possible to avoid waking Miss Eleanor. You were wearing that coat again, the one with the red fur trim. You were wearing your sunglasses. You were laughing at some sort of impression Angela was doing, waving her hands about her head. When you laugh you always cover your teeth, try and hide the gap, which is stupid because the gap is the most unique and amazing part of your smile. That's the third day in a row you two have snuck out through the gap in the hedge. Only sixth-formers are allowed to leave the grounds during school-time. I guess you know that.

I haven't always hidden away in the library. I used to sit out at lunch, on the wall over by the Lipton Building. I didn't care that I was on my own because there was this family of magpies that nested just the other side of the fence and I liked to watch them, leaping out over the crowds, snatching things for their nest in the trees. Then one day a gang of Pitt kids noticed me there. One of them was your brother. (This was a couple of years back, when he was still in school.) They crowded round me and began to say things, the usual things, about my condition and my lisp and how weird I was and how pathetic it was that I was sitting out there on my own, etc. etc., but the magpies were out that day so I wasn't really paying attention, I was too busy watching them, too busy listening to that little cackle they have, that miniature machine-gun squawk. Then your brother hunched down to eye level and demanded I 'say something'. I didn't know what to say. I was straining over his shoulder to see the magpies, picking through the bin. It made me smile because it was as if they knew exactly what they were looking for. Then one of the other Pitt kids bent down alongside your brother and reminded me that your brother had asked me to say something and told me I'd better 'say something quick, or else', only one of the magpies had caught something small and wriggling in its beak and I was too busy trying to make out what it was. Next thing I knew the whole gang was screaming 'Say something!' right in my face and they were over-pronouncing their 'S's and a crowd had gathered including Carly Meadows and a couple of other Vultures from my year and some people in the crowd were calling me a psycho and chanting, 'Say "psycho", say "psycho",' because they knew 'psycho' was a word I couldn't say properly. It was at this point I realised I was scratching at my arm, which is something I do when I'm nervous. I lost sight of the magpies when one of the Pitt kids reached forward and poured a can of Tango over my head. Everyone stopped shouting then, started laughing instead, staring at me and laughing as Tango trickled down my neck, soaking into my collar. A few of them pointed, which was kind of stupid because everyone knew what they were laughing at. I breathed as slowly as I could, counting each drip from my fringe as it hit the pavement. After a minute they stopped laughing and just stared. It was then that I realised there were other drips hitting the pavement, red droplets of something thicker, something that splattered as it landed. The arm of my shirt was spotted red. Some of the Vultures said I was disgusting and a few made that wrinkle-face but most just stared. Then they left. I think that was the only time I ever saw your brother in uniform.

That afternoon I kept my blazer on. I had Maths and my hair went all hard and sticky from the Tango but nobody noticed.

## TRANSCRIPT

Extract of interview between Detective
Sergeant Terrence Mansell (TM) and Gregory
Hall's classmate, Ian Connor (IC).

TM: Thank you for agreeing to talk with me.

IC: S'all right.

TM: As you probably know, we're here to
discuss Greg.

IC: Um . . . well, yeah.

TM: How well do you know Greg?

IC: Well, he's in my class.

TM: You sit next to him.

IC: In a few lessons, yeah. English. A few
others.

TM: Would you consider him a friend?

[IC laughs.]

IC: God, no.

TM: So, what do you think of him?

IC: Same as everyone else.

TM: Which is?

IC: He's nuts.

TM: Can you elaborate?

IC: He's psycho nuts.

TM: What makes you say that?

[IC laughs nervously.]

IC: Erm . . . ?

TM: I mean aside from the events of the past few days. I mean, what gave Greg this reputation?

IC: It's just how he is.

TM: 'Is'?

IC: The way he walks. The way he . . . watches. And there's the scratching. The mumbling. He's on meds, too. Did you know that? We found them, me and Goose. 'Antipsychotic'.

TM: Right.

IC: And then there's the way he is with girls. He's always, like, looking at the girls in class. You know? Like, staring at them.

TM: You never look at girls?

IC: Not in that way. Not, like, creepy, like he does.

TM: Are you aware you feature in his journal?

IC: Me?

TM: You.

IC: What's he say about me?

TM: He alludes to your . . . involvement
. . . with certain girls from your year.

IC: Really?

TM: And girls from younger years.

IC: Younger?

TM: Angela Hargrove?

IC: I had nothing to do with that.

TM: With what?

IC: New Year's. I know she was saying stuff
when the police showed up. Stuff about Goose
and Darren. That had nothing to do with me.
I was passed out.

TM: This is the party at Wallaby Drive? The
Lamberts'?

IC: Goose's, yeah.

TM: Did you see Greg that night?

IC: Not that I remember.

TM: But he was at the party?

IC: He might have been. I didn't notice.

TM: You didn't notice?

IC: He's very unnoticeable. That's part of his

creepiness too. His psycho-nuttiness. And,
as I said, I was out of it that night.

TM: We're getting off topic here. I'm just
trying to get a feel for Greg. What he's
like as a person. You've sat next to him
for, what, three years? Isn't there anything
you can tell me?

IC: Only what I've told you already. He's a
creep.

TM: Nothing else?

IC: It's the way he looks at you. That's it,
it's the eyes. It's all in the eyes.

TM: The eyes?

IC: Exactly. Just look into those eyes.
Everything you need to know's right there.
In the eyes.

TM: That's all you've got to say?

IC: Sorry. I'm not trying to waste your time
or anything. It's just, I don't really know
the guy. I don't remember ever even having
a conversation with him.

TM: Well, who does know him?

[Pause.]

IC: I don't know. He didn't have any friends,
as far as I know. I guess nobody knows him.

That's the thing. You could interview the
whole class and you wouldn't find a single
person that knows him. Not really. I guess
that's what makes him creepy. I guess that's
what makes him psycho, really. How alone he
is.

TM: Right.

IC: That and the eyes.

TM: Thanks.

Saturdays I work at Hampton's in the square. Your dad might have mentioned the back-lad? Probably not. I work alone in the kitchen, tucked away between the industrial freezers. There's a metal basin, a worktop for dishes to dry on and a single shelf with a kettle and tea bags and soft crumbly biscuits. The air in the kitchen is even colder than inside the freezers. I try not to breathe through my mouth because the cold hurts the hole in my tongue.

Your dad works with Phil on the fresh-meat block. They're obscured from the front of the shop by the chicken oven. I guess the customers don't like to see all that hacking and tearing. Their block is only metres from the kitchen so I always hear them joking around. Phil gives your dad a bit of stick for his ponytail but Phil's only twenty-two and he's going bald, so he's not really qualified to be making hair jokes. Sometimes your dad snatches Phil's hat and holds it in the air and Phil jumps up trying to reach it, one hand over his bald spot. Your dad just laughs. He's got one of the biggest laughs I've ever heard.

He laughs 'Heh' instead of 'Ha'. 'Heh heh heh'. All day long.

Sometimes your dad talks about you in work. He tells Phil about how you're into art, how one day you're going to university. He never talks about your brother. This morning Phil was discussing baby names and your dad said he named you the morning you were born. He'd overdosed on Dutch courage and spent the night watching a VHS of *Alice in Wonderland*, over and over, rewinding and playing it till the birds starting singing and the telephone started ringing and he found out you existed. I wonder if you know that story? Whenever they're talking about you I tend to turn off the kitchen tap and just stare at the bubbles in the water.

There's an older butcher called Charlie who works on the fresh-meat side, slicing ham and cooked chicken. His face is shrivelled to a point and he looks a lot like a chicken himself, especially with those little round glasses. (I know chickens don't wear glasses, but if you saw him you'd know what I mean.) He's always telling Phil and your dad to grow up and calling your dad a hippy. They call him the Miserable Old Cunt. Sometimes they shout back to me, 'The Miserable Old Cunt needs a fresh bucket,' and I have to fill a bucket with soap and steaming water and bring it out to him. I feel guilty responding when they call him the Miserable Old Cunt, it's like I'm agreeing with them. He never even looks at me when I deliver his bucket. I guess he is a bit miserable.

There's also this pack of four Vultures that serve out front in the shop. They're in your year, which means it's technically illegal for them to work, but it's money in an envelope so I guess it doesn't matter. Most of them take dance class with my sister and have the same bleached hair, long nails and powdery orange skin. They smell like cherries.

And then there's me. The back-lad. I just keep my head down, concentrate on my work. In the morning I have to wash the walls and the floor and the insides of the fridges. It's blood, mainly. Fresh blood wipes off easily but as soon as the cold gets to it it gets all hard and sticky and needs bleach and boiled water. They have all kinds of meat hanging in the fridge and I have to shift it around to clean. Sometimes there are cow legs or whole ribcages hanging there. Sometimes there are pig heads, with hardened snouts and icicles for eyelashes.

Twice a day I have to empty the fat from the chicken oven. It gathers in this large metal tray underneath. It's very heavy and hard to manoeuvre. I have to slide it all the way out, till I can feel the heat of the fat on my face. I have to unscrew the stopper and let the molten fat dribble into a bucket, then empty the bucket into a bin out the back. Molten fat looks and smells like thick pee. The Vultures hate it. Their noses wrinkle in disgust. They don't have a problem with meat and blood, just fat.

I make tea and coffee too, when they ask me. I have to make

drinks for everyone and it's awkward because the Vultures have never told me their names so I have to just wait for them to stop serving and notice me before I can ask what they want to drink. Sometimes they just ignore me, or do that wrinkle-face and giggle to each other.

I spend the rest of the day in my kitchen, watching the tap. I can watch that tap for hours, the water gurgling, steam in my face, warmer and warmer as the surface rises. I used to love baths when I was little. My sister and I had to share. We had this toy boat she was obsessed with. We've got some film of it somewhere, us both in the bath, playing with that boat. My sister never wanted the bath to end, she'd just refuse to get out. Maybe that's what dried out her skin so much. That was before Finners Island, before I moved to Nan's. I think about the old days when I'm watching the tap. I think about all kinds of stuff. The kitchen gets all foggy with steam.

It's not too bad, really, being the back-lad. I keep to myself. I have my own kitchen and nobody bothers me. I've heard them talk about me a couple of times but nowhere near as much as they do in school. The only thing that bothers me is when the Vultures come out the back for their buckets. They need buckets to clean the counters and the only tap's in my kitchen and the kitchen's only really big enough for me, which means they have to stand right next to me, so close I can feel their warmth. It takes a long time for those buckets to fill so usually I close my eyes. I try and think about all the pigs and chickens in the freezer, how cold they are. I try and just listen to the rushing water.

Sometimes I don't even realise they've gone until I can't smell cherries any more.

My bedroom window's the fire-escape window. It's the window that, in the event of a fire, my family would supposedly crawl out of onto the safety of the roof. A couple of years ago one of my favourite things in the world was to open this window as wide as I could on rainy winter nights and feel the chill of the rain battering the roof tiles just an arm's length from my face. Sometimes I used to reach my arm out into the night and let the rain patter and pool into the palm of my hand, numbing it out of all existence and, when it was so numb I could no longer even feel the rain, when with a reach and poke of my warm and living hand that white-dead hand felt like a hunk of frozen pork thawing in the fridge, and when the white-dead hand couldn't even feel the poking of the warm and living hand, I would pull both hands down under my bed sheets and curl my whole body around them and the white-dead hand would burn back to life. On those nights I'd always have the best dreams. I'd dream I hadn't even been born yet.

Then this one night I woke and saw it was raining and

decided to have a go at my arm-reaching-out thing but I must have been very tired because after what must have been only a minute of hand-numbing I fell asleep, my arm still stretched out on the window ledge. By the time I woke the rain had stopped. The sun hadn't quite risen and the garden was filtered with that golden light they film Corn Flakes adverts in. My hand was numb, resting there on the window ledge, and my first thought was to drag it into the warmth beneath the duvet. But, before I'd even had the chance to drag it into the warmth beneath the duvet, one of **Them** had dropped from the sky, right through the window, dropped right into the palm of my hand and just sat there, perfectly still, its legs spread wide in its landing.

Later, after my fitting and my vomiting and the seemingly impossible task of regaining my breathing, my father had said that they can sometimes ride their webs like paragliders, floating for miles on the wind. He saw it once in a documentary. He said they were fascinating creatures. Then he saw Mum and I staring up at him and he stopped saying things and went back to bed.

My window's been locked ever since. Mum's always searching for the key. She says it's dangerous. We could all burn to death. And anyway, my room smells like teenage boy. I'm used to it. I keep the key in with my secret things, in my *Casablanca* video-case. I used to keep my secret things in my *Brief Encounter* video-case but last week I finally watched *Casablanca* again and immediately swapped them because *Casablanca* became my new all-time favourite and therefore has to be my Secret Case. I designed the cases myself, during Retro Hollywood Season on Channel 4, when my video recorder pretty much constantly had its REC light showing. I wrote the name of each film on the sleeve of each case in my best cursive handwriting – drawing two thin lines in pencil, making sure the top of each letter touched the top line and the bottom touched the bottom line and waiting for the ink to dry and rubbing out the pencil and being left with titles both neat and straight. They look great on my shelf, lined up in their cases. At first I enjoyed the prospect of browsing the neat and straight titles and deciding which film to choose, but then the first film I chose was *Brief Encounter* and it instantly became my favourite film of all time. I couldn't stop watching it, over and over. Every time I came to choose a film I would start out wanting something new to watch and then think of Alec and Laura standing on that platform and Alec giving Laura's shoulder a squeeze and that shoulder-squeeze being the only way he could ever tell her that she's his one true love, his run-away-together kind of love, and that he's sorry that they'll never be together and how getting on that train is the saddest thing he'll ever have to do but he has to do it anyway, and it gave me a kind of inflation in my chest, a kind of beautiful indigestion, and I ended up choosing *Brief Encounter* every time.

I've since devised a brutal-but-fair rule for film-watching. I am absolutely (under no circumstances) allowed to watch the same film twice in a row. It's a hard rule to stick to but it's the only way I can stop myself watching the same ones over and over. I've also decided to store my videos in the wrong cases, so whatever film I choose is not the film I watch. This means every film is watched a relatively equal number of times. It also means (as the videos are no longer assigned to specific cases and as there is always a video in the VCR) that there is always an empty video-case. This video-case is my Secret Case. At the moment my Secret Case is *Casablanca*.

The other things I store in *Casablanca* are as follows:

- Nan and Herb's wedding photo.
- The ticket stub from a bird-watching walk on Finners Island. (It's years since we've been to Finners Island. I don't even know if they have bird-watching walks there any more.)
- The black button-eye of Mr Snow, my old white bear (which luckily came off before I buried him in the sand on Finners Island, losing him forever).
- The spare key to my father's study.
- Money.
1. The slick black feather of an American bald eagle.

Apart from my video shelf, my bed, my wardrobe, my TV stand and my brown and green striped draught-excluder snake 'Sammy' that lies over the crack at the bottom of my door, my room is virtually empty. Mum calls it minimalist. I just don't like clutter. I like to be able to see every possible inch of my bedroom at all times. I also like parcel tape and have used it extensively, taping the edge of my carpet to my skirting board and the foot of my bed to my carpet and taping all the cracks in all the walls and even taping over the air vent, leaving my room pretty much impenetrable.

Nan and I always used to tape the cracks back at Kirk Lane. We'd do it every winter because winter's when they come inside, trying to escape the cold. Nan called it the Great Influx. She'd say, 'We need to prepare for the Great Influx.' To be honest the term 'Great Influx' probably didn't help reassure me, but the parcel-taping did – it let me relax a little. She used to collect conkers, too, down at Crossgrove Park, scatter them all over the house. Apparently it was meant to scare **Them** away. I don't know, it's not something I've carried on since moving back because rummaging through leaves on the ground is the last thing I want to be doing if I'm hoping to avoid **Them**.

Mum won't let me parcel tape downstairs so I seal myself into my bedroom. It's the one place I don't have to worry about **Them** so much. I don't have to shake out my bed sheets or shine a torch down the back of my desk or check the insides of my slippers before use. I still do these things, but more out of routine than anything. It's just nice to lean my head against the wall without worrying about anything dropping down the back of my neck.

Sundays are hard. Saturdays are OK because I'm with your dad and occasionally he'll talk about you, but Sundays I have to just sit here with nothing to do all day but think. I think of our bus rides. I think of the times I've seen you in school, laughing out on the field with Angela Hargrove. I think back to under the bridge, back to the first time we met. Sometimes my thoughts stray to bad times, unwanted memories, and I try and think about nothing instead, try and just clear my head.

Today I watched *Gone with the Wind* (one of Nan's old favourites – a lucky selection from my random video system). Trust me, there's nothing like a four-hour-long epic romance to clear your head. Especially when there's Vivien Leigh and Clark Gable up on the screen with all their quick one-liners and chemistry, Clark clutching Viv in that kissing-embrace of his, all slicked-back hair and moustache. That's the thing I love about old movies – they had taste back then. They knew that all they needed was a kiss, an occasional shoulder-squeeze. That's the difference. In old movies, whenever the characters are kissing, it always cuts to black. A kiss is enough.

The rest is left to the imagination. In modern movies a kiss is never enough. They never cut to black. Nothing is left to the imagination. It's like that's the whole point of the film: the non-cut-to-black parts. It's disgusting.

I'd just fast-forwarded through the intermission when Sarah woke up. Sarah's time is spent sleeping or dancing. I can tell when she's awake by the dull thud of bass through the wall. She only leaves her bedroom for school and dance-rehearsals. (Sometimes she comes out at night, too, to do whatever it is that keeps her out past 04:00 and makes her fall asleep on the stairs with lipstick smeared down her chin.) Her room is like a house of mirrors in a fairground – if you peer through the crack in the door, fifteen other yous peer in from fifteen different crack-in-the-doors all over the walls and ceiling. A dancer needs to make sure they look good from every angle.

Sarah's been dancing to a new song this week. It goes:

> *Ooo you got me screamin' boy,*
> *Eat me like a cannibal.*
> *Butt in the air boy,*
> *Take me like an animal.*

It's the song she'll dance to at the Christmas Dance Fantastical. She's working on her routine. She's decided that, until that night, she's going to use all her available time to practise.

By 16:14 the dull thud of bass was giving me a headache. It was impossible to concentrate on *Gone with the Wind*. I went down to the dining room, huddled on the window seat. Mum was preparing dinner. A few years ago Mum knocked down most of the ground-floor walls. ('Open-plan.') It's pretty draughty but it means I can see right through to the kitchen from my place in the dining room.

Mum doesn't suit the kitchen. Her hair kept slipping from its bouffant and she spent several minutes tutting and fiddling in the crème brûlée mixture with a bread knife, trying to pick out what I assume was a chipped nail. Mum doesn't suit doing many things any more. Except drinking cocktails. She can stand and drink cocktails better than anyone I've ever met.

Mum's worried because the Hamptons are coming over in a couple of weeks. Ken and Ursula Hampton are Mum's best friends. Ursula Hampton uses words like 'Golly' and 'Jolly', which makes her hard to trust. Ken Hampton has a stake in several of Skipdale's most successful local businesses, including my father's clinic. He owns several sports cars and sometimes goes to parties with the mayor. It was Ken who gave me the back-lad job. He told Mum I needed to socialise more, that the work environment of the butcher's would be good for my confidence. It'd turn me into 'one of the lads'. Ken Hampton's about five foot tall. He used to be ginger, properly carrot-coloured, till one day his hair just turned black, overnight, which we're not allowed to mention.

The Hamptons come over from time to time for meals. My sister and I make ourselves scarce. Mum has to cook. My father has to socialise. I don't think they enjoy it, no matter how much they pretend to. Every meal tends to serve a purpose. This time it's to show the Hamptons the new white Italian leather couch. It also pretty much guarantees Mum a place at the Hamptons' New Year's bash, which is a hotbed of social activity. Today Mum tried out her latest menu: blackened fillet of salmon with chipotle squash purée and mango rice. For dessert Mum baked individual crèmes brûlées with cranberries and orange cream. Crème brûlée is Mum's signature dish. She has her own blowtorch.

My father spent most of the day in his study – a room he refused to let Mum de-wall in her open-planning. He has a heavy oak-effect door he keeps locked at all times. He doesn't know I have his spare key. My father is a surgeon and a part-owner of Burke's Clinic. (Who 'Burke' is, I've never found out. I think they just made the name up.) He helps lift people's confidence through surgical improvement. Burke's Clinic has pictures of all their employees on their website. (It is important for a business to have a public face.) In my father's photo he is standing in a white surgical room in blue cap and gown, a facemask hung round his neck. He is smiling, one hand holding a raised scalpel, the other giving a thumbs up. Beneath it says: 'Howard Hall: Breast Man'.

My father's latest secretary is called Joanna Hewitt. He calls her 'Jo'. Joanna's Burke's Clinic picture is cut from a group holiday photo. She has long blond hair and a low-cut top. She is both pouting and winking at the camera. There is a definite resemblance to a young Pamela Anderson, especially the breasts (which I'd guess to be at least a size DD), and also the nose, which is narrow with that distinctive bump at the end. I'd love one day for my father to employ a male secretary, flat-chested with natural black hair and a fat nose. I think it'd stop Mum getting so tense.

At 17:02 Mum shouted that dinner was served. I switched from the window seat to my seat at the table. Mum laid out four plates of blackened salmon. She was wearing a blue strapless dress with earrings: diamonds. Her nails were also blue, as were the heels she was trotting around the table in. She laid out napkins beside each plate before taking her seat, to the left of me. She smiled, not at me but occasionally glancing over to me. Sundays are becoming kind of a big deal because it's the only night my father eats with us.

After a few minutes my father emerged from his study. He took his seat beside me, opposite Mum. My father is an extremely handsome man, especially for someone in his fifties. He's well groomed. He still has all of his hair, which he gels daily. When I was little I remember it being longer and blacker and always slicked back, and over the past couple of years his hair has not so much greyed, as silvered. At one of their dinner parties, whilst complimenting his work on Ursula's implants, Ken Hampton described my father as 'the George Clooney of breast augmentation.'

Tonight he was holding a collection of photographs of inframammary infections, which he set out on the table to browse through whilst he ate. He was also nursing a glass of either whiskey or Scotch (I've never worked out the difference). He smelt of cigarettes, which is what he usually smells of nowadays, since he promised Mum he'd quit and so has to kneel on his office chair, smoking out of the study window. As soon as he'd sat down my father started on his salmon, separating the blackened and non-blackened parts with his fork, scooping the least burnt bits to his mouth. Mum frowned. She asked if maybe we could have some manners for once and wait until everyone's seated before stuffing our faces? My father sighed and let his fork fall to the table. It landed with a sort of semi-silenced clatter, speckling the tablecloth with salmon crumbs. My father didn't seem to notice, he was still looking at his photos. Mum's eyes stayed fixed on the fork for a good thirty seconds before she turned to shout for Sarah again.

Then Mum turned to me, as if she'd just remembered something of great importance. She asked if I'd taken my pill today.

I nodded. She always asks at dinner whether I've taken my pill and I always nod because I take it first thing in the morning. I used to take it at school on my lunch break but then Goose found them in my bag and showed them to Ian and he stood up and read the label out in front of everyone and so now I keep them at home. They're powdery, horrible-tasting pills and I have to let them dissolve on my tongue, so I take one just before I brush my teeth. I don't know why Mum feels the need to keep asking me about them at dinner. I think maybe she's just making conversation.

After a few minutes my sister came galloping down the stairs. She was wearing her dance leotard, earphones tap-tapping away. She took her seat opposite me, between Mum and my father. She smelt like dancing.

Mum gave a single nod and we began. The salmon tasted charred. I tried my best to eat it but the blackened parts were hard and reminded me of burnt toast. Sarah picked at her rice. She nodded a beat as she ate. Sarah is a slave to the rhythm.

My father continued one-handed. Mum always sets him a knife out just in case but I've only ever seen him use it once, on a particularly well-done piece of steak, and he sighed and muttered the whole time as if he wasn't sure how to use the thing. This uncertainty with knives is odd, considering his profession. It's possible my father's not-using-a-knife is to distance the concept of food from that of surgery. Or, more likely, my father's such a busy person he can only dedicate one of his hands to the task of eating. Mum kept smiling, watching him sip from his tumbler, watching him turn a page, watching him scoop and swallow his salmon.

Mum was the first to speak. She asked my father what he thought. He said, 'About what?' and she said this was her Hamptons meal and my father nodded and said, 'Very good.' He lifted a photograph from the bottom of the pile. It showed a woman with two different-sized breasts, one red and bulbous, far beyond the level of regular post-op swelling. He put his fork down and reached into his top pocket to retrieve his glasses.

Mum turned to Sarah. 'What do you think?'

'What?' she shouted.

'Do – you – like – it?'

She pulled out one of the buds of her earphones.

'What?'

'Never mind.'

I waited for Mum to ask me. I had all these answers prepared in my head about how delicious it was. About how flavoursome the blackened parts were. About how it was definitely not weird to mix mango with rice. But Mum didn't ask me. She just smiled at her salmon.

She said, 'I bet Ursula Hampton doesn't even know what a chipotle is.'

And I knew then, that this was not the end. That this was one of her long-term projects. That every night until the Hamptons' meal Mum will cook blackened fillet of salmon with chipotle squash purée and mango rice and will want to know if the salmon tastes any more perfect and, even if she asks me, I won't know what to say, because to me it will taste exactly the same. My favourite meal is Waitrose Maple Triple Nut Muesli (with the clusters). My favourite drink is the sweet milk that's left at the end, the odd raisin floating in it. I eat breakfast alone so I can drink it straight from the bowl.

My sister swallowed a couple of forkfuls of salmon before excusing herself and bounding back upstairs. I ate as much as I could but I never have much of an appetite and it put me off altogether when she starting heaving in the bathroom. Sarah always forgets she shouldn't dance straight after eating.

My father frowned at one of his photographs. He turned it upside down. Then his BlackBerry began to hum-hum and he stood and said, 'Hey, Jo,' and Mum looked down at her plate again. Mum rarely challenges my father's work. Once or twice I've heard her comment on his long hours but he just sighs and gives her that glare over the top of his glasses and says, 'Credit cards have interest, Deb,' and Mum looks around at her house and furnishings and the vases of black glittering twigs and nods and carries on smiling.

I tried my best to show Mum I was enjoying the salmon. I

smiled and hummed a few yummy noises. I even waited around after I'd finished, waited for the crème brûlée. I'm not sure she noticed. She was too busy nibbling and staring at her plate. She said the rice needed more mango. I don't know if she was talking to me.

Not a single person in my set has a surname beginning D, E, F or G, so for a lot of lessons I sit next to Ian Connor. I was there the time he snorted four lines of pepper in Media Studies. I was there the time he chewed that massive golf ball of sugar-free gum, telling everyone that the sugar equivalent was a laxative and having to run home with his hand down the back of his trousers. I was even standing at the window the time he rode the cafeteria trolley down that slope by the Lipton Building and crashed into Mr Cullman's Ford Capri, littering the bonnet with chocolate éclairs. Although we've never actually spoken I still know Ian better than Goose or Sam Johnson or any of those skater kids that follow him around at lunch. I know that he draws bar codes on the back of all his exercise books and writes swear words as their ISBNs. I know that at the start of every lesson he biros over the lines of the smiley face on the palm of his hand, so hard that by now it's tattooed into the creases of his skin. I know that at least twice a day his mum texts to see if he's OK and that, although he takes his time reading the texts, he never responds.

Ian and I sit on the back row in English Lit. Goose sits on the table opposite. I don't really get why they call George Lambert 'Goose'. I used to think it was his laugh (quite nasal and quack-like) but once I heard Ian say it's because he looks like someone in the year above whose nickname is also Goose. Nicknames are funny things. There's this one kid in class, one of the Oxbridge kids that sit at the front: 'Eggy'. Apparently he farted once in assembly in year seven. That's it. Now he's 'Eggy' for the rest of his life. I'd like it if someone just called me 'Greg'. 'Psycho' is a hard nickname to live down.

Today Ian and Goose spent English Lit passing notes. Ian scribbles notes to Goose on scraps of paper, usually ripped from the book we're studying and chucks them across to his desk. Goose scribbles a few lines and throws them back. It's like very slow tennis. When most people read or write notes they tend to cover what they're reading or writing with their arm, but Ian doesn't bother. He writes about girls a lot. Today the notes were about Ian and Lucy Marlowe getting together at the Halloween party a few weeks back and Ian not remembering and Goose saying Lucy must have slipped something into his drink and taken advantage of him. They didn't use terms like 'getting together' or 'taken advantage of' though. I still remember Lucy Marlowe from year seven, sitting out on the steps of the Lipton Building with her glasses and her *Star Trek* lunchbox while the boys kicked their football at her. I wouldn't have believed it was the same girl if I hadn't stayed in her set through school. If I hadn't witnessed the slow transformation: the fake tan, the contact lenses, the pink fur-collared coat. If I hadn't been there the day she came to class with an explosion of dyed-blond extensions and heard Mr Cullman say, 'Well, Lucy, it's nice to see you've finally found yourself.'

Lucy's been absent since Thursday. Goose wrote that last week he and Sam Johnson snuck into the girls' changing rooms during hockey and painted 'Flat-Chested Slut' in Tipp-Ex on the back of her blazer. Apparently Lucy spent all last lesson without even realising the sniggers were about her (and it was History with Mr Finch so he wasn't likely to notice). She probably walked all the way home without realising. She probably sat down and relaxed and watched TV (maybe even the odd episode of *Star Trek* for old times' sake), completely oblivious, until her mum arrived home from the health spa and screamed at the flaky white letters dried into her daughter's back . . . hand to her mouth . . . face Tipp-Ex white . . .

The notes became a discussion of the possible reasons for Lucy's absence. Goose's theory was that when Ian had had intercourse with her he was so big he'd ruptured her ovaries and over the last nine days bits of her insides had been slipping out when she peed and this morning she woke up screaming in a bed of blood with the remainder of her womb smeared across the mattress. Ian giggled at this. I had to look away, had to scratch at my leg under the table. It makes me sick, that kind of talk.

Neither of them has yet considered the possibility that Lucy is pregnant. Teenage pregnancy statistics are high in the Pitt but I've never known a pregnant teenager in Skipdale. I wonder if it's because in Skipdale we don't have as much of that stuff going on, or because our parents have enough shame to march the kid straight down to the appropriate clinic and get it dealt with.

I didn't get a chance to read the last note Goose threw over but it must have been hilarious because Ian spent the rest of the lesson giggling with his head in his hands. Miss Hayes carried on reading. Miss Hayes once intercepted one of Ian and Goose's notes. It was one of Ian's girl stories and was full of swearing and graphic sexual imagery but Miss Hayes read it out to the whole class the same enthusiastic way she reads *An Inspector Calls*. I think she wanted to embarrass Ian but he laughed louder than anyone. He said, 'Don't worry, Miss, I'll give you a go too, if you want.' He got two weeks' detention for that. He still passes notes but Miss Hayes tends to ignore them.

After English was lunch. I went to the library again. I was going to spend the hour writing but then I saw you and

Angela sneaking out across the field. I'd spent all weekend without you and this time I just had to follow. I waited till you'd disappeared through the gap in the hedge before hurrying out through the fire door after you.

You crossed the carriageway to the estate behind the square. By the time I caught sight of you again you were stepping through the gate of what must have been Angela's back garden. It was hard to make out, through the trees, but I could just about see you, the two of you, laid out on the wooden skeletons of her parents' sun-loungers. You were giggling and passing a rolled-up cigarette, letting smoke crawl out amongst your white and steaming breath. I sat in the bus stop across the street, hood up, hugging my parka shut. I ate my tuna sandwich. I found that, if I tapped my feet together, I could keep them from going numb.

It's strange to think that a few months ago you weren't a part of my life. That I only knew you vaguely, as The Girl In The Shades or Miss Cool or (through Ian and Goose's notes) as a little coloured-in symbol the shape of a pair of sunglasses. I knew you in the same way I know the names of the TV shows or songs people talk about, without having seen/heard them. I must have seen you around school once or twice but I'd never really registered you. Not until under the bridge. Not until your smile.

It's hard to remember now what Goose and Ian used to

write about you in their note-tennis. They haven't written about you recently so I've not been able to properly pin down your social status. You're just one of those unpindownable people. If you were popular I'd know who you were, I would at some point have been pushed to the ground or had Tango poured over me or have been asked to 'say something' in front of you in some kind of attempt to impress. But if you were unpopular then I would have more than likely witnessed you as a victim of similar pushings-over/Tango-pourings. So I'm guessing you lie somewhere in Skipdale High's social middle class. Therefore it's pretty impressive you've landed a friendship with Angela Hargrove.

When Sarah first started at Skipdale her form teacher had asked the class what they wanted to be when they grew up and Angela Hargrove said she wanted to be 'Every man's wet dream'. My sister retold this story that night at the dinner table. Mum was so shocked she let a half-chewed forkful of cannelloni fall from her mouth onto the tablecloth. I think that's what my sister loves the most about Angela – her ability to hang-mouth adults. Sarah's never actually managed to make friends with her, instead becoming one of her crowd of backing dancers at school dance shows. (Angela Hargrove is the Dancing Queen. She moves like silk. My sister says Angela has her own fifteen-minute dance solo in the Christmas Dance Fantastical and my sister, whose own part is five minutes, at the back, along with three Vultures, says this with genuine, head-shaking admiration. Awe even.)

How have you managed to get in with Angela? I bet she doesn't know you live in the Pitt, does she? No way would she hang around with anyone from the Pitt. She pulls her disgusted wrinkle-face if she sees a Pitt kid the other side of the playground, never mind sharing a cigarette on adjacent sun-loungers. The two of you seemed pretty merry with each other at lunch. You couldn't stop laughing. In the end Angela laughed so much she slid off the front of her lounger, disappearing from view behind the tree stumps. Then you started your own giggle-fit, rocking too far on your lounger and tumbling right off the back. I had to climb up on the bench to see you. You didn't seem to be hurt, though. You were still laughing.

You remained on the ground, then, the two of you. You left your sun-loungers with their legs in the air and just lay there, mumbling and smoking and giggling. I decided to head back to school. I wanted to get back to the warmth of the library, but it was starting to rain by the time I reached the dual carriageway and I knew better than to linger in the rain – it was lingering in the rain that made me sick a few months back. So I climbed down to the canal path, took shelter under the bridge instead. Usually I do my best to avoid bridges, or archways, or anywhere else one of **Them** could suddenly drop down upon me, but the canal bridge is different, I like it under there. I feel safe. Sometimes, if I don't want to go home between school and our bus, I go there and wait for you to finish work.

Today was particularly cold and parts of the canal had frozen into these little white islands. There were half a dozen ducks perched on the bank, inspecting the water like it was some lifestyle choice they'd yet to decide on. I balled into my warm-position: legs tucked into chest, coat over knees, hood pulled tight. I wondered if the ducks were cold. They seemed perfectly happy standing there, aiming their beaks at the surface of the water.

I closed my eyes and thought of you. I imagined you and Angela, lying there on your sun-loungers. Pictured you, staring up into the sky, raindrops speckling the lenses of your sunglasses.

By the time I opened my eyes again I was late for form. All the ducks had snuck off and left me.

## DATE UNKNOWN

A couple of months ago I got sick. Like, really sick. Like, spend-three-days-rolled-up-in-my-duvet-like-a-frozen-sausage-roll sort of sick.

I got sick because back then I always waited in the library after school for the crowds to disappear before walking home and so by the time I was ready to leave the sky had gone black and the wind had picked up and I had trekked across the field and out through the gap in the hedge onto the dual carriageway to avoid your brother and the rest of that gang of Pitt kids who had nothing better to do than hang around the gate after school and throw stones at the orchestra who had stayed late to practise and I had walked down towards the square and I had put my bag on both shoulders because it was really heavy because at lunchtime I had gone down to Waitrose and bought three 4-packs of videotapes to record old movies that were showing that week as part of Channel 4's Retro Hollywood Season and I had had to carry them around all day and my shoulders were really aching and the skin where my neck joins my shoulders was really stinging from the pulling and scraping of my shoulder straps and I was cold because I couldn't hug my coat together to keep warm that day because I had to keep my thumbs under my shoulder straps to keep my bag hoisted on my back to stop one of the corners of one of the 4-packs of videotapes from nuzzling my spine and the wind had been hissing at me that day like Nan's cat Mr Saunders used to hiss when I would try and move him off my bed so Herb wouldn't catch him and literally kick him off the bed instead and the wind had been getting right under my shirt that had untucked and was flapping against my skin that was all tight and goose-pimpled and there had been a mist of ice-water in the wind and it had stuck my shirt to my skin and my hood had blown down so the mist of ice-water in the wind had got into my eyes too and made them water which I had been glad of in a way because at least the tears on my face were warm and I hadn't been able to cross the dual carriageway because I couldn't see properly and it's dangerous to cross a dual carriageway when you can't see properly so I had half stepped half slid down the embankment to the canal to take cover under the bridge so that I could reposition the videotapes in my bag so that I could release my thumbs and put my hood up and walk with my hands in my coat pockets and wrap my coat around myself and hopefully stop the icy mist of rain getting in and also cover my nipples which were sharp and straight like drawing pins but in the end I hadn't been able to fix my bag or my coat or my nipples because instead of finding peace in the-safety-and-solitude-of-under-the-bridge I had stumbled down to find you waiting in the-safety-and-solitude-of-under-the-bridge and I had had to just keep on walking with my head down and pretend that I was just passing through the-safety-and-solitude-of-under-the-bridge because your big eyes were there and they were unsunglassed and blue and aimed right at me and I'd had to try my best to not look at them whilst trying to work out who you were and what year you were in because you were wearing Skipdale uniform but I hadn't recognised you at the time without those thick dark glasses and I had kept walking and the wind hadn't hissed under the bridge like Mr Saunders because it had been sheltered and silent under the bridge and for some reason as I passed you I had lifted my head which had been a very strange thing for me to have done because when I'm walking past people I always just watch my shoes and count to ten and I'm still not entirely sure whether I did in fact lift my head or whether I might have just imagined lifting my head and imagined seeing that your hair was wet and imagined that the dye had streaked red lines down your face like blood and imagined that your big eyes had fixed on mine and imagined that smile that smile and I can't remember if I had smiled back or if I had even imagined smiling back if in fact your smile had just been imagined by my imagination because all I can remember is how much I had concentrated on walking because walking had seemed only possible if I concentrated very carefully on it and I had managed one step at a time to keep walking through the rest of the-safety-and-solitude-of-under-the-bridge until I had come out the other side onto the canal path again and that's where I had stopped and I hadn't been able to walk any more and I'd sat down in the icy mist of the rain and watched the ducks for a while and then watched the ducks for a while longer until I was very cold and very wet and sick.

And even if I didn't smile back at you at the time, imaginarily or realitarily, it didn't really matter, because even through my sickness and my shaking and my headaches and my chattering teeth I kept smiling for the next three days.

Miss Hayes has a new theory. She thinks I'm not reading enough. Today she brought in two handle-stretched Waitrose bags bulging with books. It was hard work heaving them to the bus stop and the bus was so packed with rush-hour commuters I ended up having no place to store them but on my seat, which meant I had nowhere to sit but on top of them, which is why I may have seemed taller today.

Miss Hayes thinks reading will help me interact with my peers. If I made more of an effort to fit in then maybe I could make some friends. If I had some friends maybe I could stop thinking about **Them** so much. I did have a friend once, back in St Peter's. His name was Andrew Wilt. I used to stay in the classroom at lunch and play chess with him. Everyone else was out playing football but he had to stay inside because he had leukaemia and his body was weak. He was a bastard. He used to jab me with a pencil and call me Freak Boy. I guess he had the right to be a bastard, what with the leukaemia, but he'd always sharpen the pencil before he jabbed me and once the tip broke off and stayed in my hand, a little grey freckle I have to this day. The teachers thought I was very noble to stay with Andrew at lunch but he said I was just a freak with no choice. He always went on about how bad I was at chess. Then, when no one was looking, he'd jab me. In year six Andrew Wilt finally died of leukaemia and from then on I sat alone at lunch and played chess on my own. I actually preferred it that way.

I didn't tell Miss Hayes any of this. She was sitting there smiling, just waiting for me to talk, but I didn't know where to begin. She asked if I'd written anything in my journal this week and I nodded. She grinned and leant forwards, so far I could see the white of her bra. She asked if it had worked, if I felt any different. I wanted to say yes, especially with Miss Hayes literally perched on the edge of her seat like that, but I couldn't think of any effect it had had on me (except for cramping my hand a little) and I didn't want to lie, so I just shook my head and watched Miss Hayes' smile disappear, watched that frown crawl back as she slouched into her seat again. She tapped her pencil against her lips.

She said these things take time. She said I need to be more honest in my writing. She said: 'Remember, nobody will read it.' I promise that I'm being as honest as possible. I'm writing as much as I can but it's hard when you don't know what to write. I never know if I'm writing the right thing.

That's when Miss Hayes went out for the books. She had to go to her car to get them and when she got back her hair had frizzed in the rain. Her blouse was stuck to her chest and I could see her bra without her even having to bend over. I tried not to stare. I could feel this pressure, building inside me. My head ached. I was scratching my arm. She put the pencil to her lips again. I tried to concentrate on the books, tried to read the titles, but I couldn't seem to focus.

Miss Hayes said I was very lucky to have someone lend me all these books. She said that when she was my age she was good at English too and if her English teacher had given her time and encouragement and a big pile of books like this she would have found her calling earlier on in life. She said books can save people. She said books can change the world. I can't really see how a book could change the world – nobody even reads them any more. Everyone in class talks about music and TV, not books.

Miss Hayes said it was Mr Cullman who introduced her to books. She said that Cullman may teach Geography but his real passion is literature. He has a library in his house. She said she's only marrying him for his library and winked. By the time I realised I was meant to laugh it was too late.

Then she asked if I had 'someone'. I wasn't sure how to answer, so I didn't.

'You know, like a girl,' she said. 'A girl you like? Or likes you?

It's important, you know, to have someone. Even a boy . . .'

I stared at the carpet.

'You need someone you can confide in. Someone you can love. It's important to find a home for your love. Do you understand? These books are a start, but you'll need people, too. We all need people.'

Now I'm back home. Miss Hayes' books are stacked in the corner of my bedroom. They're adding an uncomfortable level of clutter to my room. I might stash them away, at the bottom of my wardrobe. I can always pretend I've read them.

## TRANSCRIPT

Extract of interview between Detective
Sergeant Terrence Mansell (TM) and Gregory
Hall's teacher, Miss Rachel Hayes (RH).


TM: Thanks for coming in.

RH: That's OK.

TM: I presume you know why you're here.

RH: I've read the newspapers. I don't exactly
know the details.

TM: I can't discuss details anyway.

RH: Right.

TM: All I'm after here is some basic information.

RH: Mm-hm.

TM: Stuff on your relationship with Greg.

RH: OK.

TM: So, tell me about your relationship with
Greg.

RH: Well, I'm his teacher.

TM: What subject?

RH: English.

TM: And you also spent time together outside of school?

RH: You know, it'd be easier all round if you didn't make me answer questions you already know the answers to.

TM: I'm just trying to establish the facts here.

RH: You know the facts. You know I saw Greg outside of school. That's why I'm here. That's why you've brought me in.

TM: To be honest, Miss Hayes, it'd actually be easier if you just answered the questions. Then I can tick them off my list. Then you can go home.

RH: Fine, yes, I saw Greg. After school. Every Tuesday.

TM: Why?

RH: The idea was that he could discuss any problems he was having. In school, at home. Whatever. But he stopped coming. A few weeks ago.

TM: Why was that?

RH: I don't know exactly. There was the stuff

61

with my fiancé, I don't know if that might
have scared him off.

TM: Right.

RH: A lot of people were . . . different
after that. It's stupid, though, really. I
mean, with Greg. It had no bearing on our
meetings.

TM: When did these 'meetings' first start?

RH: A few months ago. October, I think.

TM: And you knew about his condition?

RH: Yes.

TM: And that he was on medication?

RH: Yes. Well, I learnt about everything, you
know, the phobia and everything, from the
school nurse beforehand. I found out about
the pills in class, actually, when one of
the other pupils stole them from his school
bag. Showed them to everyone.

TM: That must have made things difficult for
him.

RH: To be honest we never really talked about
any of that, the bullying. There was a fair
bit of bullying, it's true, but I didn't
want to fixate on that.

TM: What did you talk about?

RH: Not much, really. He wasn't one for baring his soul.

TM: Right.

RH: I tried all kinds of approaches but it made no difference.

TM: What did you try?

RH: Well, I'd ask him questions. Tell him things, about me, about my life. I wanted to just make some sort of connection, you know? I gave him some books once, some of my fiancé's. Of course that's probably the last we'll see of them.

TM: But you never made this 'connection'?

RH: He was unreachable.

TM: Disconnected.

RH: Right.

TM: What was it exactly that made you want to set up these meetings?

RH: What do you mean?

TM: Well, why did you want a connection? What did you hope to get out of it?

RH: I just wanted to help him. I thought he was intelligent. Misunderstood. I thought eventually he'd open up. Obviously at this point I didn't know, you know, what he was capable of.

TM: It had nothing to do with your own
personal history?

RH: No. I mean . . . what's that got to do
with anything?

TM: Just a question. It's not important really.

RH: Well, I mean, I did have a tough time
growing up. And he seemed to also be having
a tough time. So there was that, yes. I
wanted to help. I felt compelled to help.

TM: Right.

RH: But the emphasis was always on Greg.

TM: Of course.

RH: What do you mean, anyway — my 'own
personal history'?

TM: Just referring to what I've read. The
parts Greg's mentioned.

RH: Mentioned?

TM: In the journal.

RH: Journal?

TM: His journal. That was your idea, right?
You gave him the journal?

RH: Yes, I gave him a journal. In one of our
sessions. I didn't think he used it much.

TM: Oh, he used it all right. There're
hundreds of pages' worth back at my office.

RH: Really?

TM: It took me all night to read through
them. Not to mention the stuff transcribed
from the walls.

RH: The walls? It was that bad, huh? I mean, I
read the stuff in the papers. About the house.
I didn't know how much to believe . . .

TM: Let's just stick to the journal. You
didn't know he was using it?

RH: No. But, well, I'm glad he did. That he
found some use for it. I was seeing him
regularly by the time I gave him that. He
came voluntarily, so he obviously wasn't
opposed to the idea of sitting with me. The
idea of help. It was speaking he had a
problem with. I think he was embarrassed,
you know, about the lisp? I thought that if
he wouldn't talk to me, maybe he'd talk to
himself, you know? Write to himself. You
know what I mean? It's a fairly common
technique.

TM: Common?

RH: Yes.

TM: To whom?

RH: Well, psychiatrists.

TM: Right.

RH: Writing as a sort of therapy.

TM: Yes, I get the concept.

RH: Obviously it worked on some level. I mean, it clearly sparked something inside him.

TM: Do you have any prior training in this field?

RH: Psychiatry?

TM: Are you qualified in any way?

RH: I studied psychology.

TM: Where?

RH: Sixth-form.

TM: So, like, A-level?

RH: Look, to be honest I've had just about enough of these interviews recently, OK?

TM: I believe this to be your first with me.

RH: I'm talking about my fiancé.

TM: That's a separate case.

RH: Still.

TM: I'd like to stick with Greg if possible.

RH: I'm getting a little tired of the accusatory tone.

TM: I'm not accusing you of anything. I'd like to be clear on that. It's just that you're mentioned frequently in the journal and I need to work out whether what's written there is accurate or not.

RH: Accurate?

TM: I need you to shed some light on a few things.

RH: Well . . .

TM: Several of these extracts have been disputed.

RH: Really?

TM: I just want to clear a few things up.

RH: Fine. Let's clear this up first, then: the whole time I was meeting with Greg there was never any indication he was violent. If there had been, I would have told someone. I would have asked to speak to his parents, his doctor, whoever. As far as I was concerned he was just a mixed-up teenager who needed a friend. Someone to talk to. And that's what I was trying to be. A friend.

TM: And Greg saw you as a friend?

RH: I hope so.

TM: Do you think he ever thought of you as more than a friend?

RH: More?

TM: Do you think Greg may have found you sexually attractive?

RH: What's that got to do with anything?

TM: It's a straightforward question.

RH: I couldn't really say. He was never one to announce his sexuality. Not like others in his class. I thought he might be gay, actually, at one point . . .

TM: You never picked up on anything? Any . . . feelings?

RH: Well, I noticed him looking at my chest a couple of times. But all teenage boys do that. They're fascinated by that stuff. You know, stuff they don't have. I'm aware that I'm young and therefore attractive, by teacher standards.

TM: He alludes to your breasts at one point, in the journal.

RH: Oh?

TM: He describes how he can see your bra. Due to the wet nature of your blouse.

RH: Well, OK, but I'm not sure that's important. I mean, I fancied my teacher once. I remember what it's like. It doesn't mean anything.

TM: So you did nothing to encourage this
behaviour?

RH: Excuse me? You're telling me that's not
accusatory? 'Encourage'? No, I encouraged
nothing of the sort.

TM: But you admit to the possibility that Greg
could have been attracted to you? Could have
been repressing some sort of sexual urge?

RH: I don't know. It could have been a part
of it. I didn't get that . . . erm . . .
vibe, myself. But as I've said, I didn't get
much of anything, other than silence. It
could have been a part of it, yes, I
suppose.

TM: Did he ever mention Alice to you?

RH: Not to me, no.

TM: How about her father?

[RH shakes head.]

TM: Could you answer? For the tape, please.

RH: No.

TM: How about his sister? Did he ever talk
about a place called Finners Island? About
the troubles with his family?

RH: I know it's not very helpful, but he
didn't really speak, like, at all. We'd just

sit together. That was the relationship we had. I'd try and help him and he'd just sit there.

TM: Right.

RH: Sometimes he'd nod. Or he'd answer 'yes' or 'no', but apart from that . . .

TM: OK.

RH: I mean, can you understand how infuriating it was? I tried to help him, I really did. And when he stopped coming, you know, near the end, when he started avoiding me, it was a real slap in the face. Like, we were just on the brink of making real progress and he decided to pull the plug. It was ungrateful, is what it was.

TM: I can imagine.

RH: And it's hard not to blame yourself. I mean, you read about stuff like this all the time, but to be a part of it . . . To know him. To have played some part in his life. I just wish I could have helped, you know?

TM: It's not your fault.

RH: I know, but still. I just wish he would
   have listened.
TM: Right.
RH: I just wish all of this could have been
   avoided.

Mum cut my hair last night. She used to be a full-time hair-dresser, back in the Pitt. She worked at a salon called Ahmed's Boutique, just round the corner from Kirk Lane. It's shut now, boarded up, like most Pitt places. We pass it every night on the bus but by then you're always asleep.

Now Mum does part-time, mobile hairdressing instead. It started with Mrs Jenkins next door. Mum doesn't really like Mrs Jenkins because she's old and smells like pee and some-times spends days at a time in the loft. She does like Mrs Jenkins' old-lady-conversational-streak though because a few years ago Mrs Jenkins recommended Mum's hairdressing skills to Karen Mosley in church and then Karen Mosley recom-mended Mum's hairdressing skills to Sandra Peterson and Sandra Peterson recommended Mum's hairdressing skills to Sally Anderson and Sally Anderson's gym buddies with Ursula Hampton and so now Mum's going round to Ursula Hampton's every week, styling Ursula Hampton's hair in all kinds of fabu-lous curls and inviting Ursula and Ken around for meals and over the last couple of years Ken has invested heavily in my father's clinic and this year they may even get an invite to the Hamptons' famous New Year's bash, which makes Mum truly, truly happy. Mum has friends, not customers. Hairdressing's a hobby and she enjoys it. It's not like we need the money. (These are the first things she tells Karen or Sandra or Sally or Ursula or any other friends whose hair she cuts.)

She cuts her friends' hair in the kitchen. Sometimes I sit on the stairs so I can listen to them. It's amazing how much they can talk, how they can keep thinking up things to say. As soon as they perch on that stool in the kitchen their words fill the house, echoing through the open-plan downstairs. Sally Anderson likes to talk about Karen Mosley and Karen Mosley likes to talk about Ursula Hampton and Ursula Hampton likes to talk about Sally Anderson. They talk about how such-and-such's new carpet is awful and how such-and-such has the worst dress sense and how such-and-such's nephew is getting a sex change in the summer and wants to be called Rennet and they never should have let him have that Barbie when he was a child. Her friends must know Mum talks about them with her other friends but that doesn't stop them talking about each other. It's like Mum has some kind of hold over them. Maybe it's the scissors. If Mum does get an invite to the Hamptons' New Year's bash then the Mosleys and the Petersons and the Andersons are all going to be there. I don't know what they'll all talk about.

I never know what to say when Mum cuts my hair. Last night she asked how school was. I told her it was OK. She asked how my after-school lessons were going. I've never told Mum I have after-school lessons. A few weeks ago I mentioned the meetings with Miss Hayes and since then she's assumed that's where I've been going every night. I didn't want to lie so instead I changed the subject. I told her I've been doing well with my *An Inspector Calls* essays, that I got an A- for one of them. She said, 'Very good,' and nodded. Then she asked what subject my *An Inspector Calls* essays are for and I told her English and she said, 'English?' and I said, 'Yes,' and she nodded again, smiling at me in the mirror. She asked if I want to do something English-related when I leave school, like become an English teacher or something. I said I didn't know.

Then Mum stopped talking so she could concentrate on my hair. My hair is Mum's greatest challenge. Its default setting is Scruffy Bowl. Mum says she tries her best to make me look good, with the haircuts and the clothes she buys me, but somehow I always manage to look a disgrace. She says I have a 'Natural Trampness'. I closed my eyes, felt Mum's nails navigate my scalp. Listened to the hum of the fridge, the rain on the window. The whispering snips of the scissors.

Right now I'm sitting on the bus. Even with last night's haircut my hair's still quite long, and long hair's kind of nerve-racking out in the Pitt. I know your dad's got a ponytail but he's a big bloke, he can get away with it. I'm just a kid and Pitt kids don't have long hair. There's two slouched at the back of the bus right now, heads shaved to the bone. Just enough hair to scratch your fist on. Every time I look up they're staring at me.

Now, this is a bit embarrassing, but I did some looking in the mirror this morning. Just a quick look, while I was getting washed. My new hair's about the same length as Ian's – just long enough to nibble my fringe. I stroked it down over my face the way he does, a kind of moody artistic way, like a rock star. It could never look exactly like Ian's but it was a start. (Ian scrubs his hair with shampoo, then doesn't wash it out, so it's always a bit crunchy and straggly looking. He likes it when he's walking down the street and it starts to rain and his head starts foaming.)

I had to fix my hair back to its scruffy bowl before school, so nobody would notice it'd been cut. I tried to rearrange it as I waited with the ducks but the canal isn't very reflective so I couldn't be sure whether I looked like a rock star or not. I always keep my hood up and head down on the bus, so nobody usually sees my hair, but tonight I'd planned a lean-back-with-my-fringe-over-my-face pose. I'd planned to give you a bit of a smoky-eyed glance, too, but it's hard to do anything when you step on board, my head fills with static. Did you notice? You looked over but only in that glance-around way that people assess their situation. Those vinyl-black glasses don't give much away. I think you gave the Pitt kids at the back quite a stare. Does the fact that your dad has long hair make it more or less likely for you to like it? I wish I knew psychology.

You kept your head down the rest of the journey. The Pitt kids kept playing that thud-thud music (although it was more like a tap-tap through their phone speakers). They kept staring at me, I could feel it. I wanted to turn around and tell them to shut up. You were trying to sleep.

Today the church sign said:

**JESUS**
**LUVS**
**U**
**(EVEN WEN NO 1 ELSE WILL)**

You pressed the STOP bell and we pulled up round the back of the Rat and Dog. You rubbed your eyes and stepped off without even a glance back at me and my hair. You just left me here with these Pitt kids and nothing to do but write and writing on the bus is making me sick.

I wish I could have gone with you.

Today was one of my bad days. One of my neck-rubbing collar-brushing goose-pimpling web-tickling shaking kind of days. One of those days when every time I close my eyes – every time I even blink – I see **Them**, hundreds of **Them**, massing in my head. At lunch I couldn't sit still. I kept jumping up every time my hair brushed my neck and the scraping of my chair kept waking Miss Eleanor and she kept shushing me with that big librarian finger of hers. In the end I had to go down to the toilets and sit in a cubicle in my balled-up position and stare at the wall. I had to picture your face. I knew that, if I saw you, everything would be OK.

And it was. For the whole bus ride I sat and stared at your red curls and didn't think about **Them**. I didn't even think about the fact that I wasn't thinking about **Them**. But then you got up to leave and it ached me to see you, clutching the rail, rocking from side to side as we slowed outside the Rat and Dog, knowing that any second you would step off the bus and disappear into the darkness and I would have to wait all weekend to see you again. I found myself sliding to the edge of my seat, I found myself clutching my bag to my chest, and as Man With Ear Hair and Woman Who Sneezes both stood and blocked you and I could only see a tiny patch of your hair in the driver's mirror, I found myself standing and joining the queue. It felt like the first time I'd ever used my legs.

We shuffled along the aisle of the bus, past the fat and frowning face of the driver (a face that said, 'This is not Green Avenue, this is not your usual stop') and down the steps to the pavement. For a second we stood, watching the bus pull away. You lit a cigarette, cupping your lighter to protect the flame, a yellow flash that soon flickered and faded in the darkness. I wondered how you could see with your sunglasses on.

The crowd dispersed. Man With Ear Hair and Woman Who Sneezes disappeared up the side of the Rat and Dog. My breath was steaming and my feet were numb but I still felt that warmth inside to know you were there, to hear the click of your heels as you hurried up the street. I waited till you were a black and red figure, too far away to hear my footsteps, before I began to follow.

Once my father had a bump in his company Audi and he had to drive Mum's BMW over to the garage to collect it and I remember Mum muttering the whole journey about a 'two-second stopping distance' between vehicles. The two of them sharing polite gritted-toothed words about what a 'two-second stopping distance' actually was – the disagreement, we found out eventually, caused by my father's use of 'and' to separate seconds differing from Mum's 'Mississippi'. I tried to use a similar distance-method for our walk, maintaining a twenty-second stopping distance (using Mississippis), which I think is an appropriate translation from car to foot.

It was hard maintaining the twenty-second stopping distance, though, because you kept turning corners and disappearing from view and I kept having to hurry to the corner and wait, lingering in the scent of your cigarette, watching you gain enough distance before I could start walking again. A couple of times you stopped and I stopped too, begging you not to turn around, because if you turned you would see me and I might scare you. I pleaded with you to keep on walking, to just let me follow, let me watch the swaying curls of your hair. Both times you did.

It was strange, walking through the Pitt again. It seems different now. Most of it's unchanged, really – St Peter's still looks the same (except for those tall green fences around it) and Crossgrove Park still has the swings and that rusted old climbing frame. Maybe it seems different because it's winter and it's dark or because it's even scruffier and even more over-grown with even more misspelt graffiti, or maybe it's because I know that Nan's not there any more, not really, not the Nan I knew. We walked all the way down Brook Road and through the park to the estates. I didn't see or hear a single other person, just you and your heels, echoing up each empty street. It was as if we were the only two people in the whole Pitt.

And then you disappeared. This time where I couldn't follow: up your driveway. I crossed the road and quickened my pace but by the time I reached your house your peeling red door had slammed shut. I remembered where I was, out in the furthest reaches of the bus route. I remembered the gangs of Pitt kids I'd seen from the window, pitching stones at the cars on the carriageway. I could hear laughter, somewhere, a couple of streets away. I didn't even know if I'd remember the way back.

But then I noticed something: a thin thread of smoke, rising from the end of your path. Your cigarette butt, lying there, smouldering. It gave me the same feeling of dread I get when I see a snail in the middle of the road. A cigarette that had been sitting in a packet in your pocket all day, that had travelled the bus with us, that had been to your lips and felt your suck and burnt down for you – it was just lying there, dying on the cold pavement. I glanced around but the street was deserted. I picked it up, held it in my pocket.

I ran back to the bus stop. I didn't try to remember the way, I just remembered, instinctively. It was only seven minutes till the next bus so I sat and listened to my breathing, the butt burning into the palm of my hand. I didn't dare remove it from my pocket, didn't dare examine it in case, in the yellow light of the bus stop, I realised it was just a cigarette butt, and threw it away.

Later, when my sister was thudding away in her room and Mum had taken up her nap-position in the lounge, I crept out into the garden and sat on the edge of one of Mum's plant pots and took the butt from my pocket. It was smaller than I remembered, smaller than it felt. The tip of the filter was crumpled pink from your lipstick. I smelt it, thinking it would smell of something other than cigarettes.

I held it in my lips. I clicked the trigger of Mum's crème brûlée blowtorch (the only light I'd been able to find). Its flame was blue and extremely hot and it was hard to light the butt without singeing my nostrils. I breathed deep, sucking the heat into my chest. I don't know what I was expecting – something smooth, maybe. Cigarette smoke always looks so silky but it felt more like gravel clawing down my throat. I coughed and dropped the butt into the flower bed.

It was hard to find in the darkness. Mum's blowtorch doesn't give much light. It was only as I crouched there, searching, that I noticed the burn on the palm of my hand, the weeping pink hole the cigarette had left when I grasped it.

I found the butt, eventually. It was lodged under one of the plant tubs, speckled with soil. I slipped it back into my pocket and came inside.

By the way, I wouldn't let your dad find out you smoke. Whenever Phil smokes, your dad gets very upset. He says, 'You're sucking the dick of death, man.' Phil sometimes offers him a cigarette as a little joke but your dad never laughs. He just gives Phil that stony-faced look.

This morning Phil was helping your dad carry some dead pigs to the freezer. Your dad lifted them no problem, hoisting them over his shoulder like a fireman, but Phil's small and skinny and by the end he was panting his way past the kitchen like a wounded solider carrying a comrade.

Afterwards Phil was exhausted. He wanted a smoke. He looked everywhere for his tobacco pouch but it was gone. He got pretty angry, in a breathless sort of way, and kept asking your dad where it was, but your dad just gave one of his heh-heh-heh laughs and said he didn't know and that smoking was the reason Phil was out of breath in the first place. He said, 'You're sucking the dick of death, man. Do you want your kid to grow up without a daddy?'

They didn't speak for a while after that. Phil just hacked away at the meat. The Top 40 Chart Show was playing on the radio, that song my sister's always dancing to. 'Ooo you got me screamin' boy . . .' Eventually your dad took the tobacco pouch from his pocket and slapped it on the block and Phil snatched it and hurried out the back of the shop. I just kept my head down, mopped out the fridge. This week the Top 40 Chart Show was sponsored by Burke's Clinic: 'THE place for your boob job'.

After lunch Phil came into my kitchen, smelling like a whole lot of smoke. He gave me a handful of coins and a slip of paper and told me to go to the bookies for him. I said I was too young to go the bookies and he said not to worry, I looked old enough, and if there was any trouble to just say his name. He said not to tell anyone (meaning your dad) where I was going. I went out the back door. It was busy in the bookies so I had to queue. I handed the slip of paper and the coins to the guy with the beard behind the counter and he gave me a different slip of paper without even looking up and I went back and gave Phil the new slip of paper and he tucked it into his pocket. Nobody asked where I'd been.

In the afternoon the Top 40 Chart Show finished and there was football instead. Phil stood by the radio, scratching at his neck with mince-covered fingers. The commentators were angry with the players, shouting and calling them a disgrace. It got me thinking about Lucy Marlowe again. I remembered those times she'd sit on the steps to the Lipton Building, trying to eat her lunch in peace, whilst the boys took it in turns to kick their football at her. How they'd snigger and ask her to throw it back. How she'd still always throw it back. I remember once they hit her *Star Trek* lunchbox and it clattered down the stairs and smashed open and her ham and ketchup sandwich landed in the gutter and she ran inside crying and nobody even picked up her sandwich and it lay there all day soaking up rainwater until the bread had melted, ketchup veining out across the playground. The boys used to say Lucy Marlowe was a nerd because she was passionate about *Star Trek* and wore this baggy Mr Spock T-shirt on own-clothes day that would probably still fit her now. I didn't understand because they all wore matching football shirts on own-clothes day and I think football's much nerdier than *Star Trek*. It's not like *Star Trek* host radio shows every weekend with phone-ins and episode-by-episode analysis. It's not like *Star Trek* fans stand by the radio scratching their necks and chewing their lips, looking like the entire world depends on what the commentator says next.

Someone scored and Phil jumped and punched the air. He kept grinning till the match was over. Then he winked at me and went back out to his block. I didn't wink back but I couldn't help smiling when he started singing. He danced around your dad. He gave him a big kiss on the side of his stony face.

Your dad just laughed.

'Heh-heh-heh.'

Miss Hayes has a new theory. She thinks I'm not really scared of **Them**. She thinks they're just something to blame my anxiety on. She thinks I hide my real fears behind Metaphorical Phantoms. Miss Hayes said when she was little her dad gave her a ventriloquist's doll, a clown, called Mr Fungal. Mr Fungal was her favourite toy in the world. Her and Mr Fungal used to joint-host shows for her mum and she'd swear she couldn't see her lips move. She said that when she was a little older her and her dad had a falling-out. Well, she said it was like a falling-out, only secret. She couldn't tell anyone. She said she fell out with Mr Fungal, too. She'd wake up in the night crying and Mr Fungal would be there, grinning away from her bedside table. She hated him. She couldn't even stand to be in the same room as him. She wanted to throw Mr Fungal out but then her mum would want to know why she didn't like him any more. Mr Fungal belonged to her dad and by this point her dad had gone and her mum liked to keep the few things he'd left behind.

Miss Hayes said that she stuffed Mr Fungal right down at the bottom of her wardrobe, under her boxes of books and cuddly toys and shoes. She ignored him for a while but in the back of her mind she always knew he was still there, grinning. By then she was becoming a teenager and going through a rebellious time, so she took Mr Fungal out to the woods. She walked for hours without even thinking. She came to a clearing and sat Mr Fungal right in the middle, on the dry grass, and poured a bottle of methylated spirit over his head and set fire to him. She said he gave off a lot of smoke, a big column of it pointing into the sky. She said he crackled. She couldn't leave till she was sure he was all burnt away, till she was sure he wouldn't end up back on her shelf the next day, grinning with his lips all blistered and popped.

By this point in the story Miss Hayes' voice was breaking. She clutched her skirt. Her hands were red but for a thin border of white round her engagement ring. There was silence – and not a nice silence. Miss Hayes wiped the side of her face. She said that sometimes our Metaphorical Phantoms can seem like the root of all evil but they're not, they're just a barrier between us and our real problems. She said that even if there was some natural phenomenon and all of **Them** were wiped out forever, I still wouldn't be happy. She said they're just a symbol.

I've heard similar theories. A couple of years ago when my phobia was getting out of hand again Mum took me to see her doctor, Dr Filburn. Dr Filburn was different to the other doctors I saw because he was a doctor of the mind. He wasn't like the others who just palmed me off with pills. Dr Filburn was going to cure me.

Dr Filburn said it was the concept of **Them** that scared me. He said I could happily coexist with **Them** if I could just overcome my irrational brain. Dr Filburn also used the term 'Metaphorical Phantoms', only he said I needed to face my Metaphorical Phantoms head-on. Dr Filburn was old. Not age-wise – he just looked like he belonged in the past. He had a moustache. Mum seemed to like him, though. He really helped her when she went through her sick stage. The whole time I lay in that comfy white chair Mum stood there, smiling back and forth between us. It was that same smile she dons while showing off a new item of furniture – the smile that forces you to smile right back.

Dr Filburn told me to close my eyes. With the click of a remote his office was engulfed in low, moaning whale music. After a few minutes he began to speak, softly. He told me to imagine a mountainside, shrouded in mist. He told me to pretend I was walking through the mist, searching for something, an animal. He told me to find the animal. I found an American bald eagle. It was perched on a rock overlooking a misty beach. Apparently this was my 'Safety Animal', and Dr Filburn told me to approach it, which I did. Then he told me to stroke it, which I also did and which, I have to admit, felt relaxing. Its wings were spread and I could feel the ribbed bones beneath. It made me feel light-headed.

Dr Filburn told me to open my eyes. He placed my right hand on his desk, which was empty apart from a pen, a pad and a picture of a blonde lady that could have been his wife or his daughter. Then he left the room, returning with a little plastic one of **Them**. He told me to maintain the peaceful state of mind I'd created stroking my Safety Animal. Mum was still smiling.

Dr Filburn placed the plastic one of **Them** on his desk. He asked if I was OK with the plastic one of **Them** on his desk and I nodded. He told me to close my eyes and imagine my animal. When he asked me to open them again the plastic one of **Them** had moved across the desk, a little closer to me. He asked if I was still OK. I nodded again. He told me to close my eyes again.

This continued until the little plastic one of **Them** was perched right in front of me. Then Dr Filburn lifted the plastic one of **Them** and placed it in the palm of my hand. He asked if I still felt scared. I wanted to explain that I'd never been scared of the little plastic one of **Them** because it was plastic and right at the start I could have just walked over and picked it up, Safety Animal or no Safety Animal. Instead I just shook my head. Dr Filburn nodded and left the room again.

He returned with a jar. Before the lid was even off I was clutching the leather and starting to fit. Everything went cold and dark. Mum was screaming. That was the day I bit the hole through my tongue. I never saw Dr Filburn again. I remember how angry he was when I bled all over his comfy white chair.

But anyway, they're not real. I guess that's the point. That's what I have to remember.

They're just Metaphorical Phantoms.

They're not real.

It hurts because you are still there and I know you are there and I don't know how to take you away. And it's not your fault but you could have come to school. You could have to come to school anyway and just worn your glasses and nobody would have known and I would have walked you home and everything would be the same.

But nothing is the same.

And it was hard for me. I waited for you. At 08:18 I was pressed against the gate, holding my breath, watching your bus arrive. I was examining each Pitt kid as they stumbled from the steps. By the time the last kid had departed and the bus had pulled away I'd nearly forgotten how to breathe.

And I waited again, at lunch, in the library, staking out the hole in the hedge. But Angela Hargrove crawled out through it alone and returned, an hour later, still alone.

And all I could think about was you. The lack of you.

So at 15:30 when the final bell rang I waited one more time, in my usual waiting-place, with the ducks. I waited for the

17:32. I guess some part of me still expected to see you, shivering at the bus stop outside the Prancing Horse, but you hadn't gone to work either.

But I stayed on our bus. I rode it all the way out to the Pitt. I closed my eyes and pictured your sleeping face in the driver's mirror. I told myself you were OK. You were fine. You were at home. You had not been hit by a bus. You had not been attacked by a gang in the Pitt. You were not at the hospital having contracted cancer from all that smoking and you were not going to die like Andrew Wilt, shaky and milky and bald. I got off at our usual stop, walked our usual route. I watched my feet. That way I could pretend you were up ahead of me. I could imagine the click of your heels on the pavement. I could even sniff for your cigarette – I swear at one point I could even smell it. But you seemed further ahead than usual. I couldn't keep up with you. Every time I lifted my head you'd disappear again and I'd be alone again and in the end I started to run, up all the dark and empty streets, run with the cold air biting my face.

By the time I reached your house I was panting. I sat on the wall opposite. The air was cold and stung the hole in my tongue. I focused on your red and peeling door. Your curtains were drawn. Your father's car sat outside, rusted browny-green, its backseats packed with Hampton's cardboard boxes. I could hear a sound, a voice. Canned laughter.

Your house backs onto Crossgrove Park. I hurried across the field, counting the houses till I reached your back hedge. Your garden was overrun with weeds, foot-long grass, white plastic patio furniture. Any intentional plant life was dead – the hedge patchy, the few scattered plant tubs at the back housing only shrivelled brown remains. Your father was spread across the couch in the lounge, lit by the TV. Laughter murmured behind the glass. Your father wasn't laughing, he was swigging from a bottle. His eyes were shut and he was swigging from a bottle.

There was a shed in the corner: shelter from the light of the house. I found a gap in the hedge just behind it. The shed itself was rotten. There were several crooked or missing planks. The roof was held up by four wooden beams, one in each corner, planted into the surrounding mud.

A strip of light shone from the first floor of the house. A bedroom. The curtains were thick and purple, giving nothing away but a thin square of light round the edges. Every few seconds a shadow passed over it, flickering, back and forth. Back and forth.

That's when I heard a growl – deep, nearby. I was leaning on the shed and I assumed it was the boards creaking but as I turned the growling increased, snarling and guttural. I turned too sharply, slipped in the mud. The wet grass broke my fall. A sharp pain spread from my palm – the burn, the scab from your cigarette butt, I'd grazed it on the side of the shed and now it was bleeding. There was mud and blood on the arm of my coat. I tried to wipe it but my hands were muddy too, even muddier than my arm and all I could do was make things muddier and bloodier and worse.

That's when the barking started. I could see it now, the dog, through a gap in the shed. Its head was long and snouted, just a foot or two from mine. Its breath was hot and smelt like boiled ham. The only thing holding it back was a length of chain, knotted round its neck. I don't know one breed of dog from another but it was a pretty mean-looking dog. It had lots of teeth, most of them yellow with black bits in between. Its gums were the colour of chopped liver.

I was halfway to standing when the back door opened. Your father's voice echoed out across the garden. I dropped to the ground, once again facing the roaring stinking dog. Your father shouted for a minute, stuff like 'Shut up, Scraps' and 'I'll give you something to bark about' but the dog didn't shut up, if anything it got louder. I closed my eyes. The barking stabbed into my ears. Everything was wet and tasted like soil.

And then there was you. All it took was your mumble across the garden and the dog stopped its barking and turned to face the house. It whined from deep inside itself. You told your father to go back indoors. Liquid clunked from his bottle. He coughed and swallowed and breathed.

He said, 'If you don't shut it up, I will.' And the back door slammed shut.

I tried to catch a glimpse of you then, strained to see over the long grass. Your feet rustled past. They slowed to step over the patio furniture, slapped the concrete steps up to the shed. The dog scrambled over to greet you. I glanced at the house. Your father was across the couch again, head back, swigging at his bottle.

Your footsteps creaked into the shed. I saw you then, kneeling beside the dog, scratching its ears as it whined. You had your back to me, your hair tied in pigtails. You wore a pink dressing gown, a pair of black Wellington boots. You rubbed the dog's head, pulling the skin back to show the red of its eyes.

You told it, 'There-there.'

Then you stood and reached, high up into the shed, returning with a clear plastic bag of bone-shaped biscuits. You rattled a few into your palm. The dog chewed noisily. It drooled onto your dressing gown. When it'd finished it rested its head on your lap. You stroked its belly. Rubbed its ribs.

You said, 'Good boy, Scraps. Good boy.'

You lay its head beside me. Facing me. It breathed, soft and warm. The boiled ham smell was stronger than ever, probably because of the biscuits.

It closed its eyes, let its tongue loll onto the shed floor. Its ribs rose and fell in time with my own.

I closed my eyes.

You locked the shed. You crunched across the lawn, back to the house. I waited till I heard the kitchen door, then climbed to my feet.

You had stopped in the doorway. You were staring over at the shed, right at me. I hunched down. You mustn't have seen me because a second later you turned and disappeared inside, locking the door behind you.

I can still see you now, that image of you I glimpsed for just a second. Your red hair parted, your eye all swollen and black.

This morning I watched your father through the blinds of the back fridge. He hacked at the hunks of meat on his block. He sipped tea and read the paper. He joked with Phil, holding his hat in the air with that big hand of his, too high for Phil to reach. Always with that laugh: 'Heh-heh-heh.'

I only realised how long I'd been standing there when Phil stepped in and asked me to go the bookies. I was shivering but he thought I was nodding so he just placed the money in my hand and gave me a thumbs up.

It was 09:55. I had to sit on the step and wait till 10:00 for the bookies to open. The square was empty. There were two pigeons hopping around the car park. One of them was missing a leg. The other was missing an eye. They picked at a carton of chips. When the man from the bookies opened the door they scrambled into flight, landing the other side of the square. Pigeons never fly very far.

When I got back to Hampton's your father was in the kitchen. He was enormous in my tiny kitchen, his head right up near the ceiling, where the steam gathers. He smiled down at me. I smiled back. I was numb and empty and smiling back seemed almost natural. He asked me to make him and Phil a tea. Phil shouted back that he wanted a coffee. Your father said cheers and called me 'mate'.

In Hampton's we use T-Rex Bleach. It's 'The wild way to clean'. The bottle has T - R E X written across it in jungle-style font, a teeth-marked chunk missing from the T as if an actual T-rex has taken a bite. Bleach is something I've got used to, working as a cleaner. It stings my nostrils and makes my fingers peel and sometimes at night I can still taste it, burning the back of my throat, but it's the only way to shift real grime – the kind of grime that's hard and black and no longer resembles what it used to be.

I put half a teaspoon of T-Rex Bleach in your father's tea. Mum uses bleach to keep her mugs white and I know from experience that it's only after a few sips the burning taste is noticeable and you realise you should have washed the cup more. I'm guessing T-Rex Bleach is stronger than the spray Mum uses. It says I N D U S T R I A L across it. The lid is childproof, with a black and yellow X on it. I can't help but wonder why, if they didn't want children to play with it, they put a T-rex on the front of the bottle.

Your father was over at the mincer, one hand shovelling hunks of steak down the funnel, the other covering the plate where the mince worms out. It's important to cover the mince as it worms out or else it can pop and splatter the walls. I placed his tea on the block. I waited for him to notice me, so I could point to the mug. Eventually he did and I pointed and he nodded and pushed the big red STOP button and lifted the mug with his enormous mince-covered hand and slurped in the newfound silence. He coughed. He slurped again. Then he sat the mug back on the block and the whirr of the mincer started up again. He didn't look up so I went back to my kitchen.

In *An Inspector Calls* there's a character called Eva Smith who kills herself by drinking bleach. I think you'd have to drink a lot of bleach to kill yourself. If you brewed a tea bag in bleach and added milk and sugar and heated it in the microwave till it was steaming and gulped it down, that might kill you. I doubt half a teaspoon of T-Rex Bleach could kill anyone. Especially not someone as big as your father.

It was only after I'd delivered the tea that I remembered my first day at Hampton's – your father showing me the racks at the back where the cleaning stuff's kept, pointing to a white plastic dish containing green, plastic-looking pellets on the floor right at the back and telling me never to touch it, telling me it was rat poison. How many teaspoons of rat poison would it take to kill someone? How many to just make them really sick?

Your father didn't ask for another cup of tea.

Today I walked down to the canal. I needed to be somewhere I could think. I took some bread because all last week as I waited for our bus the ducks came venturing over the ice to peck at my feet. I guess when the canal's frozen they don't eat. They went crazy at the sight of bread. I only had four slices (all that was left in the bread bin) and they gobbled it up in no time. Then they stood there, glaring at me. It was kind of awkward, like they were weighing up my edibility.

At 15:15 I heard mumblings from above. I recognised the voices: Ian and Goose. Their feet were hanging over the mouth of the bridge. Ian wears these black trainers with luminous shoelaces and they glowed like green dangling worms. The ducks waddled out, staring up at them. I guess they thought they were food.

Ian was talking but I couldn't hear what about. The usual stuff, probably. Girls. Parties. At one point he flicked a cigarette butt down onto the ice and the ducks went crazy again, swarming and pecking to the squeals of Goose's high-pitched laughter.

I huddled into my warm-position and waited. I figured they'd leave soon and I could be alone with the ducks. Be alone to think. Only the longer I sat there the less I could think about anything other than **Them**. It was different, with Ian and Goose there – I couldn't seem to summon the usual safety-and-solitude feeling of under the bridge. Instead I was very aware that I was under a bridge – that normally that'd be the kind of place that would terrify me. That there was a very real chance one or more of **Them** were above me, in the darkness, waiting to descend. I began to panic. I thought I might even have one of my attacks. I tried to picture you, but each time I'd see that eye of yours, all black and swollen.

After ten minutes or so Ian and Goose left and I was able to climb up to the carriageway and head home. I don't think either of them saw me.

I got home just as Mum was serving dinner. My father wasn't there. I didn't ask where he was but I assume the answer would have been that he was working. Who has breast augmentation on a Sunday afternoon? We ate our salmon in silence. Then Sarah and I went up to our rooms. Sarah was dancing to that song again. 'Ooo you got me screamin' boy . . .'

I waited till 21:30, then crept down to my father's study. Sometimes at night I sneak down there for internet research. Mum's always had an issue with closed spaces and locked doors (she pretty much knocked down half the house under

Dr Filburn's guidance to make it 'an open and honest place to live'), so she definitely has a problem with my father's locked study. I don't know what upsets her more, the thousands of photos of women's breasts he has stashed away in there or the fact that she can't get in to polish the woodwork, but each time my father clicks that lock Mum's lip does some serious twitching. It's as if, for a split-second, the left half of her mouth is trying to out-smile the right.

I happen to know that my father has little of interest inside his study. There's a desk, a filing cabinet, a black leather chair and a bookcase. The bookcase contains six shelves of breast augmentation journals and one shelf of *Baywatch* videos. The filing cabinet's scattered with plastic models of different-sized and -shaped breasts. There is a large poster of Pamela Anderson pinned over the desk. My father says Pamela Anderson is an icon of his generation. He says it's a shame that all our generation has in the way of a strong female role model is Katie Price.

It's the click of the study door unlocking that I always think will wake Mum. Occasionally her sleeping face twitches but that's it. Mum's an expert napper. She can nap through anything. Her usual nap-place was the couch but, as we're still waiting on the white Italian leather couch, we're now in a transitional period couch-wise, and so Mum has taken to napping on the lounge carpet instead, her body horizontal across the floor, her head vertical against the white-painted wall. Tonight I stood outside my father's study for a few minutes, just watching the light of the television flicker across her, sometimes lighting her legs, sometimes the rise and fall of her chest beneath her dressing gown, sometimes the sag of her cocked, unsmiling head. Mum never smiles when she sleeps.

Tonight's internet research was a regular of mine: Finners Island. Finners Island's a dot on the map just off the southern coast of England. We used to go there when I was little. Half the island's wetland and my father was a big fan of its constant photo opportunities. There were all sorts of beautiful birds there. There were a lot of ducks, too, but my father rarely took photos of them. There was a bald eagle there, somewhere, according to legend. My father never managed to get a photo of the bald eagle, which to him was proof enough of its non-existence. But Nan and I knew better. We saw it.

I've tried to find the Finners Island photos many times over the years, but I think Mum must have thrown them out. She doesn't want to be reminded of it – of what happened to Sarah. Now I use the internet for photos. Of course none of the internet photos of Finners Island include Mum or Nan or Sarah and I (or the bald eagle – even Finners Island's official website seems to doubt its existence) but there are some of the ducks and the woods and the beach. It's nice, clicking through the photos. Finners Island has always been a place I can go to when Skipdale gets too much, and it's nice seeing that there's this one little part of the world that never changes.

Mum was still in her nap-position when I relocked the study, the light of BBC News 24 washing over her. It was 22:10. The earliest my father's arrived home from work in the past six months is 23:07. By then I'm always well out of his study and up in my room and Sarah's thudding has usually stopped and all he has to do is unplug the TV and fireman's-lift Mum upstairs to bed. Some nights my father doesn't arrive home from work at all. He's a very important man. Mum says that Burke's Clinic wouldn't be half as successful if it weren't for my father's mix of long hours and surgical expertise. My father's patients are more like friends than clients.

I crouched there with Mum for a while. The lounge seems so empty, couchless. So cold. The whole house seems cold since she had it open-planned. I sipped her glass of wine. I'm not meant to drink, really, because of my medication, but I thought I'd try a sip. I wish I hadn't – I can still taste it now. Wine tastes like blackcurrant and perfume.

BBC News 24 was all about this winter and how it's going to be the coldest in thirty years. It showed footage of Scotland covered in snow, kids sliding down hills on bin bags, a woman falling over in the street while people carefully hurried by. Mum likes to keep up to date with the news for when the Hamptons discuss current affairs. Ken Hampton reads the

*Guardian*. I don't think Mum's ever watched a full report before drifting off.

I put down the wine and unplugged the TV. I left Mum laid out on the lounge carpet, ready for when my father gets home.

Today you still weren't in school so I had to catch the bus alone and walk to your house alone and climb in through the back hedge. Your father was drinking in the TV light again. Scraps was snoring in the shed. I knelt till I could make out his sleeping head through the missing-plank gap. I whistled. He raised an ear but the rest of him stayed asleep. I whistled again and tapped the side of the shed and he yawned and turned to me. He scrambled to his feet to bark but before he had the chance I reached in with a bag of leftovers: yesterday's blackened salmon. He stopped and sniffed and trotted towards me, as far as his chain would allow. He picked the salmon from my hand and carried it to his corner.

It was a tight squeeze through the missing-plank gap. The shed shuddered so much I thought it might collapse. Scraps tilted his head to watch me. I told him 'there-there'. I tickled his ear. He whined and carried on eating. The shed smelt of metal. The only light came from a shaft of moonlight, spilling through a gap in the ceiling. Various rusted garden tools hung from various nails, their shadows dancing up the walls.

We used to have a shed. Nan called it 'Herb's pigeon coop' but I never saw any pigeons (and besides the Herb I knew didn't go near the shed – he spent the whole time in his chair). I used to have nightmares about that shed – the webs in the corner, scattered with dead flies and egg sacs and **Them**. My father called it 'The Lair'.

Of course your shed was a lair too. I could feel **Them** – their many eyes watching from the top shelves, where the moonlight doesn't shine. But I concentrated on you. I sat on the tool chest by the window. I could hear **Them**, their usual whispers. I just ignored **Them**. The window was stained and murky but I could still make out the glow of your bedroom.

Scraps finished eating and lay beside me, head on my lap. He sniffed at my pocket. I apologised, I didn't have any more salmon. I imagined Scraps sitting there, every night, staring up at your room. I rubbed his head the way you did, dragging his eyelids back. I didn't rub his belly because it was all black and bruised.

There was a tool hanging by the window, the size and shape of a gun only with a cartridge at the bottom, packed with nails. I remember Miss Hayes once saying that a gun is an omen. If there's ever a gun somewhere in a story then by the end one of the characters will be dead. I don't know if this applies to nail guns. I unhooked the gun and held it on my lap. Your father lay, flat out, on his couch. His bottle slipped to the carpet, rocking in the cradle of his hand.

I wrapped my arm round Scraps, hugging his head to my chest. It's usually hard to see stars in the Pitt because of the light pollution but tonight it was so clear we could make out each and every one. I pointed them out to Scraps. His mouth opened and for a moment I thought he was awestruck but then he closed his eyes and sneezed on my hand.

We watched and waited. Your curtains remained shut. At one point I thought I saw a shadow pass over them but it didn't pass again. I thought Scraps might have kept me warm but he turned out to be even colder than I was. I'd have been better off hugging the tool chest. I began to tremble and eventually he stood and stumbled away, curling in the corner, just to get some rest.

When it reached 21:00 I hung the nail gun back in its place and crawled over to the plank gap. I promised Scraps I'd be back, I'd bring him more blackened salmon. When I reached the hedge I looked back one last time. Your father was spread across the floor in the lounge. His bottle had rolled to the other side of the room.

On the bus back I thought about your father. I thought about you, up in your room, waiting to make your escape. I thought about Finners Island. I'd always planned to live on Finners Island. I never thought what I'd actually do there – there are only six or seven people who live on the island and they all work for the National Trust. I don't think I'd be very good at working for the National Trust. You would – you like animals (well, you like Scraps). You could paint, too – there are plenty of picturesque landscapes. Perhaps I could work on the mainland. Become an English teacher. We could walk Scraps in the woods.

When I got home Mum was asleep on the lounge floor. I heard voices coming from Sarah's room. A girl said, 'You just need to curve your back more, pretend you're liquid.' Sarah said, 'OK.'

Sarah's door was ajar. I could see her reflection in the large ceiling-mirror, her and one of her Vulture friends. It could have been one of the Vultures from work, there's no way of knowing. They were both in their Dance Fantastical leotards, a violent glittering red against the orange of their skin. My sister reached for the remote. Music burst from the TV.

I stepped closer till I could make out the reflection of the screen. There was a music video playing. The singer was scrawny. Blond hair swayed around her body as she moved. It was that song again: 'Ooo you got me screamin' boy . . .' The singer's legs were sliding about in black latex trousers, skintight, glistening like oil. On the line, 'Butt in the air boy', she crawled onto her knees, sliding her rear up towards the camera. The air was warm and sweet like cherries.

The song finished. My sister and the Vulture were staring at me. My sister told me to get the fuck out of her room.

Miss Hayes has a new theory. She hasn't told me it yet, but she has a brand new set of questions, mostly about my relationship with my parents. She asked if I think I'm a good son. I didn't really know what to tell her. I don't smoke. On the other hand I don't do the washing-up (I'm too scared of breaking the china). I can't be a bad son because I don't really do anything. I'm a nothing son. It's like in Chemistry when we studied acids and alkalis, dipping those purple strips of litmus paper into beakers of vinegar and lemon juice to determine their pH level. I am the tap water. I am pH7. Neutral. I remain purple.

In the end I couldn't decide what to say and too much silence had passed to say anything, so I said nothing.

I didn't go to the bus stop afterwards. I couldn't face the ride without you so I just walked home. Mum was on the floor in the living room, reciting a shopping list she was writing in permanent marker on the back of an old *House Proud Magazine.* The list consisted of more salmon and more mango and more rice and more chipotle and more butternut squash

111

and more of pretty much everything else needed for the Hamptons' meal. The big night's getting closer and not only is Mum's starter not quite perfect but the new couch still hasn't arrived. I'm not sure if Mum invites the Hamptons over because she's decorated or if she decorates because they're coming over. I don't think even she knows.

I didn't like the thought of Mum having to cart all that rice and mango and fish around Waitrose alone so I collected the reusable bags and waited in the car. I used to go shopping with Mum when I was little. We'd go to the outlet store. They had jars of mayonnaise the size of my head. I haven't gone with her the past few years because she always goes to Waitrose and it's so cold in Waitrose. It's like every aisle's the frozen aisle.

It was another ten minutes or so before Mum tottered across the driveway. Her heels caught in the cobbles and she had to keep reaching out to maintain her balance. Mum says a girl should always wear heels because she never knows who she might run into. (Mum can't run anywhere in heels.) I think Mum got a bit of a fright when she noticed me, sitting there in the passenger seat. She gave me a glance of The Eyebrow. 'No after-school classes tonight?' I shook my head. She sighed and pressed the start-engine button and Elvis swooned into life with 'Are You Lonesome Tonight?' Mum skipped to 'Suspicious Minds'. 'Suspicious Minds' is Mum's favourite. It's the only time I know for a fact that her smile's genuine – when

Elvis announces he's 'caught in a trap'. Halfway down the avenue Mum got all bouncy and turned the volume knob, round and round, again and again, even when it said VOLUME MAX. By the time we reached Derby Lane Elvis was roaring and Mum was singing along, aiming too high and holding the notes for as long as she could, which didn't really suit 'Suspicious Minds'. I'm not too big a fan of Elvis myself but I like his effect on Mum. Ken and Ursula listen to slow jazz covers of 'Singin' In The Rain' and 'Feeling Good'. They'd never listen to Elvis.

Waitrose is always the same level of busy: not very busy at all. Mum says that's why she likes it. She says high food prices are worth the exclusive shopping experience. This is why Mum hates the Waitrose Essentials range. She says Waitrose shouldn't down-market their produce to people who can't afford to shop there. My problem with the Waitrose Essentials range is that it includes stuff like couscous. I don't think couscous is very essential.

Mum set about replacing the food for her dinner party. Mum shops in the order in which her food will be served and a good dinner party always starts with nibbly bits, which are the far side of the shop. Salted chilli almonds, marinated onions, bean dip with crudités. Waitrose is nibbly-bit heaven. It has its own olive bar – tray after tray of rubbery black grapes that taste like the sea. Mum says appetisers are imperative. A guest should be greeted with something to eat so that they're not just standing there, having to talk to each other. Nibbles are foreplay.

Mum's starter is baked aubergine, stuffed with rice and blue cheese. Aubergines, rice and blue cheese are situated in different corners of the shop so Mum had to hurry back and forth between aisles, leaving little black heel-scrapes wherever she went. She was constantly mumbling but I was trailing behind with the trolley and couldn't hear what she was saying. By the time we reached the seafood counter Mum was out of breath. The fishmonger was nice enough to wait. Mum leant on the glass, gulping down that icy air, the fish glaring up at her, their mouths gaping. Eventually Mum coughed and sighed and smiled and said she would like the finest Scottish salmon the fishmonger had to offer, please. She said that the salmon needs to be the climax of her meal. It has to be perfection. Mum's favourite phrases are: 'Immaculate', 'Perfection' and 'Wow Factor'. The fishmonger was only a teenager and didn't really know how to reply. He just kept saying, 'It's good fish, this. It's fresh.'

Once the trolley was stacked with salmon we hurried over to the drinks corner. The floor of Waitrose's drinks corner is wooden to give it the look of an authentic wine cellar. Ursula Hampton only drinks champagne (other drinks give her heartburn) so Mum collected a few bottles and slotted them into the front of the trolley. Finally, the Hamptons are to be served coffee. Mum says a person's coffee tells you a lot about them. Mum has a large machine that grinds beans and froths cream. She polishes her cafetière daily. Waitrose has an unprecedented range of coffee: Brazilian Daterra, Colombian Supremo, Kenya AA, Kwonggi Mountain, Monsoon Malabar, Colombian Reserve, Sumatra Mandheling, Mocha Sidamo. Mum had to try and figure out which flavour of coffee was most appropriate. She kept muttering, 'I just don't know, I just don't know.' She lifted a packet of Colombian Supremo and sniffed it. She examined the description on the back.

I wished she would relax about the whole thing. I kept thinking about the Prancing Horse around the corner and wondering if they served cocktails and if they'd serve me. I wanted to ask Mum if she fancied a cocktail, to relax her. I know she prefers places in the city with leather seats and atmosphere but I thought I might as well ask. I didn't know what we'd talk about. I wasn't giving much thought to it at all, actually – my mind was full of Elvis. I just wanted to buy her a drink so she wouldn't go home and cook another blackened salmon, tottering around the kitchen in her heels, whilst all the time smiling and smiling. It must be exhausting. In my head I kept saying, 'Do you fancy a cocktail?' I thought, 'I'll say it on three,' and counted 'One' and counted 'Two'.

But then Mum dropped the Colombian Supremo and pushed the trolley into my stomach, forcing me back behind the bread stand. She shushed me, even though I wasn't saying anything. She peered around the corner. After a minute I peered too. Ursula Hampton was at the olive bar, a basket hung over her arm, spooning olives into a little plastic tub.

'I can't bump into her,' Mum said. 'Not like this.'

I couldn't work out why. Mum was wearing her heels and her hair and makeup were perfect. She looked beautiful. She kept repeating the word 'No,' over and over, under her breath. 'No, no, no, no, no.' Then she turned to me and said, 'Just promise me, if she sees us, just promise me you'll try and be normal.'

I didn't reply to that because I didn't know how to reply. I didn't know how I could promise something I had failed to do my whole life. Ursula flipped through a couple of magazines, then headed to the checkout. A man came up behind us wanting a baguette and Mum apologised and passed him the largest one she could find. We waited until Ursula was out into the car park before making our way to the tills.

At the checkout Mum's cards kept beeping. She kept rummaging in her bag for card after card, her protests quietening as the queue grew. In the end she split the bill over four cards and we left without looking back.

She didn't play any Elvis on the way home.

It's been a long day. I've spent the past ten minutes or so sitting here in the snow, trying to remember how exactly it all began, and it's just come to me. Of course: the Italian leather couch came. This morning was the last possible morning it could arrive in time for the Hamptons' meal. And this morning it arrived.

I waited until the van had rolled off down the avenue before I left my room. Mum was so excited she'd forgotten to pour the Colombian Supremo for the delivery guys and the cafetière was still steaming on the dining-room table. I headed straight to the front door but she rushed out of the living room, grinning and whispering to 'Come and see, come and see.'

The living room looks much smaller with the couch. It's a leather corner-suite. White. Mum kept stroking it with the tip of her finger. I know she wanted me to comment on its beauty, on how the white leather matched the white walls or something, but I don't know about that stuff and I can never think of what to say at the time. In the end I just nodded

117

encouragingly. Then she got all serious and told me under no circumstances was I to sit on it. I nodded again and stepped out to the hallway. She didn't follow so I left for school.

First lesson was Geography. Ian and Goose were passing notes again, which is more geographically difficult than in English Lit., since Ian and I sit front left and Goose sits back right. It means that sometimes Goose's notes (which he scrunches into tight little balls) land in my collar or bounce off the back of my head. They were discussing Lucy Marlowe again. Goose's latest theory was that, after Ian had shown her the 'magic of sex', Lucy had realised how much she loved it. How much she needed it. He wrote that since Halloween she's been out every night picking up guys just to try and relive the experience. He wrote that she's now quit school to pursue a career as a prostitute.

Before Ian could respond the door opened at the back of the class and Lucy entered and Mr Cullman stopped explaining the possible outcomes of the collision of tectonic plates and just stared at her, every member of the class straining over their shoulders to join in with the staring. Lucy lingered in the doorway, one hand on her hip. Goose whistled. Lucy stepped past him to the front of the class and sat at the table alongside Ian. I didn't want to stare like everyone else because I know it's not nice being stared at, so I kept my head down. I just glanced up occasionally.

At first it seemed as if Lucy had stuffed two footballs down her blouse, but on closer inspection the tops of the footballs were bursting from the top of the blouse and they were clearly not footballs as they were covered with skin and frilled with the pink lace of a bra. Lucy kept her head up. She looked serious and sophisticated. After a minute Mr Cullman managed to look her in the eye. He muttered a welcome back and turned to the whiteboard.

Ian continued to stare. Eventually Lucy turned to him and said, 'Do you mind?' and Ian grinned in response, not looking up from her chest. She tried to carry on looking all pissed off and sophisticated but she couldn't help smirking. She took a deep breath and her chest swelled, almost bursting from her blouse. Ian let out a squeal of excitement. I felt sick, light-headed. I don't think Lucy's Mr Spock T-shirt would fit her any more.

After lunch was English. We were studying act three of *An Inspector Calls*, which is Miss Hayes' favourite part. Miss Hayes got excited reading it to us. She folded the book over, holding it with one hand so she could convey the words with the other. She circuited the room, stopping at her favourite passages to gauge our reaction. She adopted different voices for each of the characters. Ian and Goose were passing notes again but Miss Hayes just ignored them and concentrated on her reading.

I tried to concentrate on her reading too but it became hard not to glance at Ian and Goose's notes. They were still discussing Lucy. Goose asked if Ian'd had a go on her implants at lunch but Ian wrote back that she wouldn't let him because they were in school and if he got caught fondling they might get suspended. He could look at them as much as he wanted, though. He drew a picture of them. He wrote that after school he was going to Lucy's house and he was sure they'd get up to you-know-what and he'd have a proper go on them then.

Then Goose started drawing pictures. The pictures were of the possible scenarios you-know-what might entail. In most of them Lucy was bent over, screaming with her eyes closed while Ian stood behind her, a big smile on his face. I felt that pressure building inside me again. I tried to concentrate on picking my fingers. It takes a few days for the effects of T-Rex Bleach to show on my hands but when it does they're plagued. It's like picking glue except it stings, the skin underneath's so soft and pink and raw.

Then Goose's notes were about you. About how you've also been off the past couple of weeks. He thought maybe you'd gone in for surgery, too. He drew more pictures, this time with your screaming face. He even drew your sunglasses. Ian just replied 'Haha' but Goose carried on, note after note after note. My head ached. I picked and picked till my fingers bled, till my copy of *An Inspector Calls* was patterned with bloody prints.

The bell rang. Everyone hurried from class. Miss Hayes smiled over at me, as if she wanted one of our little chats, but I kept my head down and left. Goose and Ian set off over the field. Last period was P.S.H.E. but Ian and Goose never go to P.S.H.E., they always sneak off somewhere, usually with a couple of girls.

Lucy was waiting for them, over by the sandpit. When Ian saw her he ran and hoisted her into the air. She screamed and laughed and slapped his shoulders, shouting for him to be careful: 'They're still sensitive!' They sat together in the sand. Goose sat with them. They started kissing and Goose just sat there, watching.

I waited over by the bins. Eventually Ian leant over and whispered something to Goose and Goose nodded and stood and retreated to the hole in the hedge. By the time I crossed the field he'd disappeared onto the dual carriageway. Ian and Lucy were laid out, kissing in the sand.

It was 14:36. The dual carriageway was dull and empty. The sky was thick like cream. Goose was sitting on the wall of the canal bridge, his legs dangling over the edge. He was smoking a cigarette.

I put my hood up. I placed my hands in my coat pockets and crossed the carriageway. There was no wind but the air was very cold and each breath stung the hole in my tongue. I wrapped my coat as tightly as I could but the cold was somehow still seeping inside, clutching my bones and making me shiver. I tried to think of you, but all I could see was the version of you in Goose's drawings, bent over, screaming.

I reached the canal bridge. I could just make out the tapping of Goose's earphones. I gripped the insides of my pockets. My entire body was trembling. I thought any second he'd hear me, the slight swishing of my parka as I edged towards him, but he was too busy nodding his head to the music. There were strips of web hanging from his hair, clinging to his left shoulder, dancing in the air.

Whatever Goose was listening to was tap-tapping into some sort of climax. I took my hands from my pockets. My finger-tips ached in the cold. I leant forward, till I could feel the warmth of his fleece on my face, till I could smell the sour mix of sweat and cigarettes.

That's when I saw it: one of **Them**, emerging one leg at a time from the collar of his fleece. It wasn't a particularly large one – about the size of a two-pence piece, including leg-span – but I froze all the same as it scurried down his back. It drew to a stop between his shoulder blades, level with my face. The earphones ceased their tapping. There was a silence in the air.

It perched there, still for a second, before extending a leg out towards me.

I pressed my hands into Goose's back. The soft fleece burnt my stinging fingers. I half expected the fall to be in slow motion, like a fall in a film, but Goose barely had time to lift his arms before he hit the ice. The ducks scattered, squawking in alarm. Goose's body lay there, arms spread, like he was making snow angels. Blood veined from his mouth across the frozen canal. The ducks watched him. I watched him. They moved in slowly, pecking at his sides and his back. I breathed.

Then I ran. My feet were numb and ached in the cold but I just kept on running. I must have kept running for nearly an hour. There weren't many cars about and for a while I ran right along the middle of the carriageway, but then the school traffic started and I carried on along the pavement. I ignored the pain of my breathing, the stitch in my side. I ran the bus route, all the way down the Social De-cline. All the way out to the Pitt. I needed to see you. I knew that once I did, everything would be OK.

By the time I reached the church it was starting to snow. I leant against the wall, breathing deeply.

The sign said:

## FORGIVE AS THE LORD FORGAVE YOU

I passed the Rat and Dog and turned, heading down towards the park. I crossed over to your estate.

And then I stopped. Scraps was there. He was standing in the middle of the road, sniffing at a pigeon that was spread across the tarmac. He stared at me for a second, recognition in his eyes. He bounded over.

I knelt to him. We were both panting. He sniffed at my pocket, licked my hands. I told him I didn't have any salmon, sorry. I asked what he was doing out in the street.

Then I looked up and saw you, standing at the corner. I stepped back from Scraps. He woofed at me.

'There you are,' you said. You were talking to Scraps. He trotted over and you took hold of his collar and rubbed his head and told me you were sorry, glancing sideways through your red curling hair. You weren't wearing your sunglasses.

In my head I said, 'Say something, say something, say something,' but I didn't say anything.

Then you walked away. I thought maybe that was it. I was too scared to speak but inside I was aching for you to say something else, anything else.

You'd nearly reached the corner again when you stopped and turned to me.

You said, 'You're in my school, aren't you?' and I nodded and you smiled and said, 'I've seen you on the bus. You live round here?'

I nodded again. It's not lying, really, it was just nodding.

You asked my name and I told you.

You said, 'I'm Alice.'

I tried my best to think of what to say next but my mind

wasn't processing anything. The snow was getting thick. It gathered in your hair.

'Well, see you around.' You walked to the corner, holding Scraps by his collar. Scraps looked back over his shoulder a few seconds before turning back to you. I just stood there, watching through the snow.

At the corner you turned back one last time. You said, 'By the way, you shouldn't stand there.'

I swallowed.

'On three grids,' you said.

I looked down. You were right – I was standing on a set of three grids. I stepped off onto regular plain pavement.

'It's unlucky.'

## DATE UNKNOWN

So Mum and my father and Ken Hampton and Ursula Hampton are sitting at the dining-room table with knives and forks and big white plates of blackened salmon and mango rice and chipotle-whatever-it's-called and they're smiling and there are trumpets sounding softly from over in the lounge and nobody's talking because everybody's politely waiting to see who'll be the first to take that first bite of delicious-looking salmon and Mum thinks but isn't sure that one of the Hamptons should be the first to take a bite because after all they're the guests but Ursula Hampton is sure that Mum should be the first to take a bite and 'lead the meal' because after all she's the host and the only sounds are the long swooping trumpet-notes as they glide from Mum's subwoofer in the lounge, past the vases of glittering black twigs and tall glass candlesticks supporting thick purple red-grape-scented candles to harmonise over the heads of the four diners, who still sit and still smile and still wait for someone to start eating and in the end it's Ken Hampton who takes the initiative and under the polite-smiling gaze of

126

the other three diners cuts a small slice of salmon and spreads it with mango rice and chipotle-whatever-it's-called until his fork is loaded with an even mixture of the textures and flavours compiled on his steaming plate, nodding in turn to each of the diners before raising his fork to his lips, however as he does so there's this small but audible clink, Ken's fork stopping dead before his face, Ken's red and bushy eyebrows crawling into a frown upon his forehead and as a third trumpet joins the two soft trumpets playing a slightly louder, slightly sadder note it becomes clear that although Ken's smiling lips have parted, his white wall of smiling teeth beneath have not and no matter how much Ken strains against the locked hinges of his jaw he cannot seem to part his teeth, cannot allow the blackened salmon and mango rice access to his mouth, cannot experience that smoky Mexican chipotle flavour, cannot do anything in fact but let the forkful of food slip back to his plate, splattering amongst his rice and splashing mango sauce up onto his salmon-pink shirt and by now several more trumpets have joined the increasingly sad trumpet music, this time playing even lower and more sustained notes, thick and deep like subtle but relentless foghorns and the focus of the diners has shifted to Ursula who's attempting to take some of the limelight off Ken by slicing into her own plate of blackened salmon and mango rice and chipotle-whatever-it's-called, delicately arranging a mixture of fish and rice on her fork before lifting it to her still-smiling lips, but as Ursula attempts to take a bite she too is met by a small but audible clink and she too finds her teeth unopenable and she too strains against her jaw-locked mouth but cannot get a single ounce of Mum's delicious-looking blackened salmon past her gleaming white teeth and so she too finds her forkful of salmon splashing back into the mango sauce, speckling the tablecloth with a scattering of sauce spots and so as the trumpet music squeals ever louder from the subwoofer speakers in the lounge the focus of the four smiling diners turns to Mum who, even through her beaming smile, is clearly so appalled and embarrassed at her disaster-of-a-dinner-party that she has no choice but to take control, to 'lead the meal', to politely smilingly dig into her own plate of blackened salmon, mango rice, chipotle-whatever-it's-called and show them how it's done but as Mum obligingly slices into the food on her plate it becomes pretty obvious before she even raises her fork that her chances of success are likely to be similar to Ken and Ursula's, that Mum is more than likely also going to suffer the inevitable clink, the inevitable jaw-lock, the inevitable slip-of-food-from-fork, yet still Mum persists, still raising her fork, still parting her lips, still trying her best to jab that fork through her still-sealed teeth and by now several more trumpets have joined the increasingly loud trumpet music, squealing chaotically and distorting harshly and far surpassing the appropriate volume for background music and my father is also trying to join in and eat some salmon and so now all four diners are attempting to open their jaws, to break past their smiles, to eat the food that Mum has spent so long preparing but no matter how much they fork, how desperate their eyes look, how many drips of sweat fleck the plates before them, they can't seem to manage to stop smiling long enough to get a single forkful of salmon into the warm wetness of their mouths and the trumpets are wailing now, sustaining unmatching notes for far longer than any trumpeter could possibly blow and the diners are practically stabbing the cutlery into their faces, my father resorting to holding his fork towards him like a samurai when they stab themselves in old movies and he's thrusting with all his might at his mouth and Ursula Hampton's hair has slipped down over her eyes and she is hack-hack-hacking away at her face until eventually she misses her teeth and hacks off a hunk of the side of her cheek and Mum is now trying to pry open her jaw with her stainless steel knife and Ursula's blood is staining the tablecloth and the jazz is building into a sort of swarming buzzing free-style-jazz frenzy and as Ken Hampton finally breaks through his two front teeth two long curling black legs begin to wriggle out through the gap and

II

It's official: Christmas is coming. Mum's decorations arrived this morning. We have two new artificial Christmas trees. Mum buys new trees every year. She says she can tell when a tree's spent eleven months in the loft.

Mum's down in the dining room, singing 'Suspicious Minds'. She got the call from the Hamptons yesterday: she and my father are invited to the New Year's bash. Mum's been singing Elvis non-stop all morning. Every so often she comes up to show me a new bauble or strip of tinsel or the various twinkle-settings of her White-Gold Icicle fairy lights. My father hasn't been home since Tuesday.

I feel better today but Mum won't let me out of bed. She says she wants me strong for work. She doesn't want to let Ken Hampton down. I doubt Ken Hampton would care if I wasn't strong for work (I've never even seen him set foot in the butcher's) but it's not bad spending a few days in bed. I haven't had to get dressed or eat at the dinner table. I haven't had to wade out through the snow to school. All I do is lie here, watching film after film from my Retro Hollywood video collection. This morning I watched *Breakfast at Tiffany's*. I snuck a box of Waitrose Maple Triple Nut Muesli up to my room and crunched my way through two hours of 1940s-New-York-related bliss. That final scene gets me every time: Holly and Fred and the little wet cat in the rain. Audrey Hepburn clutching the collar of George Peppard's coat. I think you're prettier than Audrey Hepburn.

Mum's spent the last few days looking for my window-key. She wants to air my room before the sick-smell contaminates the rest of the house. She says a house should smell like nothing but fresh air. It was fresh air made me sick in the first place. On Monday, after you spoke to me, I spent hours out in the cold. I was out in the Pitt all alone and I needed some time to think.

I thought about going to Nan's old house, on Kirk Lane, but sometimes my father goes there with his secretaries and in the end I decided against it. I walked to the church instead. I sat on the wall outside. I wrote in my journal. I watched the snow transform the Pitt around me, cars and walls and bins and cans and bottles becoming shapes, carpeted in white.

At one point a gang of kids emerged from the houses up the road, their upturned faces amber in the street lights. They set about building a snowman – some rolling the snow while others ran home to collect the facial fruits. They constructed it out on the corner, a mountain of a thing with two cooking apples for eyes. It was only when they'd finished that I realised the snow was covering me, gathering in my hair and the fur of my parka. I was becoming a snowman myself. I stood and shook off and one of the kids pointed and screamed and turned and ran and the others followed, disappearing into the ever-whitening Pitt.

I waded back to Skipdale. The snow was up to my knees. It twirled around me like leaves in a breeze. The cars on the dual carriageway were rolling along the same speed I was wading. I don't know what time it was when I arrived home. As I stepped into the hallway I heard mumbling voices, clinking cutlery, slow jazz. I heard the correctly pronounced 'ha-ha's in Ursula Hampton's laughter. I heard the door slip shut behind me. I heard the slow jazz end and the talking cease and then silence, real silence.

I swallowed and stepped into view. There they were: Ursula, Ken, my father, all perched in the candlelight with wide eyes and smiles and plates of blackened salmon. Mum had her back to me. She kept her head down. I was glad in a way because even if she'd turned I don't think I'd have been able to look her in the eye. The slow jazz started up again – a trumpet wailing.

Ken Hampton said my name. He said it as if it were a question, raising his eyebrows, closing the gap between them and his thick black hair. He was wearing a pink shirt, the three undone buttons causing it to clash with the fuzzy layer of orange on his chest. He said he didn't know I was joining them this evening and my father immediately said that I wasn't, that he thought I was at a friend's, why wasn't I at a friend's? My father's voice was loudening. This was a bad sign. He kept glancing at Mum, chewing the inside of his cheek.

'Beautiful night,' Ursula said. I nodded. I was still shivering from the wade back. The bottoms of my trousers were caked in snow. The smell of salmon churned my stomach. It dawned on me that my current symptoms – nausea, shivering, tight-locked jaw – were the same ones I get as a result of seeing one of **Them**. It further dawned on me that I had in fact seen one of **Them**, only a few hours earlier, creeping down the back of Goose's fleece and that I hadn't yet experienced any of the usual effects. I waited a few seconds, breathing deeply, staring at the floor, unsure whether to continue upstairs to my room.

Somebody spoke. At first the words didn't register and I glanced from face to face, waiting for whoever it was to repeat what they'd said. We'd entered into a conversation now and I knew I'd have to wait there, under the Hamptons' gaze. Wait until they deemed it fit to let me go, until they gave me the opportunity to run up to my pretty-much-impenetrable bedroom, to close my door and position my brown and green striped draught-excluder snake and crawl into my bed, safe and warm and alone.

It must have been Ken who'd spoken because he repeated his question. He asked how I was finding things at the butcher's. In my head I told him I hated it. I told him I didn't even need his money, that it was just building up in a video-case in my room. I told him, 'Shove your job up your ass.' The whole time I was in my head telling him these things there was slow jazz and smiling faces. Ursula sipped her champagne. My legs were trembling. I wasn't saying anything. I was just standing there not saying anything. Mum raised her hand to her forehead.

Then Ursula asked me how school was. I nodded an 'OK' and tried to smile but I couldn't tell if they even noticed my smile because they were all already smiling, even my father, who never smiles.

'He's doing very well at English, aren't you, Greg?' my father said.

Ursula Hampton repeated the word 'English' and asked if I wanted to be an English teacher when I grew up and I nodded again, like it was appropriate to just stand there and nod at everything they said, which, by the look on Ursula's face, it wasn't. Ken also nodded for a few seconds, his brow creasing into three distinct lines like the claw of some wild animal, whilst he thought of something else to say. He asked what I thought of the new couch. Ursula shot him a frown. She turned back to me and smiled.

'Lovely, isn't it?'

I wanted to say that I loved the couch. I wanted to say it was the most beautiful piece of furniture I'd ever seen, that it was even more white and pure and beautiful than the snow outside. I wanted to tell them about its Italian origins and how it complements the curtains and prove to Mum that all this time I have been listening, I've just never known how to reply. But I didn't. I just stood there wondering how long it would take them to notice my trembling legs. Wondering how I could leave without making things worse.

That's when I vomited. It started as a cough – it was only after three or four coughs that I could taste the thin, hot bile, a similar taste to mum's chipotle squash purée. From then on memories are vague. I remember sinking to the floor but that's when I must have blacked out because next thing Mum was kneeling over me, her nails scratching my neck in search of a pulse, probing my mouth to scoop out sick, pinching my skin as she struggled to lift me. I heard my father telling the Hamptons to sit, finish their meal. I heard him remark on the blackened salmon.

The voices faded. Mum carried me up to the bathroom. At the time I was certain it was you carrying me. Each time I opened my eyes I saw that image of you, out in the snowy street with Scraps by your side. I don't remember much of Mum undressing me, just the cold sting of bathroom tiles, the rumble of the bathtub filling with water, my head rocking as she peeled off my sick-covered trousers. I didn't regain full consciousness till I was in the bath and even then it came more as a slow realisation that I wasn't dreaming.

Mum was kneeling beside me, holding my head above the surface of the water. Her dress was wet, clinging to her arms and stomach. She wasn't smiling. I didn't know what to say so I just lay there, staring back at her. The water felt like a blanket. Sweat or steam gathered into a droplet at the end of my nose. I was very aware of being naked.

'I'm sorry,' I said.

Mum shushed me. She slicked my fringe out of my eyes. She told me it'd all be OK.

I didn't let Ken Hampton down. I got up extra early and waded to work. It was easier wading in the road because the snow wasn't as deep but every so often a car would approach and I'd have to clamber back up onto the pavement. I don't think I stepped on any sets of three grids but it was impossible to be sure. I was eighteen minutes late. As I arrived your father cheered and called me a 'Snow Hero'.

I spent most of the morning making coffee. Phil's got a night job driving up to the woods in his brother's van to collect Christmas trees. He said that, what with the new baby, he's saving for the best Christmas ever. I made fresh coffee every half-hour, using twice the normal amount of granules, like my sister does when she wants to maintain her dancer's energy. I didn't want Phil to lose concentration and cut off one of his fingers.

The coffee-drinking played havoc with Phil's waterworks. He was rushing back every ten minutes to empty his bladder. The pipes had frozen and the toilet wouldn't flush, so all day the aroma of coffee and urine lingered in the back of the shop. Every time the Vultures came out for a bucket they'd frown their wrinkle-faces and Phil'd just laugh and say, 'Merry fucking Christmas.'

Eventually home time came. I'm meant to finish at 17:00 but I never get out till at least 17:15 because I have to wait in the safety and solitude of my kitchen until the Vultures (who also finish at 17:00) have vacated the premises. The Vultures take their time vacating the premises. Since Ken Hampton insisted every employee wear a black Hampton's Butcher's cap the Vultures have ended their Saturdays gathered in the cloak-room, trying to fix their hat-hair. They do this with a mixture of combing and spraying and applying metal clips. They like to talk about their night ahead: which bars they will go to, which songs they will dance to, which boys they will kiss. I stand in the kitchen and pretend to be mopping the long-since-clean 5ft$^2$ tile floor. Once I tried running the tap to drown out the Vultures' giggling but one of them appeared at the kitchen doorway and reached in and turned the tap off and said, 'Do you mind? We're trying to talk here,' so now I just stand there and wait for them to leave.

Once they'd gone I stepped out front for my wages. Your father and Phil were sitting on the counter. Your father asked if the cleaning was all done and I nodded. He said he had one more job for me.

He took me out the back to the car park. There was only one car – ploughed bonnet-deep in the snow. Your father said he'd had a little trouble getting into his usual parking space this morning. He grinned and handed me a shovel.

The snow had hardened to ice in the darkness. I hacked away, piling shovelful after shovelful by the bins in the alley. It was getting on for 17:30 and I knew I was no longer being paid but still I shovelled, all around the car and behind the four wheels. I even cleared a path to the street so your father could reverse out easily. My feet numbed and my hands stung and the ice lost all texture. I could hear your father and Phil, laughing inside.

It was just as I was finishing, hacking the snow out from under the exhaust, that I smashed a tail light. I don't know what happened, my arm just suddenly jerked. The force of it ached my hand (the palm's still sensitive from that cigarette burn). The bulb was bare and broken and there was red glass scattered over the ice. I considered running home, abandoning the snow and the shovel and the envelope with my wages that lay on the counter inside. I even dropped the shovel. Then I picked it up again. I buried the shards and went back inside.

The lights were off. Phil had gone. Your father was waiting in the darkness.

'All done?' he said.

I nodded.

He took the shovel and rested it in the corner with the brushes. He padlocked the back door and led me out into the shop. I stepped into the square and hugged my coat around myself.

He handed me my wages.

'See you next week.'

It's hard returning to school after an absence. It's only when I reappear that people realise I've been gone. People notice me. People talk.

There was more pressing news this morning, though. Cullman was off. According to the whispers of the Vultures in form, he's been suspended. Ian and Goose were also absent so I wasn't able to obtain any further details via their note-tennis.

At break I went to the library. As soon as I entered I knew something was different. It was the smell. There's normally that book smell of ink and dusty paper (which is what Miss Eleanor smells like too, I've noticed, when passing her in the corridor) but today the air was sweet and thick, like Mum's chipotle squash purée. Miss Eleanor was nowhere to be seen.

There was mumbling from the bookshelves at the back. I knew it'd more than likely be other pupils up to no good.

I'd half retreated to the door when I heard your laugh.

You were in the Fiction aisle. When I knelt I could see you, through a gap in the shelves, cross-legged in the corner by

Poetry. It's days since I've caught your bus, days without even a sight of you and now this – you – here in my library. I couldn't imagine what would happen if you saw me. Would you recognise me again? Would you speak to me? Your head was back as if in mid-yawn. Smoke rose from your mouth, a great curling mist of it, growing and gathering at the duct-taped fire alarm. Angela's head rested on your shoulder, glaring at the cigarette between your fingers.

'Holy shit,' she said.

You took another drag. The two of you began to giggle but I couldn't work out why.

Then came Ian's voice.

'My turn, ladies.'

I crawled along the aisle. Ian was over by the audiobooks, leaning back on his elbows, tie round his head, Rambo-style. Goose was beside him, grinning, waiting for his turn with the cigarette.

'Just a second, babe.'

Angela slid down into your lap for another drag. The tip flared in your sunglasses.

I huddled against the bookcase. I shut my eyes. I pictured Goose as I'd seen him last, laid out on the canal, ducks surrounding him on the ice. I felt the static of his fleece on my fingers. Now here he was, here in my library. Not a scratch on him. Grinning away without even a chipped tooth.

Here you all were, you and Goose and Ian and Angela, here in my library.

This is what happens when I don't see you. This is what always happens to pure perfect things, given time. Circumstances change. People change. The world moves on and I am left behind. I wanted to rewind to when it was just me and you, standing in the street. Me, you and Scraps, in the snow.

I tuned in and out of the conversation. You remained silent but Angela spoke of several things: the quality of the cigarette you were smoking, an upcoming party at Goose's, the Christmas Dance Fantastical. Angela ranted about Cullman. Apparently he's been suspended for having indecent images on his computer. Angela says the images were of Lucy Marlowe. She says Lucy sent pictures of her post-op breasts to Cullman in an effort to secure herself a place in the Fantastical. She said Lucy was a little bitch for trying to muscle in on her dance show. Now there are rumours the Fantastical's been suspended, that they may be reorganising it after Christmas. Whoever heard of a Christmas Dance Fantastical after Christmas?

Angela snorted. I turned back to the missing-book gap. She was kneeling on all fours in the aisle, her face twisted in a state of extreme silent laughter. She looked like Nan's cat Mr Saunders used to, coughing up a fur-ball.

Ian said, 'What?' He started laughing too. 'What?'

'It's just Cullman,' she panted between giggles, 'the old paedo. I can't believe he finally got caught!'

Angela dropped head first into Ian's lap. Ian took the opportunity to lift the cigarette from her fingers. He inhaled. You were slumped back against the bookcase, that smile still over your face. Goose shuffled over and sat beside you. He kept staring at you. You were wearing your sunglasses but I could tell from the tilt of your head you were sleeping.

'Fuck Lucy,' Ian said, letting the smoke crawl out with his speech. 'I don't even care about her and her tits. She never even let me touch them.' He held the cigarette out. Goose took it without shifting his gaze from you.

'Younger girls are more fun.' Ian lifted Angela's hand and kissed it like a gentleman.

'Is that right?' she said.

That's when Ian and Angela started kissing. I turned away again. All I could make out was the wet popping and peeling of lips. Angela moaned. The bookcase wobbled. A hardback of *Pride and Prejudice* tipped onto its side. The smoke was giving me a headache. I shut my eyes.

Then Angela said, 'I'm bored, let's go get some food,' and climbed to her feet. She must have used the bookshelf to balance because it wobbled again and this time *Pride and Prejudice* slipped from the shelf, landing corner first on my knee. I huddled up against the wall, over by History, trying to rub the pain away.

You appeared one by one, stumbling down the aisle to the fire escape. Ian was holding Angela's hand. Goose was holding yours. You spilt out through the doorway into the playground.

Your laughter grew quieter and quieter and quieter. Then it disappeared.

I waited in the library till the bell sounded. Then I went to English. Ian and Goose didn't show up. They must have stayed with you and Angela. Miss Hayes didn't show up either. The rest of us waited fifteen minutes, then left. The rule (for our year at least) is that if a teacher hasn't shown up for class within fifteen minutes, the class is allowed to leave. I'm pretty sure this is not an actual Skipdale High rule.

I went to Miss Hayes' office. The door was closed. I knocked but there was no answer. I checked the car park – her car was still there.

I went and knocked again.

'What?'

I told her it was me. I asked if I could come in. She didn't say no so after a few seconds I entered.

Miss Hayes was at her desk. Her mascara had run, gathering in the wrinkles under her eyes. I asked if she was OK but she didn't respond. I took my usual seat.

'What are you doing?' she said.

I told her I'd come for our meeting. I'd missed the last one because I was absent, I was sick, and for that I apologised.

Miss Hayes laughed. Not a proper laugh, just a single 'Ha'. She stared at her hands, one holding the other on her lap. She'd placed her engagement ring in the middle of the desk.

'I guess you've heard the rumours,' she said. 'You're here to see if they're true.'

I shook my head. I told Miss Hayes I had come for me. I needed her help. I asked if she had any new theories.

'What's the point?' she said. 'I'll sit here and try to help you and you'll sit there and won't say a word.'

I didn't know what to say to that so I just sat there and didn't say a word.

'Have you even read any of those books I lent you?'

I stared at her engagement ring.

'Thought not.'

I wanted to show Miss Hayes my journal. Show her how I've used it. Show her how it's so filled with words that the pages can't take it any more. Show her how the spine is so cracked and worn I have to hold it together with an elastic band. I wanted to explain that it didn't matter if I answered or not when she spoke to me, that it was OK for us to just sit in silence.

But I didn't say anything. I just stared at the desk.

'Just go away,' Miss Hayes said.

So I did.

This morning as I came down for breakfast Mum was kneeling on the dining-room window seat, splitting the blinds with her thumb and finger. She was shaking her head.

'Have you seen this?' she said. 'Have you seen it?'

I didn't need to split the blinds. Even through the frosted glass of the porch I could make out the outline of the seven-foot inflatable Father Christmas Artie Sampson had erected on his front path. It grinned proudly. It nodded in the breeze. I wondered how he'd get his car in and out of the garage.

'We all agreed,' Mum said, 'but he just couldn't stick to it, could he?'

Mum's Christmas light petition started in August. Everyone in the avenue agreed on the same White-Gold Icicle fairy lights with the same product number from the same catalogue, agreeing to hang them from the same points on the arch of their roof. Even Mrs Jenkins next door agreed. But Mum knew Artie Sampson was up to something. She knew it from his vacant smile when she showed him the pictures in the catalogue, from his assurance he'd remember the product number and didn't need to write it down. Mum had told him how she just wanted the avenue to look nice for the festive period and Artie Sampson had nodded and winked and said, 'Oh, don't worry, it will,' and Mum had just known he'd pull a stunt like this.

Mum finished her Christmas decorations last night. Our house is near enough a replica of the *House Proud Magazine* Christmas special. The magazine calls it 'modern-traditional' – traditional lights, garlands and presents juxtaposed with an enormous porcelain snowman and wire-figure nativity. In the centre of the lounge ceiling hangs an upside-down Christmas tree. Mum spent over an hour on the stepladder, gluing each decoration onto its PVC branches. She says it has Wow Factor.

Mrs Jenkins next door hasn't put her White-Gold Icicle lights up yet either. I was the only one dressed, so Mum sent me round this morning to see if she needed any help nailing them to her porch. There was no answer. She was probably in the loft. Mrs Jenkins spends days at a time up in the loft, playing the piano. Every so often, late at night, I can hear her, the tinkling of her piano keys. I knocked four or five times, then retreated down the path. Artie was standing on his door-step with his wife, admiring the Father Christmas. He shouted over, 'Good morning!' then noticed Mum, kneeling there at the dining-room window and waved, gesturing at the inflatable figure on his path with a grinning thumbs up. Mum smiled and waved back. As I entered she turned from the window, rubbing the image from her eyes.

She frowned at the floor for a few seconds. Then she shook her head and said, 'It'll take more than Artie Sampson to ruin this Christmas,' and disappeared into the lounge.

I carried on through to the kitchen. Sarah was there. She was over by the cafetière. Normally Sarah won't leave her room till she's all made up and lacquered and squeezed into her uniform but this morning she was still in her dressing gown, hair tied back, face pale and clean. She looked like a child again.

I went to the cupboard for a bowl and began to fill it with Waitrose Maple Triple Nut Muesli. Sarah was getting her usual morning coffee-shot. She spooned some Colombian Supremo beans into a mug, waiting for the kettle to boil. Her eyes were narrow. There were a couple of angry spots on her forehead. The kettle clicked and she quarter-filled the mug, swilling the beans, softening them in the water. I offered the milk but she ignored me, draining the beans over the sink, knocking them back, chewing them noisily as she hurried upstairs.

I left my muesli and followed. Mum was in the living room, scrubbing at the couch. Her latest enemy is gravity, which was littering the white Italian leather with glitter and PVC pine needles, courtesy of the upside-down tree. She was too busy scrubbing to hear me tiptoe upstairs, to hear the creak of the floorboards as I knelt at Sarah's door.

Sarah was at her dressing table, frowning at her pale clean face. She reached for her vanity case and began dabbing foundation, powdering herself a blank canvas. I never thought Sarah'd be able to wear makeup. She got into Mum's blusher once, when we were little, and had to be rushed to A&E. It was her skin, she had a reaction. She was always having trouble with her skin. It was too dry. It was always peeling. The kids at school called her 'Flake'.

Dust was the problem, that's what the doctors said. Dust was the enemy. Dust made her scratch and when she scratched her skin it turned to dust. It was a vicious circle. Mum used to tell her off for scratching, used to make her wear oven mitts to bed, but there was no stopping her. I'd often hear her in the night, that sht-sht-sht of her little claws as she shed into her bedspread. I still remember the two of us, jumping up and down on her mattress, watching the particles of dust, Sarah's skin, dance in the sunlight around us.

That was before the time on Finners Island, before I moved to Nan's. When I came back there was a different Sarah, a popular Sarah, who wore makeup and danced on stage and was never called 'Flake' by anyone. I sat in the hall and watched her this morning. I had to see the transformation for myself, had to witness her paint herself into a woman again. Otherwise I'd never have believed it was the same girl.

## TRANSCRIPT

Extract of interview between Detective Sergeant Terrence Mansell (TM) and Gregory Hall's sister, Miss Sarah Hall (SH).

TM: I promise this won't take long.

SH: That's OK.

TM: I just need to talk. About what's gone on with your brother.

SH: I figured.

TM: How are you dealing with everything?

[SH shrugs shoulders.]

SH: OK, I guess.

TM: OK?

SH: I mean, I don't know. I suppose. What do you want me to say?

TM: Just the truth.

SH: Well, Mum's having another breakdown.

Everyone at school now hates me, so there's that.

TM: Because of Greg?

SH: They call me 'Psycho Sister'.

TM: Nice.

SH: This girl in my year, Angela, she came over and spat on me the other day. Actually spat on me. On my neck.

TM: Kids can be . . . you know.

SH: Yeah.

TM: I guess you're right then. 'OK' probably is the best word. 'OK' under some very difficult circumstances.

SH: Right.

TM: Have you seen Greg at all?

[SH shakes head.]

TM: You don't want to?

[SH shrugs shoulders.]

TM: What's your relationship like?

SH: With Greg?

TM: Yeah.

SH: Well, he's my brother.

TM: And?

SH: That's about it, I guess.

TM: You aren't close?

SH: He's a bit strange. Like, creepy. I mean,
he can't help it, it's not his fault. It's
just the way he is. He never says much.
He's always just there, lingering.

TM: I believe you lived apart when you were
younger?

SH: He lived at Nan's.

TM: So you didn't see each other much?

SH: Mum wouldn't let us. She went over to see
him at weekends but she never let me go
with her. She said it was because of the
cat. I had eczema. She said the cat was bad
for my skin.

TM: You didn't believe her?

SH: Well, that never explained why Greg
couldn't come here, did it?

TM: I guess not.

SH: It never explained why we'd have to go on
separate days out. Why we never went on
holiday any more. Why, during the odd time we
were together, like Christmas or my birthday,
she'd sit us at opposite ends of the table.
Like, what, he had too many cat hairs on
him? Like, they couldn't just brush him off

156

or something? I mean, I was allowed to go to
Nan's for New Year's, to watch the fireworks.
But even then I'd sit one end of the kitchen
and he'd sit the other. Everyone just acted
as though it was, you know, normal.

TM: Why do you think she wanted to keep you
apart?

SH: Because of how he was. Because of the
whole Finners Island thing. Although if you
mention that to Mum, it's like there's no
such place. She's so fucking repressed.

TM: Enlighten me, what's 'the whole Finners
Island thing'?

SH: Some place we used to go when we were
little. I can't really remember.

TM: But something happened there? There was an
. . . incident?

SH: I think I was like eight or something. I
remember I wanted to go in a boat, but they
wouldn't let me in the boat. And then Greg
took me out in the boat. I don't remember
much after that, just being in hospital.

TM: And that's when Greg moved away?

SH: Yeah. Suddenly it was like, 'Oh, he's just
going to Nan's for a bit'. And then, 'Oh,

they're having so much fun he's going to
stay'. And then, five years later, when Nan
went cuckoo, when she had to go in a home,
it was like, 'OK, well look who's back'.

TM: Was that strange, having him back?

SH: Well, yeah. It was weird. Because I'd
still seen him, every so often, but then
suddenly he was there, like, all the time.
Like I said, lingering.

TM: You'd prefer he hadn't come back?

SH: No. I wouldn't say that. I mean, he's my
brother. I just don't know him. And he
never, you know, tried to get to know me
either. We just steered clear of each other,
when he came back. We were used to steering
clear of each other.

TM: What about when he went missing?

SH: What about it?

TM: How did you feel?

SH: Well, I saw him. You know, that night? At
the party? I was the last one to see him.

TM: This is the Wallaby Drive party? The
Lambert house?

SH: Right. So I told Mum and Dad and they
were all like, 'What? A party?' And I was

like, 'Yeah'. I actually thought it was
pretty cool he came to the party. I mean, I
never thought he would. It took some balls,
with his reputation.

TM: What time did he get there?

SH: It was about eleven when I saw him, I
think.

TM: And how was he?

SH: Alone, as usual. He said he was looking
for someone. I think we can all guess who
that was. And he was drunk, I think. They
made a big deal about that. The drinking.
Because he's not meant to drink, you know, on
his meds. But I didn't think it could hurt.
I mean, he's got to get drunk sometime,
right? He's a teenager, for god's sake.
That's what he's supposed to do.

TM: Did you speak to him at the party?

SH: I told him to go home. I felt bad about
that afterwards, but what was I supposed to
do? I thought he was going to get himself
beaten up.

TM: And that was the last you saw of him?

SH: Yeah.

TM: You didn't see him take the knife?

SH: I didn't see him take anything.

TM: And what about the accusations?

SH: What about them?

TM: Do you think he's guilty?

SH: No.

TM: How come?

SH: Well, I mean, I guess he is. But not like properly guilty. It's a disease, right? How can he be guilty of a disease? If you're looking for someone to blame, you should blame us.

TM: 'Us'?

SH: All of us. We should have been keeping an eye on him. We should have been dealing with it. Instead we were ignoring him. Hoping it'd all just go away. That's what I was doing, at the party.

TM: It's wrong to blame yourself.

SH: Yeah, right.

TM: I'm serious.

SH: Well I blame the disease, then. I blame the pills. Whatever.

TM: Just don't blame yourself. You're too young for that kind of guilt. It eats you up, that kind of guilt.

SH: Right.

TM: You've done nothing wrong.

SH: Whatever.

TM: I promise.

SH: Can I go now?

I haven't been to the library since Monday. At breaks I sit on the steps behind the technology block. I ball into my warm-position. Nobody ever goes back there.

Today I watched the rain out over the field, dissolving the last of the snow. My mind must have wandered because I didn't hear the bell and ended up late to third lesson.

Third lesson was also last lesson, with it being the last day of term. We had English Lit. As I arrived Miss Hayes was waiting in the corridor. She was soaked from the rain, her bra showing through her blouse again. She told me she was sorry for being so rude the other day. She said I could stay behind after English, we could talk. I nodded. She clutched my arm. Her hand was cold and wet and she was wearing her engagement ring and it had turned on her finger so its diamond stabbed into my wrist. She told me she really was sorry. I nodded again, then pulled away and hurried inside.

The class silenced as I entered. They watched me cross the room to my desk at the back. Only half of them were present

– a typical turnout for the last day of term. Most had abandoned the seating plan and were sitting with friends. A gang of Vultures were gathered in the corner: Lucy Marlowe, Carly Meadows, a few others. They'd formed a circle with their chairs and were whispering amongst themselves.

Miss Hayes kept her head down as she entered. She avoided eye contact with Lucy and the Vultures. She also avoided my corner – she was probably scared of seeing Ian and Goose there, grinning from the back of the room, but they never come in for half-days. I took my copy of *An Inspector Calls* from my bag. Nobody else had taken their copy of *An Inspector Calls* from their bags except for Eggy and Dan Bradey. Eggy and Dan Bradey always have their copies of *An Inspector Calls* out well in advance so they can get a head start with the reading. They like to make notes and ask Miss Hayes questions about Priestley's socialist principles. They're going to Oxbridge.

Miss Hayes sat at her desk. She glanced over at the door, or perhaps the clock above it, awaiting any latecomers. By 11:30 no one else had arrived so she began to read.

Miss Hayes was quiet today. She stumbled on words and had to repeat them. She kept her eyes on the page, not once adopting any character voices. There were twenty pages remaining of *An Inspector Calls*. We'd reached the climax, where Inspector Goole shouts at all the other characters for being so nasty to Eva Smith. On paper the speech is strong and passionate and Miss Hayes' mumbling didn't really do it justice. Most of the class were sleeping or watching raindrops snake the windows. Sam Johnson was picking shards of soil from his trousers. The Vultures were whispering in their corner. The only people paying attention were Eggy and Dan Bradey.

I tried to concentrate on *An Inspector Calls* but my mind kept drifting. I kept thinking of you, that image of you, cross-legged in the library with Goose and Ian and Angela. I tried to remember happier times – our bus rides, under the bridge, the time you spoke to me in the street – but all I saw was Goose, leering at you in the Poetry aisle. The flare of your cigarette in vinyl-black lenses. Ian and Angela's wet-sucking kisses. Miss Hayes' voice was breaking. I glanced up at first but soon learnt to keep my head down. I couldn't stand it, watching her. Her hair was still wet and it might have just been the rainwater lining her face, but it looked like she was crying. Carly Meadows soon noticed and muttered to the other Vultures. Lucy snorted, stifling a laugh. Miss Hayes just ignored them, carried on reading.

I followed her reading in my book. I underlined each word with my finger as she read it. I thought that maybe if I showed Miss Hayes how much I was concentrating, she'd realise that she was doing a good job and become a more confident reader. It was just as Goole's speech was ending, just as she stopped to turn the page, that I glanced up at Miss Hayes again and noticed one of **Them**, at the front of the class, descending from the ceiling above her.

I haven't had many attacks at school. There was the time in P.E. with the one of **Them** in my trainer and the time I felt a web brush my face in the stationery cupboard but apart from that school's been relatively fit-free. In the winter they tend to inhabit warm places (i.e. the Great Influx) and – with its high ceilings and un-double-glazed windows and constantly left-open double doors – Skipdale High isn't exactly warm.

Today was different. Today one had crept into English Lit and was hanging there, right at the front of the class. At first I didn't know how to react. It was so out of place, so alien, dangling there over Miss Hayes. It was its blackness that struck me – maybe it was just the contrast between it and the white-board behind it, but its blackness was almost a void, like a hole in the fabric of reality. The Vultures were still giggling in their corner. Sam Johnson was still de-soiling his trousers. Even Eggy and Dan Brady – who were both staring right at Miss Hayes, so it was clearly in their sightline – just carried on jotting notes in their copies of *An Inspector Calls*.

Miss Hayes kept on reading. Her words were just noise now, a slow hum to accompany the descent. Little by little it closed the gap between itself and her head. It drew to a stop, inches above her. It hung there for a second, rocking in the breeze, front legs twitching in anticipation. Then it dropped into her hair.

My fits tend to come in stages. First my body seizes up. The term 'frozen to the spot' is pretty accurate because the seizing has a coldness to it, as well as a prickliness that gathers at the base of my spine. Sound fades. Blood pulses. My head aches. It's often worse when I can't actually see the one of **Them**, when the one of **Them** is there one minute, then suddenly hidden from view. Like the one in Miss Hayes' hair.

I tried to fix my mind on the play but by then my copy of *An Inspector Calls* was shaking violently. I shut my eyes. I breathed. I followed Miss Hayes' words in my head. Word after word after word. The only other sounds were the hiss of the rain, the Vultures' occasional giggling. Then Miss Hayes stopped to clear her throat and I couldn't help but glance up at her again, couldn't help but notice it, creeping out across her forehead.

That's when Lucy and Carly Meadows turned to glare at me. Carly muttered something to Lucy and Lucy snorted and I realised I'd clenched my fists, ripping a handful of pages from my copy of *An Inspector Calls*. My breathing was fast and probably loud. I dropped the book and clutched the sides of my desk. Each time I closed my eyes I kept seeing you, sitting in the poetry aisle with Goose, only now it was Goose kissing you. Now it was yours and Goose's lips, popping and peeling. The one of **Them** crawled further down Miss Hayes' forehead. It slowed, struggling to clamber over her eyelashes before scurrying down the left side of her nose. The desk rattled from my trembling. Others were turning. Sam Johnson abandoned his mission to de-mud his trousers and just glared at me. Even Eggy and Dan Brady glanced over, muttering to each other, tutting. Miss Hayes just kept reading, reading and reading and reading, all those words that had long since lost all meaning, as it sat there, balanced upon her lip, bouncing to the rhythm of her speech. She stopped to turn the page and it finally disappeared, slipping out of sight into her open mouth.

I must have toppled my desk when I bolted because there was a sudden scraping and a clattering and my copy of *An Inspector Calls* skated out across the classroom floor. Somebody laughed. One of the Vultures screeched the word 'Psycho'. I ran down the echoing corridor of the Lipton Building. I ran out across the field. I kept running, through the gap in the hedge and up the dual carriageway. The rain fell in sheets, drowning the world around me. A river cascaded the pavement. When I reached the relative dryness of the bus stop I just sat, hugging myself into my warm-position.

I threw up. It was phlegm, mostly, plus a couple of raisins from breakfast. I felt better after that. I sat, shivered, watched the rain wash the phlegm away. The whole time I sat there I half expected to see Miss Hayes, skittering up the carriageway after me. But she never came.

At 12:02 the bus pulled up and I climbed on board. I took my seat at the back. I concentrated on the view, the rainy blur of the Social De-cline, the ever-rusting bridges that pre-empt the Pitt.

The church sign said:

## WHAT IS MISSING FROM 'CH CH'?
## U R

I got off at our usual stop. By then the rain had slowed to a spit. There was a mound of snow still out on the corner by the church, an apple rotting on the pavement. The remains of the Pitt kids' mountain of a snowman.

I hurried round to the park. I crossed the field to the houses at the back. I just needed to see you. Alone. Without Goose and Ian and Angela. I needed it to be just the two of us. Like before.

I counted the gardens till I reached yours. I was halfway through the hedge when a shout came from the play area. It didn't sound like any human shout – more like the angered cry of some prehistoric animal. I turned back to the field.

There was a gang of four Pitt kids perched on the bars of the climbing frame, glaring over at me from under their hoods. It reminded me of that scene from *The Birds*, where Melanie Daniels turns and sees all those crows gaping down at her.

Then, one by one, they slid from the bars, crossing the park towards me.

The leader was your brother. I could tell from that walk of his – the way he bows his head, fixes his glare, lets his arms just hang there by his sides. I should have run as soon as I saw him, I realised that, but in no time he and his friends had surrounded me and it was clear I was going nowhere.

I'd interrupted your brother mid-smoke and for a minute he just stood there, savouring the last few drags of his cigarette. The other Pitt kids waited either side, grinning to each other. One of them tossed a football from one hand to the other. Your brother flicked his cigarette into the hedge and bent down to exhale in my face. His deodorant was strong, sour in my throat.

'What do you think you're doing?'

It seemed a strange question at the time. My mind had blanked and I didn't really know what I was doing. I was in class listening to Miss Hayes reading and then suddenly I was out in the Pitt. There was no logical explanation. All I could do was stand there, trying to mouth words, but what those words were I've no idea. The other Pitt kids were still grinning but your brother's face seemed locked into a frown.

'I'll ask again,' he said, slowly. 'What the fuck are you doing sniffing round my garden?'

His eyes bore into me, the same glittering blue as yours. I

tried to concentrate on my breathing, the trembling in my ever-weakening legs. All I could think about was the time with the Tango. I'd have loved for one of them to pour Tango over me. I kept thinking 'Just pour Tango over me and leave. Just pour Tango on me and leave.'

Your brother turned to one of the Pitt kids, the one with the football. He muttered something into his ear. The Pitt kid laughed and nodded. Your brother turned back to me.

He smiled.

He lifted his hand from the pocket of his hoodie. I expected a knife or a broken bottle but there were only his fingers. His hand was bunched into a fist with his index and his middle finger pointing towards me like a gun. He turned his hand and spread the fingers into a V, so he was swearing at me. His mates giggled. My stomach quaked. Maybe that was it – he was just going to swear at me. All things considered it wasn't that bad.

Then he pressed his fingers into my eyes. I backed as far as I could into the hedge, so far that the branches were stabbing into my neck, but your brother just kept on pushing. Deeper and deeper and deeper and deeper. He hooked his thumb under my chin, grasping my head like a bowling ball.

At first the pain was sharp and stinging but the longer and harder he forced his fingers the more it swelled into a deep, brain-splitting ache. I clutched the branches of the hedge, thorny against my palms. The soft skin of my burn-wound throbbed. The warm wetness of what I hoped were tears ran down my cheeks.

The Pitt kids laughed.

Somewhere a dog barked.

Your brother hissed into my ear. I can't remember the exact words but it was the usual kind of stuff. He called me a psycho and told me I shouldn't be snooping round people's gardens and said that if I ever came back he'd more than blind me. He pressed harder and harder, in keeping with the rage in his voice. A pressure built in my forehead. Any moment my eyes would burst like ripe tomatoes. His fingers would split through into my skull.

Such is the danger of being noticed. I should have checked the field first. It was stupid not to. I would pay for my stupidity. Your brother would blind me, out in Crossgrove Park, the park I used to play in as a child. The park Nan used to take me to, to look for conkers. He would blind me and I would never see your face again. This is what I thought as I sank down into your hedge.

Only then, a voice came. It said, 'What do you think you're doing?' just like your brother's had, only softer. And I knew instantly it was you.

The pressure eased then, the fingers withdrew. I slipped down to the ground. I pressed the heels of my hands into my eyes, trying to rub out the pain. All I could see were purple and yellow shapes, swooping and popping like fireworks. I really wanted to get up and look like I was OK. But I wasn't OK.

You told your brother to leave me alone.

Laughter.

You said, 'I mean it, Sean.' You talked about whiskey, about how your brother had taken some from the shed, how you'd tell your father. You said you'd tell him about the smoking, too.

'You know what he'll do if he finds you've been smoking.'

Seconds passed. Raindrops rattled in the hedge around me.

The warmth of your brother at my cheek:

'Next time, mate . . .'

And then he was gone. The patting of feet grew distant over the field. All that remained was clean cold air.

'You OK?' you said.

I nodded. It was hard to tell how powerful a nod without being able to see. I added a 'Yes.'

'I don't think you are.'

I tried to stand up but it was hard to know which way up was, I had no idea which direction I was facing. I clutched the hedge for support but its leaves were wet and I slipped and scratched my face on a branch.

'You're definitely not OK,' you said. 'Come here.'

Your hands were small and cold in mine. You were stronger

than I expected – in seconds I was hoisted from the hedge, dragged forward till my feet found the ground. I brushed the leaves from my hair.

'It's me, Alice,' you said. 'We've met before. Remember?'

I nodded, this time it was a big nod, to be sure you saw it. My legs were still shaking. Traffic hummed from the dual carriageway in the distance. It couldn't be real. You couldn't be there, before me. I decided I wouldn't believe it till I'd seen it, till I'd seen you. I tried to open my eyes but everything was a bright blinding white.

'Come on.' You took hold of the sleeve of my coat. You dragged me out across the field. You must have been running because I stumbled to keep up. The grass was boggy and soon my socks were soaked. Somewhere along the way I'd lost my school bag, but it didn't seem to matter.

We stopped. Your hands pressed into my shoulders. You told me to sit. You guided me onto a hard, swaying seat. When I lifted my hands and found the chains I realised it was a swing. We'd reached the play area.

'Just sit here a minute,' you said.

'I'm blind,' I said.

'You're not blind,' you said, 'trust me. Just give it a minute.'

I gave it a minute. The rain had stopped. Somewhere to my right there was a panting sound.

'How many fingers am I holding up?'

I opened my eyes. The world was still a flash of stinging white.

'Three?'

'No. You're right. You must be blind.'

I couldn't see if you were smiling. I lowered my hands to my lap. Something warm slid over my fingers. I jerked.

'That's just Scraps,' you said. 'He's harmless.'

I reached and found Scraps' head. I could feel every notch and socket of his skull. You told me that he doesn't usually like strangers. I must be special. I waited another couple of minutes before opening my eyes again. This time the grass and the sky and the rows of houses were there, only caught in a bright swirling mass of colour.

I shut my eyes again.

'Better?'

I nodded.

I waited another few minutes. I could smell smoke, that sweet chipotle smoke I'd smelt in the library. You must have seen me sniffing because all of a sudden you said, 'Do you want some?' Before I'd even had a chance to say, 'No thank you,' the paper tip of a cigarette was stuck to my lips and you were saying, 'Go on, just try it – breathe it in – it'll relax you.' So I did. I took a short sharp mouthful. It caught in my throat and I coughed, so much I nearly lost my balance. I had to clutch the chains of the swing.

You snorted, trying to hide your laughter.

'Try again.'

This time I inhaled slowly. You said to hold the smoke in my chest. As I breathed out I felt a lightness crawl up through me. I opened my eyes. I could see the outline of the world around us – the park, the houses, the slide. You. The sky was bright and at first I had to squint. You said, 'Here,' and slid your sunglasses over my eyes. The world was tinted pink but it was there and in its right place and so were you, smiling from the swing beside me. You were wearing that coat you sometimes wear for school, the one with the red fur trim. You were squinting now. I realised what it was then, from that close up, what was so strange about your un-sunglassed eyes. I noticed for the first time that you don't have any eyelashes.

You lifted the cigarette to your mouth.

'Look,' you murmured. 'You're meant to hold it in your lungs. Right? I'll show you the proper way. You ready?'

You placed the cigarette to your lips and closed your eyes. The end flared, your neck flexed. You opened your mouth into an O. The faintest wisp of smoke spilt out into the air, just for a second, before you sucked it back down inside. And then time stopped. You froze. You didn't breathe. Your mouth remained O. Your eyes were shut, so pale and naked without their lashes. Slowly smoke reappeared, crawling from inside you, out into the air around us.

You smiled.

'See?'

I scanned the park. You told me to relax. You said your brother's an asshole, he'd be off playing on the railway line by now. My coat-sleeve was muddy and my hands were scratched from the hedge. My palm was bleeding again, that burn from your cigarette that just won't heal. I was shivering. Scraps bounded off across the field, chasing a flock of pigeons. They scattered into the air.

You passed me the cigarette and I took a drag. It was easier the second time but there was no way I could hold it inside for as long as you had. After less than a second it all came spluttering out.

I remembered I was still wearing your sunglasses and apologised and passed them to you. You slipped them on.

You said, 'You probably think it's pretty weird, me always wearing these . . .'

I shook my head.

'Everyone does. They call me "Miss Cool".'

'You look like Audrey Hepburn,' I said, 'in *Breakfast at Tiffany's*.'

You said you hadn't seen it.

'You have to.'

But by then you'd stopped listening. You were frowning. I couldn't tell what you were frowning at because you were wearing your sunglasses. You leant forward, towards me. You reached for my eyes, just as your brother had, only this time I didn't flinch or back away. I pressed my feet into the grass to stop the rocking of the swing. You stroked the underside of my eyelid and gently withdrew your hand. There was a single eyelash curled over your fingertip.

You held it out to me.

'Make a wish,' you said.

I didn't know what you were saying. I was too busy staring, my reflection staring back from the lenses of your sunglasses. You were still frowning.

'You have to blow and make a wish,' you said. 'Each of your eyelashes is a wish. Don't you know that?'

So I did as you said. I closed my eyes and blew and when I opened them again your finger was bare. You put your hand back into your pocket. You turned from my gaze to scan the park, the backs of the houses.

You turned back to me, frowning again.

'I have to go.'

You picked up your bag and stood from the swing.

'Oh,' I said.

'I'll see you around.'

You hurried across the field to your house, your feet patting the wet grass. You reached the hedge and called out to Scraps before disappearing down the side of the shed. Scraps glanced back once and followed. I kept waiting for you to look back but you didn't.

I stubbed the cigarette out and stood to leave. It was only then that I noticed your father, staring down from your bedroom window.

## DATE UNKNOWN

So its the middle of the night and Im huddled in bed and from the weight of my head Im certain Im sleeping when suddenly a sound like taptaptap comes from the glass of my fireescape window and at first I try to ignore the sound try to keep my eyes shut try to pretend Im asleep but as the sound persists I cant help but wake cant help but sit up cant help but notice you out in the darkness your palm against the glass your breath white and shivering in the silver glaze of moonlight and at first Im confused and a little scared because it can be a little scary and confusing to wake in the night with someones face at the window but as you raise your hand and tap once more and fix those wideblue eyes upon me all my fear and confusion subsides and turns within my stomach and I see that smile that smile and all I want is to let you in to peel back that wall of doubleglazed glass between us and admit you into the safety of my room into the softwarmness of my bed however as I reach for my fireescape windowhandle I find the windowhandle hard and immovable and my fireescape window fixed and unopenable and lockeduptight and of course my fireescape window is lockeduptight my fireescape window has been lockeduptight for years my fireescape window has been lockeduptight ever since that incident with the paragliding oneof**THEM** and so as I scramble out of bed to my videoshelf to retrieve the windowkey from my *Brief Encounter* videocase to peel back the wall of doubleglazed glass between us and admit you into the softwarmness of my bed you can imagine my shock and horror to find the videocase completely sealed in a prettymuchimpenetrable layer of crinkled brown parceltape my frustration when I cant seem to be able find any kind of seam from which I can peel back the parceltape my desperation as the taptaptapping resumes and I glance up and see you there still with those eyes fixed upon mine still with that smile that smile and all I can do is tell you that Im sorry Im sorry but not to worry not to worry Ill soon have the videocase open Ill soon have the windowkey Ill soon peel back that wall of doubleglazed glass between us and admit you into the softwarmness of my bed and everything will be OK everything will be OK everythingwillbeOK but to be honest Im not entirely sure everything will be OK in fact Im not entirely sure you can even hear me because afterall the windows doubleglazed and Im speaking fairly quietly so as not to wake any of my family and your face isnt showing any sign of having heard me and is still fixed in that same vacant smile and small white

JAMES RICE

flakes of snow are now drifting through the darkness settling
on your hair your dressing gown the black rubber toes of your
Wellington boots and youre shivering and still tapping at the
window still waving and so when I do finally discover a seam
in the parceltape seal of the *Brief Encounter* videocase you can
imagine my relief as well as my urgency and frustration when
I set about peeling and peeling and peelingpeelingpeeling only
to find that there seems to be no end to the parceltape that
no matter how much I peel the parceltape just keeps on going
on and on layer after layer like some kind of passtheparcel
parceltape nightmare gathering in reams like an enormous parceltape snake coiled on my prettymuchimpenetrable bedroom
floor and so as another taptaptap comes from the glass of my
fireescape window I glance up and see that the snows coming
down heavy now your shivering growing into a shaking and
all I want with every ounce of my soul is to unlock that window
to peel back the glass to let the ovenwarmth of my bedroom
settle upon you to hold and hold and hold you in the softwarmness of my bed but no matter how much parceltape I
tear from my *Brief Encounter* videocase I just cant seem to
get inside to that key that tiny bit of metal Ive kept hidden
away for so long without ever thinking it would be so important and unobtainable and Im clawing at the parceltape now
and biting at it and Im sweating and my hands are sticking to
the hot wet plastic and your shaking is growing into more of

181

a rattling and your taptaptapping more of a knockknock-knocking on account of the layer of ice thats hardened over your knuckles and each time I look up at your everwhitening face youre still smiling with those everwhitening lips that smile that smile that smile and Im screaming now screaming for help from anyone who can help but theres not a sight nor sound from the rest of my family and Im trying to get the box open really I am but I cant get the box open I cant get it open and your face is frosting over like one of the pig heads in Hamptons freezer and Im smashing the *Brief Encounter* videocase against my videoshelf and Im hurling the case to the ground and stamping on it and Im on my knees clawing at it and finally as I claw through the plastic your banging halts your skin white as snow your hair frozen into solid curls of ice and as I tear back the broken box with my hot and bleeding fingers all I find is **THEM** hundreds of **THEM** thousands of **THEM** spilling from the shattered shards of plastic wriggling through my fingers spreading across my bedroom floor and

The shop was empty when I arrived. Charlie and the Vultures don't get there till 08:30 but your father and Phil are usually at their block first thing, slicing steaks for the counter. I checked the kitchen, the toilet, even the freezer at the back but there was no sign of anybody.

My first job was to empty last night's fat from the chicken oven. I dragged out the fat-tray, scraped the contents into the green plastic bucket and hauled it out the back to the bins. There was Phil, sitting on the steps in the alley, smoking, counting a wad of £20 notes. He scrambled to his feet, forcing the wad down the front of his jeans. He laughed when he realised it was me.

'Gave me a heart attack.'

I lifted the lid off the fat-bin. Phil said your father had gone to the abattoir to pick up the Christmas turkeys. I tipped the bucket. I had to turn from the smell as the fat glugged out, slapping and spreading a new surface. Phil scratched his neck. He glanced over at the empty car park. He kept one hand on the buckle at the front of his jeans.

'Do you know what happens to that?' He nodded at the fat. I glanced into the bin, then back to Phil. I shook my head.

'It's taken to the rendering plant,' he said, 'recycled. Used in glue and chemicals and stuff. Makeup, too. That's why when your bird wakes up in the morning she's always covered in spots – all the grease in the makeup.'

I shook the bucket, watching the last few lumps slip into the bin.

'Did you know that?'

I shook my head. I slid the lid back and turned to the shop. Phil was blocking the doorway.

He rubbed his chin.

'You won't tell anyone,' he said. 'About me being out here?'

I shook my head again.

He looked up to the sky. He clawed his neck with his nails. The fat-bucket was sticky. It smelt like rotten chicken. I wanted to go inside and wash my hands. Phil nodded, slowly. He smiled.

'Come on then,' he said, and turned and disappeared inside.

Phil kept his head down the rest of the morning. He didn't turn on the radio or send me to the bookies or even try to wind up Charlie. I hoped that's how the day would play out: Phil at his block, me in my kitchen, your father off at the abattoir. Next Saturday's Boxing Day and Hampton's is closed and I liked the prospect of going two whole weeks without seeing your father. Then, just as I dragged off my rubber gloves and turned to go to lunch, he appeared in the kitchen doorway. He wasn't smiling.

He told me to follow him.

There was a van out in the car park, backed up to the alleyway. Your father opened the doors to reveal stacks and stacks of turkey-crates. The turkeys were enormous, especially when you consider that lumpy white carcass is just the torso. Some of those turkey torsos were as big as yours.

'Grab a crate,' he said.

They were even heavier than I thought. As I lifted a pain ached, not just in my scarred palm this time, but all the way up my arms and neck to my forehead. Your father pointed out where to stack them, up on the shelves of the big empty freezer. The freezer was misty and layered with ice. I nearly slipped as I hoisted the first turkey-crate. Your father disappeared into the shop. He returned a few minutes later with Phil, leading him past me to the van outside.

I stepped out for another crate. Your father was rummaging through the glove box. He retrieved a bottle of mulled wine – a present from the guys at the abattoir. He poured two mugs and handed one to Phil and they leant against the van, drinking, watching as I shifted the turkey-crates. A couple of times a crate slipped and I had to catch it with my knee and your father told me to be careful not to dirty any turkeys. Hampton's customers had pre-ordered months in advance and each and every turkey was spoken for.

Phil chewed his lip. He tapped the side of his mug.

'Let's give him a hand, eh?' he said. He was shaking. Sweating. He must have been up all night delivering Christmas trees.

Your father said nothing.

'Ah, come on,' Phil said. 'It'll be quicker.' He placed his mug on the roof of the van and stooped to reach inside for a crate.

Your father didn't help. He probably could have lifted a crate on each shoulder, but instead he just leant against the wall, watching Phil and I struggle up the steps to the freezer. We had to stack the turkey-crates quite tightly to fit them inside, piling them as high as possible. Phil piled his to the left, I piled mine to the right. Slowly the two piles began to join.

We got a system going, taking it in turns to grab a crate from the van. It got to the point where Phil and I only passed each other in the doorway. Where, when I was stacking a crate in the freezer, he was fetching one from the van, and vice versa.

I was out in the van when I heard the screaming. It was a squealing sort of scream. Ear-stabbing. By the time I scrambled out into the alley your father had dropped his mug and disappeared inside.

For a few seconds it was hard to tell what was happening. The freezer was narrow and misty and Phil was thrashing about, fist in the air, blood lining the front of his apron. It was only when he fainted, his body hanging there like a passenger clutching the rail of the bus, that it became clear his arm was caught on a meat hook. Your father took his legs, lifted them over his shoulder. He hoisted Phil hook and all from the freezer and carried him out to the butcher's block. The hook had pierced the back of Phil's hand, its tip jutting from his wrist. Your father wrapped Phil's arm in an apron. Blood steamed from a pool in the freezer. It had trickled down the steps, curling round the grouting of the tiles. One of the Vultures stepped out the back to check what all the commotion was. She squealed, 'Eeeee!' and ran back to tell the others.

Your father told me to clean up. Wipe the turkeys and get them back in their crates. He carried Phil to his car and sped off down the carriageway. By the time I got to the blood it had frozen and I had to scrape it away with a knife. I transported the rest of the crates on my own. It took all afternoon. I kept having to stop, leaning against the van to catch my breath. At one point I leant too hard and Phil's mug of mulled wine toppled from the roof, bouncing from my shoulder and shattering in the alley. I shovelled the shards away and carried on shifting the turkeys.

When your father returned he went straight to his counter. I didn't ask about Phil and he didn't tell me. Without the radio all I could hear was the banging of his cleaver, the laughter of the Vultures out the front in the shop.

I tried my best to finish my cleaning early so I could leave before the Vultures' congregation in the coat cupboard, but transporting those turkeys put me behind all day. At 16:55 I still had a stack of chicken trays to clean. And chicken trays are the worst – all that baked-on fat. I have to boil the kettle and leave it to soak with detergent and T-Rex Bleach and even then (even through my rubber gloves) I still grate the skin from my fingertips. 17:00 came and went and the Vultures fixed their hair and set off into the cold and I was still scrubbing at chicken trays.

By the time I went out the front for my money it was 17:27. Your father was alone at the counter, sorting through piles of £20 notes. I picked up my envelope and headed for the door.

'You going to leave without saying merry Christmas?' your father asked.

He kept his head down, counting.

'Merry Christmas.' I tried the door. It was locked.

'You'll never guess what happened to my car last week.'

He slid a rubber band round a wad of twenties. I tried to say, 'What?' but all that came out was an unrecognisable grunt.

'Some son of a bitch smashed my tail light. Can you believe it?'

Your father looked up. He smiled. He stepped round the

counter and crossed the shop towards me. His trousers were still speckled with Phil's blood.

He stopped beside me, at the door. He stared down at me for a few seconds. The keys hung there on their chain on his belt but he didn't reach for them. Instead he leant forwards, took his large hand from his pocket and placed it on my head.

'I see things,' he said. 'You know?'

The tail of a dragon tattoo was curling out from the sleeve of his T-shirt. I tried to nod but he kept tight hold of my skull.

'I know you know what I'm talking about. I saw you. You know I saw you. From now on you keep away from her. OK?'

I swallowed. I was about to say, 'OK,' when he nodded my head with his hand.

'She's very special. Too special for you. OK?'

Nod.

'I know you have your problems, but Ken gave you the job here to try to help you. To normalise you. Not so you could go sniffing round your boss's daughter. She is out of bounds. Otherwise you become my problem. OK?'

Nod.

'I find out you've been near her again, that's it. There is no second warning.'

He kept hold of my head a few seconds longer. I thought maybe he was going to pop it, like a watermelon, but the pressure eased and he let me go. I glanced over at the selection of turkeys, hanging in the window. The clock behind the counter said 17:30. Your father turned to it and grinned.

'Your mam'll be worried about you,' he said. 'Best run on home, eh?'

He patted me on the shoulder.

'You're all right really, aren't you?' he said. 'We're all right?'

I nodded on my own this time. My neck ached from his grip. He told me I was all right a few more times as he unhooked the keys from his belt. He unlocked the door and held it open. I stepped out into the darkness.

'Oh, and kid . . . ?' he said.

I turned back. He took out his wallet and removed a £20 note. He held it out to me.

'Merry Christmas.'

I swallowed.

'Go on,' he said. 'Merry Christmas.'

I took the £20 note and scrunched it in my pocket. I hurried away. I kept expecting him to call out again but he didn't. As I turned from the square I heard the bolt of the door.

When I reached Green Avenue I turned back one last time. I could still see his shape in the window, his head amongst the raw hanging turkeys.

Today started like today starts every year, with the creak of the door and the click of the light switch and Mum's grinning face: 'It's Christmas!' She sat a glass of orange juice on my bedside table and told me I'd best come downstairs: 'Santa's been!' With that she was gone, off to wake the others.

I went down to the lounge. My father was there, perched on the edge of the couch. He too was clutching a glass of orange juice. He was wearing the Ted Baker ensemble Mum bought him last year: light brown trousers, green V-neck sweater. He smelt of aftershave. Mum buys us new clothes and aftershave every Christmas but my father always makes the mistake of getting dressed and applying his aftershave before we open our presents, then has to get rewashed and redressed afterwards. In the centre of the carpet was an enormous pile of presents, neatly wrapped in white paper. Usually we store presents at the foot of the Christmas tree but this year the foot of the Christmas tree is nailed to the lounge ceiling. I took a moment deciding whether to sit beside my father on the couch, before Mum appeared behind me.

'Don't you want to sit on the floor?' she said. 'With the presents?'

I told her I couldn't sit on the floor. I had to always sit on a couch, with my feet up. Because of **Them**. Remember?

'Fine. That's fine. Sit, sit. Make yourself comfortable.'

My father slid up to make room for me. Mum lingered for a few seconds, watching as I lifted my feet to sit cross-legged.

'Just please be careful.'

Mum disappeared upstairs then, to try to wake Sarah again. I took a sip of orange. My father chewed the inside of his cheek. Mum mumbled from Sarah's room. The mumbling faded for a few seconds then started up again. Then Sarah screamed, 'Just fuck off and leave me alone,' and Mum retreated back downstairs. She stopped and smiled in the doorway before taking a seat between me and my father. The upside-down Christmas tree hung between us like a giant twinkling drill about to bore into the centre of the carpet. My father took a sip of his orange juice and from the bubbles I realised that his wasn't actually orange juice at all, but Buck's fizz, which is like orange juice only fizzed with champagne. I'm not allowed Buck's fizz because of my medication. I don't mind so much because I tried a sip once and Buck's fizz is disgusting.

Eventually Sarah limped down to the lounge and we were

able to start unwrapping presents. Mum goes a little overboard at Christmas so everyone had several presents to unwrap. My main present was a DVD player. Mum said she knew I liked watching films and it was about time I caught up with the twenty-first century. I don't actually own any DVDs, but I didn't mention this to Mum because it was still a very thoughtful gift. My other presents were the usual: aftershave, trousers, a grey Armani jumper. I folded the jumper and trousers and placed them on the floor beside me and Mum knelt and refolded them, smiling and muttering something indistinguishable. Mum had bought my father a new aftershave/trousers/jumper set too and he moaned, 'I'll have to go and get changed now,' in a fake-angry sort of way. He'd bought Mum chocolates and some new cleaning fluids for the couch. Apparently they were very expensive.

I handed out my presents. I'd tried my best to find lounge-colour-scheme-matching wrapping paper but the best I could manage was white with a scattered array of *Winnie-the-Pooh* characters. It didn't seem to matter: Mum tore the paper to shreds before it even had a chance to register. I'd bought her a box set of Elvis Presley CDs and as soon as she saw his black and white grin she gasped and told everyone to stop unwrapping while she put some music on. My father was next to open his present – a bottle of Scotch and a poster of Marilyn Monroe. I told him Marilyn Monroe was the Pamela Anderson of her day. He nodded and chewed the inside of his cheek. One

Christmas my father chewed his cheek so much he bled, spotting his new Ralph Lauren shirt with red stains. Mum used to say he'd one day chew a hole right through and end up with two mouths, but Mum never says that any more.

Sarah was the last to open presents. She had to be coaxed a little by Mum, who was rubbing her arm and whispering, 'Come on, your turn, love.' Sarah's been practising extra hard these past few weeks. Since the allegations against Cullman the Christmas Dance Fantastical's been delayed and so now Sarah has to keep practising right through till the twenty-eighth. Sarah placed her Buck's fizz on the floor and slowly peeled back the paper of her main gift: a crate of Hi-Wizz Vitamin Energy Shake. She nodded (a crate of Hi-Wizz Vitamin Energy Shake was what she'd asked for). She also received the usual makeup and pyjamas and perfume. What Sarah really wants is breast enhancement surgery but Mum says she's not allowed to until she's at least in her twenties. Apparently Mum was in her twenties when she first got her breasts enhanced. Sarah says that's not fair because there are girls in school (e.g. Lucy Marlowe) who've had the op., but Mum's word is final. I bought Sarah *Singin' in the Rain* because there's lots of great dancing in it. Sarah muttered that she didn't know we were buying each other presents this year.

By the time we'd finished it was getting light. Sarah disappeared upstairs to bed, my father to his study, Mum to the kitchen to prepare Christmas dinner. I sat on the dining-room window seat and watched her rubbing oil onto the turkey carcass. Occasionally my father ventured out of his study for some nuts or a mince pie. He opened the bottle of Scotch I'd bought him. Mum gave him a glance of The Eyebrow but my father just smiled and said, 'It's Christmas, you can start early at Christmas,' rummaging through the cupboard for a glass. He poured. He asked Mum if she wanted him to drive. She didn't reply.

'If you want me to drive I won't drink,' he said.

Mum washed her hands. She lifted a bowl of stuffing from the fridge and tipped it onto the chopping board. She shook her head.

'OK.' My father knocked back the drink, poured another and disappeared back into his study.

Once dinner was in the oven we left for Golden Pines. Mum drove. It was starting to rain. I thought Mum might have brought her Elvis CD to listen to on the way but she didn't and we listened to the rain instead.

Halfway down the Social De-cline my father got bored of listening to the rain and switched on the radio. Sarah's dance song was playing. Apparently it's called 'Screemin Boi' by someone called Miss X. According to the radio it's the Christmas number one. It thudded from the speakers the whole way out to the Pitt but Sarah didn't once try and dance. She just watched the passing cars, the rain on the windows.

Mum exited the carriageway by the industrial estate, taking the back roads through the Pitt. Mum always takes the back roads through the Pitt because it means she doesn't have to pass Kirk Lane or Ahmed's Boutique or the church or any of those old places. By the time we pulled into Golden Pines the rain was heavy. My father asked if Mum had her umbrella.

She shook her head.

'Guess we'll just have to run for it, then.'

The reception was empty. Mum stood for a while by the desk, staring at the 'Ring For Attention' bell. My father and Sarah sat on the couch. I stood beside Mum, counting the drips from my coat soaking into the carpet. The phone behind reception started to ring. It rang six times and stopped. Then it rang again. The receptionist stepped out. It was a different receptionist to the one at Nan's birthday. This one's badge said 'Evon'.

Evon led us past the TV room. The other old ladies were all together, slumped in various mismatched armchairs. A few were alone but most had family members gathered around them. Mum asked why Nan wasn't in the TV room. Evon said it hadn't been one of Nan's good days.

Nan was in bed. There was a nurse kneeling at her side, guiding her arm into a beige dressing gown. Nan's whole room was beige. There were beige curtains and beige walls. They'd tried to decorate it for Christmas, an assortment of tinsel-scraps and paper snowflake streamers hung round her window frame, but these only emphasised the beigeness. There was a small fibre-optic tree on the bedside table. Mum watched the pulse of its glow. She didn't look at Nan.

The nurse turned to us and said she was just getting Nan 'all cosy'. I recognised the nurse from last time. She was wearing a badge that said 'Jade' but I didn't recognise the name Jade so maybe it was a different nurse or maybe I just didn't read her name badge last time or maybe I've just forgotten the name Jade since then. It was a while back. Jade tied Nan's dressing gown in a double knot. She pressed her jaw closed. 'Don't want to go catching any flies,' she said.

There was a tray on Nan's knee and on the tray was a plate and on the plate was a Christmas dinner and on the Christmas dinner was a layer of gravy, long since congealed. Jade said it seemed Nan wasn't hungry. I'm not sure if Jade doesn't know about Nan's not eating, or was just being polite in not mentioning it. She lifted the tray from Nan's lap. The gravy wobbled like jelly. She wished us a merry Christmas and stepped out into the hall.

Mum sat on the chair beside Nan. She reached out and held her hand for a second, then held her own hands together on her lap. There were several tubes draped over the headboard, connecting Nan's arm to a hooked-up bag of clear liquid in the corner. Sarah sat at the end of the bed, next to the bump of Nan's toes. My father stepped over to stare out of the window. The rain hissed out in the car park, drumming the roofs of the cars.

'Hi, Mum,' Mum said.

Nan stared straight ahead. Her face was more skeleton-like than ever. It still had that thin layer of ultra-fine, white hair I could never stop staring at as a child. The tray had left a rectangle of flattened duvet on her lap. A metallic tap-tap-tap came from the corner as Sarah began to nod along to her earphones.

'We brought you some cake.' Mum took a wad of silver foil out of her bag and placed it on Nan's dressing table. She peeled it open to reveal a slice of Christmas cake.

Nan didn't acknowledge the cake. She was staring at the cross above the door. That's what she does when we visit – stares at the cross above the door. My father used to say it's because she's cross. He used to say, 'She's cross, that's what she's trying to tell us. She's cross.' He doesn't say that any more. He just stares out of the window. He stares out of the window and Nan stares at the cross and Mum stares at her hands and Sarah stares at her iPod and I don't know where to stare. Usually I stare at Nan's feet, the bump they make in the bed sheets. Today her big toe was sticking out from under the blanket. Her toenail was longer than I've ever seen it. Whose job is it to cut her toenails? Jade's? Evon's?

Ours?

'Merry Christmas, Mum,' Mum said.

Nan stared at the cross.

'Have you had a nice day?'

Nan stared at the cross.

'We went to church this morning, the whole family. We really enjoyed it.'

Nan stared at the cross.

Last Christmas, as Nan was staring at her cross, she started mouthing a couple of words, over and over. It took us the whole visit to work out what she was mouthing. At first Mum though it was 'pyjamas' and told Nan she was already wearing pyjamas, but then my father realised it was 'praise Jesus'. He was made up when he realised – we all were. We couldn't stop smiling at how clever he was.

We all sat there, smiling, as Nan praised Jesus.

Nan didn't start with religion till Herb died. That was when she began to change. Mum said she'd have been better off dying beside him that night, but I don't know if that's true. Nan and I had some of our happiest times in those final couple of years. It was me who found her that afternoon. It was back when I was living with her. Nan was meant to be picking me up from school and I thought it odd, her not being there at the gate when we finished, but she always baked on Fridays and baking made her absentminded. It was only when I got back to the house and found the milk still on the step, the paper still in the letterbox, Mr Saunders pacing the porch, crying to be fed, that I knew there was something seriously wrong.

I went round to the alley and climbed over the wall into the yard. I got in through the kitchen window. There's a way to jiggle the lock so it falls right out. I called to Nan and she called right back to me and she sounded frightened, more frightened than I'd ever heard her.

I tried my best to lift Herb off the bed but he was so stiff and cold and unmovable. I phoned an ambulance. After that we waited. At first I sat on the floor. I told Nan about my day at school. This was during the Andrew Wilt period and I knew that the best way to take Nan's mind off things was to talk about our chess games. It was only when Nan started crying that I climbed into bed with her, forcing myself between her and Herb. She couldn't get over him, that was the problem. Her side of the bed was against the wall and Herb always slept on top of the duvet. Nan held me to her chest so I couldn't see her tears but I still felt them, running down the back of my neck.

Like that we waited for the ambulance.

By the time we arrived home the rain had stopped. Mum served the turkey. Nobody ate much. Mum picked but I didn't see her actually eat any. Each time she caught me looking she smiled and I smiled back and carried on eating, trying my best to finish as much as possible. She didn't ask if I'd taken my medication. At one point a piece of turkey slipped from my fork, splashing gravy onto my new Christmas jumper, but Mum didn't even look, she just kept smiling down at her plate. Elvis crooned from the living room. The Sampsons' inflatable Santa grinned from across the street. My father ate using only his right hand, his left hand cradling the rim of his Scotch glass. He stared at the tablecloth, at the spot where he'd usually place his inframammary infection photos. The only sound was the clinking of cutlery.

After dinner Sarah went to her bedroom. My father went to his study. It was just Mum and I sitting in the lounge, at opposite ends of the couch. We watched BBC News 24. The only news was that it was Christmas. They cut to a shot of a reporter, supposedly in the North Pole, supposedly interviewing the real Father Christmas.

I waited till Mum began to snore, then retrieved my coat and your present. I took some turkey, too, and a little leftover Christmas pudding, for Scraps, and headed off down the carriageway to the Pitt.

I stopped off at the canal on the way, to see the ducks. I figured people probably don't bother taking bread on Christmas Day and it's only fair that they eat too. I could give them Scraps' Christmas pudding. He wouldn't mind – he'd still have the turkey.

The canal had melted in the rain. It had formed those little white islands again. Only today the ducks were nowhere to be seen. I walked up and down for a full fifteen minutes but I couldn't find a single one of them. Then it struck me: the ducks have left. They've given up on Skipdale. They've flown south, where it's warmer. They've finally seen sense and got the hell out of here.

I followed the carriageway down the Social De-cline. I couldn't stop smiling about the ducks, the thought of them, off some-where warm. Pitt families go all out with Christmas decorations. The boarded-up houses were still in darkness but those inhab-ited were bright enough to compensate. There were flashing lights, nativity scenes, 'Santa Stop Here' signs. Five different houses had one of Artie Sampson's inflatable Father Christmases. Even your father had made the effort. The front of your house was lit by a string of electric-blue lights, pinned along the gutter. A nodding Rudolph grinned from his dashboard.

I crossed Crossgrove to your back hedge. I scanned the field for your brother but he was nowhere to be seen. I slipped in through the hedge gap. I took the turkey from my pocket. It was only as I knelt to the missing-plank gap that I realised Scraps was missing, his chain lying limp on the shed floor. Your living room was brighter than usual due to the Christmas tree, twinkling its various light-sequences. Scraps was laid out in front of the fire. You were kneeling beside him, rubbing his belly. Your father was on the couch in his usual position, sipping from what looked like (though from a distance it was hard to verify) a snowman-shaped mug.

I crawled up into the shed anyway. Where else would I go? It was especially cold tonight – Scraps must give off more heat than I gave him credit for. I dragged the toolkit over to the window and sat, forehead against the glass. You were wearing your dressing gown. Sunglasses. Your hair was tied up, covered in small squares of tinfoil. You were stroking the side of Scraps' head, eyes fixed on the TV. Your father had freed his hair from its ponytail. It flowed down the back of the couch, right to the floor. Occasionally you'd turn to your father and say something. Occasionally he'd turn back. Occasionally you'd both burst out laughing.

I hadn't expected this. You and your father and Scraps, together in the living room. Me, out here, alone. This was new.

After a while I began to sense **Them**. I could feel **Them**, glaring down from the tops of the shelves, the dark corners. I unhooked the nail gun and held it on my lap. It helped. I realised it wasn't fear I was feeling, it was anger. There was an anger in me. I don't know if I was angry at you or your father or Scraps or **Them**, but the anger was there. This was also new.

I took the turkey and the Christmas pudding from my

pocket. I placed them over in Scraps' corner. I figured he'd find them, eventually. Then I took out your present: *Breakfast at Tiffany's*. I fixed the ribbon, brushed off a few scattered pudding crumbs. I tried to think of somewhere I could leave it for you, somewhere only you would go. I couldn't think of anywhere, so I just held it on my lap, next to the nail gun.

Soon I could hear **Them**. They hissed from the shelves at the back. I shut my eyes but I could still sense **Them**, crawling through the darkness. I held the nail gun out in front of me and squeezed the trigger. The gun jerked, cracking like a whip, spitting a glittering nail into the far wall of the shed. A warning shot. I fired again. The hissing ceased, the crack of the wood emphasising the silence.

I shot out a few more nails, just to be sure.

Then I placed my cheek against the glass. I concentrated on you. Nobody moved, neither you, nor your father, nor Scraps, nor I. I found that if I closed my left eye I couldn't even see your father. He'd disappear into the darkness. Gone in the blink of an eye. I kept my left eye shut for a while.

Then I must have shut my right eye.

I don't know how long I slept but next thing the door was creaking open, cracking as it struck the corner of the toolkit. Next thing someone was stoop-stumbling into the shed. From the snorting and grunting and the gagging whiskey smell, I knew it wasn't you.

My cheek was frozen to the glass, frosted by my breath. I knew the door must be partly obscuring me but to what extent I'd no idea. I was sure any second he would notice me, perched there in the corner. He creaked over to the back, where Scraps usually lies. As my eyes adjusted I noticed Scraps still inside the house, laid out in front of the fire. You were beside him, sleeping.

I peeled my cheek from the window, as quietly as possible. Your father was hunched, rummaging through the jars and rusted tins that layer the shed's shelves. He was grunting, shaking his head, hair dancing down his back. He dislodged a paint tin, which rolled across the floor, clinking against the toolkit between my knees.

There was a square patch of ceiling, silver-lit by moonlight. As your father rummaged one of **Them** scurried out, its shadow stretched limb-long. Your father gasped. He'd caught his arm on a nail in the wall. He examined the small patch of nails, plucked one from the wall and held it to the moonlight. I realised I was still clutching the nail gun. He dropped the nail and turned back to the shelves, reached to the back, dislodging something, a bottle, holding it up to the light to examine its quarter of amber liquid. He unscrewed the lid and sniffed its open neck.

Another one of **Them** crept out, joining the one of **Them** in the centre of the ceiling, their merging shadows creating a new, indefinable, stretched-out silhouette. Your father took a swig from his bottle. He swilled and he swallowed. He sighed. He took another swig. Another one of **Them** crawled out. Another. Another.

Then your father noticed something on the floor. He knelt, the old boards creaking with his weight. He lifted something and examined it in the moonlight. The piece of turkey I'd left for Scraps. He sniffed it, took another swig, never taking his eyes from the turkey. My shaking began to rattle the metal-flapped lid of the toolkit. I lifted the nail gun from my lap. I didn't know whether to aim at your father or at **Them**. All I could hear was their mass hissing.

More of **Them** were creeping from the shadows.

Your father took another swig.

I dropped the nail gun and scrambled to the door. The toolkit tipped, its contents spilling over the floorboards. Your father cried out, his bottle shattering as I leapt the stairs. I slipped on the grass, twisted my ankle. I stumbled down the side to the hedge and tore out across the field. It was raining. Your father shouted – slurred shouts, contradictory:

'Come back here, you little shit . . . You'd better run . . .'

I did run. I ran through the estate, up past the Rat and Dog. I ran till I reached the church, till my legs and my lungs couldn't take any more. I leant on the church wall. The rain was heavy. My ankle ached. I was shaking all over. Beads of rain dripped from the hood of my parka.

I breathed, slow deep breaths to keep the vomit down. After a few minutes my stomach had settled and the pounding in my head had stopped and I began to make out singing. It was hard to hear through the hiss of the rain, but it was there. Delicate. Choir-like. 'Silent Night'.

The church sign said:

## CHRISTMAS CHOIR SERVICE
## ALL WELCOME

Rain rippled the puddles around me. I hugged myself through my coat. Your father's words rang out over the choir music:

'You'd better run . . .'

And I knew he was right. We have to run. We have to leave, like the ducks. It's simple, really.

I waited for the song to finish, then limped back up to the carriageway. As I reached the canal bridge I checked my pocket and realised I'd left your present in the shed.

Sarah didn't go to bed last night. She danced right through till morning.

Thud – thud – thud – thud – thud – thud – thud – thud – thud – thud – thud.

At 05:32 I gave up trying to sleep and hobbled down to the kitchen. I ate a bowl of Waitrose Maple Triple Nut Muesli. I checked Mum's Colombian Supremo but there were only a few beans left so I microwaved a half-drunk mug from last night instead, being sure to wipe Mum's lipstick from the rim. I wanted to be alert for the Christmas Dance Fantastical. Sarah said everyone would be at the Christmas Dance Fantastical. This meant you would be at the Christmas Dance Fantastical. The coffee was very bitter. I added milk and sugar but it made little difference. Coffee's a taste that lingers.

Mum was at the foot of the couch, sprawled across the carpet. BBC News 24 looped the same old snow footage. The rolling news bar said: SNOW WARNING! . . . SNOW

TO RETURN WITHIN ONE WEEK! . . . The television was muted, the only sound the dull thud of Sarah's dancing. Occasionally she'd leap across her room and the upside-down Christmas tree would shudder, its baubles clinking above me.

I sat cross-legged on the couch, next to Mum's sleeping head. Sarah's music didn't cut out till 08:02. It ended mid-song, leaving a buzz of silence. Mum sat up and wiped her chin. She climbed to her feet, shuffled out to the kitchen and popped the lid from her coffee tin. She sighed. It was most likely Sarah who'd used all the beans, in her morning coffee-shots. The kettle hissed. There was the familiar rattle of the grinder and Mum returned with a steaming mug and perched on the couch beside me. She sipped.

The snow footage looped again and again. Kids still sliding down the hill on their bin bags. That green-hatted woman ever-slipping on the ice, never catching the wall as she fell, people passing by without ever stopping to help.

The rolling news bar said: . . . TEMPERATURES REACH RECORD LOW ACROSS EUROPE . . .

At 8:33 Sarah thundered down the stairs. She was wearing her Christmas Dance Fantastical leotard. She said she was late for dress rehearsal. Mum asked what time the Fantastical started and Sarah told her it was 19:30, like it said on the tickets. Mum told her to take a coat but Sarah said it was good to be cold, the colder she was the more she'd dance and the more she'd dance the more practice she'd get and after all practice makes perfect. She took a few bottles of Hi-Wizz Vitamin Energy Shake from the fridge and hurried out the door.

Soon after that the doorbell rang. It was Old Mrs Jenkins' niece, Gretna. Old Mrs Jenkins is dead. Another victim of the winter, Gretna said. Too much time in that draughty attic. Apparently Gretna comes over every year for Boxing Day supper and usually Mrs Jenkins hears her bike roaring from the dual carriageway and is waiting on the doorstep for her to arrive, but this year she was nowhere to be seen. She wouldn't even answer the doorbell. Apparently when Gretna peered in through the letterbox she fainted, right there on the doorstep. The smell just knocked her out. And Gretna's a big woman.

Mum went for a lie-down once Gretna had gone. Mrs Jenkins had been her first ever Skipdale customer, the one who'd first recommended her hairdressing skills. The two hadn't spoken for a couple of years now but Mum still had a soft spot for her. She didn't come down till dinnertime. We had turkey sandwiches. Mum laid out stuffing and cranberry and horse-radish in little bowls across the table but we both ate our sandwiches dry, with just a little salt and butter. I could tell she'd been crying but I didn't mention it.

19:30 came and went but my father never arrived home from work. Mum said we could always leave my father's ticket on the mantelpiece. He could catch us up if he wanted. If he had time.

We arrived at Skipdale High at 19:45. A group of sixth-formers manned the gates – high-visibility jackets, P.E. whistles bit between their teeth. They waved us over to a space in the corner of the field. It was a muddy patch and Mum had concerns about the BMW's paintwork but she parked up there anyway. We hurried across the field to the sports hall, as fast as Mum's heels would allow.

The hall was dark when we entered. Silent. Rows of parents stared up at the stage from a sea of plastic chairs. Mum scanned for empty seats but the room was packed. I searched amongst the crowd but it was impossible to find you in the darkness. There was a silence in the room that can only be described as The Calm Before the Storm.

The stage was T-shaped, a catwalk running out through the crowd. A spotlight flickered and there was Angela Hargrove, halfway up the catwalk, dressed as a scantily clad Christmas Fairy, perched upon a Christmas tree. (The tree was actually a stepladder with two green cardboard tree-shapes glued either side but in theatre you have to suspend your disbelief.) Angela welcomed everybody to this year's Christmas Dance Fantastical.

She said that this year Santa was going to bring a very special present for all the boys and girls of Skipdale High. (It's actually December the twenty-eighth but again: suspension of disbelief.) There was a group of sixth-formers in the corner of the hall, leaning against the monkey bars. Mum stared at each of them in turn but they were too busy glaring up at Angela to notice us. Then a dance remix of 'Santa Baby' kicked in and Angela skittered down the stepladder to the front of the catwalk-stage. Lights flashed. Six girls in C.D.F. leotards poured on from either side, strutting up the catwalk, circling Angela. It was hard to tell if any of the dancers was Sarah, they were all moving so quickly and the lights were flashing so dramatically. All I could make out was red Lycra and flesh.

'Santa Baby' ended. The audience applauded. Angela descended the catwalk, disappearing stage right. One of the sixth-formers noticed us and directed us to seats in separate corners of the back row. Mum mouthed that she'd meet me by the car after the show. Another song began, the six Vultures continuing their backing dance. I realised that none of them could be my sister because my sister's only part was during 'Screemin Boi', which was the grand finale.

I scanned the crowd again. In one particularly bright flash of light I noticed Ian, crouching stage left, glaring up at the dancers. In the next flash I saw you, sitting in the row behind. From then on I kept my eyes fixed on that point. Each time the spotlights crossed the catwalk I could just make you out, Goose beside you, whispering into your ear. You were smiling. Occasionally you were laughing.

There were themes to the Fantastical's various dances. Some were Christmas-related, others I think were popular songs, most of which I didn't recognise. The backing dancers all wore C.D.F. leotards but Angela Hargrove had a range of different costumes. 'Rudolph The Red-Nosed Reindeer' began and Angela took to the stage once again – fairy-lit antlers, diamanté-encrusted nose. Another monologue: this time about her red nose, her responsibilities to Santa, how the other reindeers never let her join in with their reindeer games. Ian was watching from the very edge of his seat. He was practically foaming at the mouth. You still had Goose at your ear, only now he'd put his arm round you. You weren't smiling any more.

Then the Rudolph remix kicked in and a swarm of dancers flooded the stage, the lights strobing on/off/on/off/on/off, transforming everything into a series of images, segmented by blackness: Angela dropping to the floor. BLACK. Angela, jerking her head back. BLACK. The swarm of backing dancers, pouring in behind her. BLACK. The backing dancers forming a line. BLACK. The backing dancers kicking their legs out. BLACK. Angela writhing across the floor, nose held high. BLACK. A sea of parents' faces, staring hang-mouthed at the stage. BLACK. Ian, grinning, straining to see up Angela's skirt from the side of the stage. BLACK. Goose, huddling close to you. BLACK. Goose, nuzzling your neck. BLACK. You, pushing Goose away. BLACK. Goose's tongue against your neck. BLACK.

You, standing.

BLACK.

You, pushing Goose down into his seat.

BLACK.

You, clutching your sunglassed eyes.

BLACK.

You, dragging your hood up over your head as you step through the crowd to a doorway, stage left.

BLACK.

And that's when I found myself standing, following. It was hard, crossing the hall in the strobing lights but at least with the dancing nobody seemed to notice me. I headed to the doorway, stage left.

The doorway led to the Lipton Building. The light was dim but constant, the Rudolph remix a dull hum.

The corridor was empty. I checked every classroom till I reached Miss Hayes' office at the end but you were nowhere to be seen.

I retraced my steps.

It was only when I'd lapped the corridor a third time that I noticed the caretaker's closet, the door slightly ajar.

I pressed my cheek to the wood. I shut my eyes. I could hear you breathing inside.

I considered going back to the hall, sitting across from Mum and waiting for the show to end. I considered going out to the car park, waiting it out with the BMW.

Then I opened the door.

There you were, huddled in the corner by the brooms, head in your hands.

'Fuck off,' you said.

I told you it was me, Greg. You shuffled a little, trying to block out the light with your folded arms.

'Oh,' you said. 'OK.'

You shuffled back a little further.

'Well, if you're going to come in, come in.'

I asked if you were OK.

'Just come in.'

I stepped inside. It was only a small closet and stepping inside meant my knees were right beside your face.

'Shut the door.'

I asked why.

'I can't deal with the light right now,' you said. 'Just shut the door.'

I shut the door. BLACK. I stood for a while. Then I crouched. I thought about sitting but there wasn't room, what with the piles of mop heads and bleach bottles behind me.

'It's just my eyes,' you said. 'The lights.'

I said it was OK.

I could feel your breath, warm against my arm. Here we were in the caretaker's closet, in darkness once again. I always seem to lose my sight when I'm with you. I wanted to ask about Goose. I wanted to ask about your father. I wanted to ask if you found your present. I wanted to tell you about Finners Island, about my plan for us to run away. But I didn't.

I don't know how long we stayed like that, you huddled there with me crouched over you. By the end my legs ached. Music hummed from the hall. I could make out the odd lyric of 'Screemin Boi'. Then it stopped. You didn't say anything, you just breathed. You sniffed a few times. Everything smelt of disinfectant.

Then suddenly you stood.

'I'd best get going,' you said.

I asked if you were OK again. I was aware of repeating myself.

'Just a migraine,' you said. 'Happens sometimes.'

Light flooded back into the room. You were standing in the doorway. You might have been staring at me. I don't know. You were wearing your sunglasses.

'Thanks for checking on me,' you said. 'I am OK. Honest.'

I nodded.

'I guess I'll see you at the party.'

I asked what party.

'Goose's party. New Year's.'

I said I hadn't been invited.

'Everyone's invited.'

I didn't know what to say to that so I just crouched there, staring up at you, not saying anything.

'Whatever,' you said. 'Might see you there.'

You turned, let the door shut.

BLACK.

It came again this morning, the rain. The steady hiss. The house has seemed so quiet since Sarah's rehearsals have finished and it was nice just to listen to it, battering the windows, gurgling over the brim of the gutter, spilling and slapping on the pavement out back.

Mum said it's supposed to rain at funerals. 'Washes all sins away.' She was fixing her fascinator in the dining-room mirror. She bought it especially – black lace, embroidered with tiny black roses. Across the road lay Artie Sampson's inflatable Santa, a crumpled red puddle on his path. At first Artie had tried to fix the gash with parcel tape, but each time he got it standing the tape'd peel and it'd bow again and Artie'd sink to his knees, clutching what's left of his hair. I considered telling him that duct tape would be a better idea (Nan and I would sometimes use duct tape on outdoor cracks, where parcel tape wasn't quite enough) but I knew Mum would kill me so I kept quiet. Since the rain came he's given up. Occasionally his face appears at the window, but that's it.

Mum asked if I was going to get ready. I told her I was ready. I was wearing my school blazer. It's the only black jacket I own. I unstitched the Skipdale badge so there's no way to tell it's a school blazer.

Mum gave me a glance of The Eyebrow.

'Wouldn't you rather wear your new Christmas clothes?' she said.

I told Mum my Christmas clothes are grey. Are you allowed to wear grey at a funeral?

Mum said grey was fine. She'd cut my hair last night, blow-dried it into a bowl, managing to keep all the curls down. She wanted me to look smart for once. Was that too much to ask?

Mum was in a good mood today. The past couple of days have been hard for her. I went over to Goose's on Monday, to stake out the place before the party, and when I got back Mum was in the car, crying, 'Suspicious Minds' roaring from the speakers. Artie Sampson's Father Christmas was half deflated over the road, still with Mum's hairdressing scissors jutting from its belly. It was only when the car battery died and Elvis cut out that she finally stumbled over to the house.

My father and I waited in the hall. For a full minute she just stood there, smiling from the doorway. My father asked if she was OK. She nodded. He asked if she'd like a cup of coffee. Again, she nodded.

'I'll make it,' she said.

She turned to lock the car. I don't know if it was the flat battery or that Mum was just pressing the wrong button on her key fob but it wouldn't lock. After four or five tries she dropped the keys on the porch floor. Two steps into the hallway she collapsed.

It turned out Mum had been to the Hamptons' that morning. Ursula bought the couch. The exact same white Italian leather couch. The exact same product number from the exact same catalogue. Apparently it looks fabulous in Ursula's living room, which is twice the size of our living room. It has more Wow Factor than Mum could ever dream of. It'll be the talk of the Hamptons' New Year's party.

My father chewed his cheek. He left Mum on the floor whilst he went to the kitchen for the coffee. There was no Colombian Supremo left so he had to use instant. He filled two mugs and brought them through to the hall. Then he knelt beside Mum, lifting her head, forcing her to sip from one of the mugs. Coffee ran down her chin, joining the trail of snot and mascara.

He told her it was OK. He told her he'd had a couple of new clients recently. He told Mum we could afford a little redecorating. She could start the room over again. She could decorate a brand new room if she wanted to. Whatever she thought best. Mum clutched the sleeves of his shirt. She sobbed into his lap. My father assured her that everything would be OK.

We left for the funeral at 15:40. The service was at St Mary's. Mum and I sat in the second row. There was only Gretna and her sister Molly in the first row but Mum said that's how it was meant to be, family only. There were others dotted around, old ladies mostly. Artie Sampson and his wife appeared, taking a pew at the back. They ignored us and we ignored them.

For the first five minutes the vicar spoke about Mrs Jenkins, about how she was a well-loved member of the community and a regular at the church and how concerned they all were when she stopped showing up for service. He said Mrs Jenkins had had a lot of tragedy in her life but she fought through it all. She was a fighter. Then he spoke about Jesus, about the tragedy Jesus had had in his life. He spoke about Jesus for about half an hour. Then the funeral ended.

It was still raining as we left. We ran to the car. I wasn't bothered about getting wet but Mum was worried about my hair and my Christmas clothes so I stooped under the umbrella with her. The spokes kept catching my scalp.

Mum said she didn't want to be the first to arrive at the wake so we waited in the car for a while, watching the rain. She switched on the CD player. I thought she was going to play 'Suspicious Minds' but instead she skipped to 'Are You

Lonesome Tonight?' She stared up at the church. I could tell she was thinking about Nan. Church always makes her think of Nan, that's why she never goes. We listened to the entire song, start to finish, twice, before she switched off the CD player and started the engine.

The wake was at the Prancing Horse. There was a table in the corner with a 'Reserved' sign and a buffet of finger sandwiches – ham, egg, cheese and pickle. Gretna was sitting at the table, chatting to two old ladies. Gretna's sister was standing at the buffet, peeling back the sandwiches to study their fillings.

Gretna waved us over. She said, 'Wasn't it a lovely service?' and Mum said, 'It was.' The old ladies smiled up at us. Gretna's sister returned from the buffet and Gretna introduced her as Molly. Molly invited us to help ourselves to a drink at the bar, there was a tab. The old ladies and Gretna and Molly were all drinking pineapple juice but Mum said we'd need something stronger. She ordered us both a cosmopolitan, which is a type of cocktail. I said maybe I shouldn't, what about my medication?

'Just one won't hurt,' she said.

We took two stools at the reserved table. At first Gretna asked about my age, my school, what I wanted to be when I grew up. Mum said I was very good at English and Gretna asked if I was going to be an English teacher and I nodded and smiled and sipped my cocktail. It tasted like cranberry juice.

For a while Gretna talked about her life on the road. She's a Heaven's Angel. The Heaven's Angels are a Christian biker gang. They travel the country, trying to recruit other Christian bikers. Gretna never said what would happen when they'd recruited enough Christian bikers. Molly was also a Heaven's Angel. They both had leather jackets hung over their chairs, a picture of a smiling Jesus stitched to the back. They held hands under the table. I couldn't help but doubt what Mum had said about them being sisters.

Mum ordered us two more cocktails, margaritas this time, which tasted like lime juice. Then Mum began to tell Gretna and Molly and the old ladies about the kitchen she's planning, how she's going to knock through the lounge and extend the back of the house to make room for it, how we're saving for an Aga cooker. She'll probably need planning permission and so Gretna might have to sign something at some point, 'But it's not going to be unsightly or anything, don't worry.' Gretna nodded and smiled and sipped her pineapple juice. I ate an egg sandwich. It was gritted with shell. I washed it down with more margarita.

I kept an eye out for you. I thought I might catch a glimpse of you in your Marigolds but I didn't. I'm not sure if you even work at the Prancing Horse any more. It didn't matter too much, tomorrow is Goose's party. Tomorrow we're going to run away together and I'll see you every day then. It's strange to think I'll probably never see Mum again. That's why I kept drinking those cocktails with her. Some of them were disgusting but I didn't want Mum to know that. I figured it was a good memory she could have of us. A good way to say goodbye.

The rain was heavy when we left, even heavier than it'd been all day. We planned to make a run for the car but as soon as we set off Mum tripped in her heels. She kicked them off and tucked them under her arm and the two of us sprinted across the car park. Mum squealed at the icy rain on her toes. I tried to protect her with the umbrella.

By the time we reached the car we were shivering. Mum set the air-con to HEAT, lifting her feet to the dashboard. There are floor heaters in the BMW but Mum doesn't know how to turn them on.

'That was pretty fun,' she said. 'For a funeral.'

We listened to 'Are You Lonesome Tonight?' again. Mum sang along. She started the engine and pulled out of the car park. It was dark by now. Even with the wipers on full it was hard to see through the blur of the rain. I put my seat belt on. Mum said she was going to make Singapore slings when we got home.

'Have you ever had a Singapore sling?'

I shook my head.

'They're fabulous.'

We pulled out of the square onto the dual carriageway. Mum

started to tell me about Singapore slings, how you shake everything up with the ice before serving, how you have to be careful
not to add club soda until after it's been shaken or else it
explodes all over the kitchen. We'd just passed the canal bridge
when we heard the squeal. The car bounced a little.

'What was that?'

I shrugged.

'The tyre?'

Mum frowned in the rear-view mirror. She pulled into the
bus stop and stared over her shoulder.

'What is that? Can you see that? In the road?'

I told Mum I couldn't see anything.

'Wait here.'

She opened the umbrella and stepped out into the rain. The
hazard lights clicked and flashed and clicked and flashed. Rain
hammered the windscreen. I closed my eyes.

Next thing Mum was back, knocking on my window.

'Greg,' she cried. 'Get out, Greg.'

I climbed out of the car. The rain washed over me. It flattened my hair. It soaked my sweater. It ran down the collar
of my shirt. I hunched, as if hunching would keep me dry. A
river of rain cascaded over the street, flashing red in the
hazard lights. A white feather floated by, disappearing under
the car.

Mum was standing in the middle of the carriageway. The

umbrella lay beside her, filling with rain. She was staring at a white fluffy ball in the road.

It was a mallard. Its neck was flattened, worms of what looked like mince smeared in all directions. One of its legs was pressed into the tarmac, the other flapping wildly in the rain.

'What is it?' Mum said.

I told her it was a duck.

'What the hell's it doing here?' she screamed. 'Out on its own? Don't they emigrate?'

I told her I thought they did. I thought they had.

'Should we kill it?'

I didn't know.

'We can't just drive off,' she said. 'We can't just leave it.'

The rain soaked through my jumper. It snaked my back, gathering at the lip of my boxers. My fringe was starting to curl. I was surprised how little blood there was, just feathers and meat.

Every few seconds the duck let out a squawk. It sounded like it was coughing.

'We've got to do something,' Mum said. 'What if I reversed over it?'

The rain lightened. Spitting. Its hiss died.

Everything went quiet.

'What do we do?'

**TRANSCRIPT**

Extract of interview between Detective
Sergeant Terrence Mansell (TM) and Gregory
Hall's mother, Mrs Deborah Hall (DH).


TM: Let's talk about Greg's condition.

DH: OK.

TM: He's schizophrenic.

DH: Apparently.

TM: You don't believe he is?

DH: Sometimes. Sometimes I'm not so sure.

TM: Why?

DH: That doctor, he . . . he just assumed
   that's what it is, straight off. That first
   time we saw him. And there's no proper test.
   It's not like they can ever know for sure. I
   . . . I don't know. It just seems too easy.

TM: Easy?

DH: It's like a cop-out. Like, an excuse for

the way he is, rather than an explanation.

TM: But his hallucinations? His episodes? This
would suggest schizophrenia?

DH: He sees things, yes. Things we can't see.
Sometimes I think he's making it up, but then
sometimes I think maybe he's just overreacting
because he's actually seen something, a cobweb
or something, and it's sent him into over-
drive. I don't know. I think maybe it's a bit
of both. He doesn't know, when he sees something, whether it's real or not. I mean, to
him it is real. I guess it doesn't matter.

TM: But that's what schizophrenia is, right?
Paranoia? False beliefs?

DH: I suppose.

TM: You're still unconvinced?

DH: There's no proper test. That's all I'm
saying.

TM: How old was he when he was diagnosed?

DH: Sarah was four at the time, so he must
have been, what, six or seven.

TM: That seems young.

DH: It is young. Very young. Dr Hughes said
it was the youngest he'd ever seen.

TM: But he was certain it was schizophrenia?

DH: He was determined. Mind you, almost everyone since has agreed. We have check-ups less regularly now, but at first we were going back every couple of months, not always to the same doctor. The only person who ever even considered another possibility, who ever considered Greg could be cured, was my psychiatrist, Dr Filburn.

TM: What about your husband? What does he think?

DH: I don't know. At first he thought Greg was just doing it for attention. Now, I don't know. You'd have to ask him.

TM: But he is a doctor?

DH: Not any more, he's a surgeon.

TM: But presumably he was? Presumably he went to medical school?

DH: Well, yes.

TM: And he didn't notice anything? Any signs? Before the diagnosis?

DH: I think he was hoping it was just a stage. I don't know. He was thinking that it was, you know, attention.

TM: It must have been hard.

DH: It is.

TM: Not just for Greg, but for you all.
There's quite a stigma.

DH: We kept it private. We keep ourselves to
ourselves. We're that sort of family.

TM: What was it that made you get him checked
out in the first place?

DH: It was Sarah. How he was with Sarah.

TM: They didn't get on?

DH: They got on fine, at first. He was fascinated
by her.

TM: In what way?

DH: Well, when we first brought her home he'd
stand at the end of the cot for ages,
staring at her. It was like he didn't
believe she was real. It was only when she
got older he started acting up.

TM: How?

DH: There were incidents.

TM: Like what?

DH: We found him in her room a couple of
times, at night.

TM: Doing what?

DH: Watching her. Crying.

TM: Crying?

DH: He said it was, you know, 'them'. He said

she had them all over her. This was the
first we heard about 'them'. To start with I
didn't know what the hell he was talking
about. By then she'd be crying too. This
was when she was about eighteen months and
he used to scare her, doing that. So I'd
lift her out of bed and I'd lift her
pyjamas up to show him how clean she was,
show him there was nothing there, nothing on
her, but it made no difference. He'd just
keep crying, telling me I had to help her.
Telling me I had to get them off her.

TM: So what did you do?

DH: I didn't know what to do. I wasn't
sleeping much. I was working at the salon
then. Howard was still planning the surgery,
so it was a stressful time. I was the one
who always had to get up in the night. But
I figured it was a stage, it'd pass.

TM: But it didn't pass.

DH: It got worse when she was about four.
That's when he started scratching at her.

TM: Scratching?

DH: Well, she had eczema. Really bad eczema.
She was always scratching, always covered in

scratches anyway, so we didn't know, at first, that he was doing it too. Then we were at the supermarket one day and I heard her screaming and turned round and she was cowering from him, and he was over her, standing over her, clawing at her. He was six so he was bigger, a lot stronger. He started saying it again, the same old stuff, that she had 'them' all over her. That he had to get them off.

TM: He thought they were something to do with her eczema?

DH: He'd muddled the two things in his mind somehow. He'd sit there watching her scratch, saying stuff like, 'Help her. Get them off her. They're all over her.' And I'd try and explain there was nothing there, but he wouldn't listen. They were real. To him they were real and that was that.

TM: So you took him to the doctor.

DH: Howard didn't want to. I don't know why. We never talked about it all that much, he just told me not to be dramatic. Told me it was just attention-seeking. He didn't witness it first hand, though, and it was hard to explain how . . . how horrific it was. How obvious it was that Greg really believed in them. Believed that they were real. Until Finners Island.

TM: Finners Island?

DH: That was when he crossed a line. When I decided to split them up.

TM: What happened?

DH: We don't know, exactly. [Sighs.] Look, I feel I'm giving the wrong impression. He's not . . . violent. He's a very peaceful person, very calm. It's just his condition. He can't seem to help it.

TM: What happened on Finners Island?

DH: He had some kind of episode. It was out on the water. Sarah always loved the boats . . .

TM: The boats?

DH: There were these boats you could go out to sea in. These little inflatable things. What are they called?

TM: Dinghies?

DH: Yeah, like rubber dinghies. Anyway, we wouldn't let her out in them because she was only four. But she really wanted to, she

kept going on about it. Then one morning
Howard and I went into the woods for a
walk. My parents were with us and they were
supposed to be watching the children.

TM: Are these the grandparents Greg went to
live with?

DH: Yeah. Don't get me wrong, they were
reliable, usually, and responsible. But
they were old, even then, especially Herb.
I think those holidays took a lot out of
them. Anyway, they must have both fallen
asleep or something because when we got
back the kids were gone. Mum and Herb were
frantic, obviously — we all were. We had
no idea where they'd gone.

TM: They'd gone out in a dinghy.

DH: Yeah. Though they weren't in the dinghy
any more by this point. I just saw this
splashing, something splashing out in the
water, and then Howard was gone, running out
across the beach like something from one of
his *Baywatch* videos.

TM: He saved them.

DH: He was the hero, yes. Sarah was unconscious

but Howard brought her round. He had to resuscitate her. That was the worst moment of my life, watching him do that. You know, that thing with the hands? The kiss of life? She was too young for all that. Her body was so small. It seemed absurd. It was only when we got back to the hotel we realised she was all scratched up. Greg was throwing up in the reception, into a bucket from this bucket-and-spade set we had. Sarah was bleeding quite a bit and it was obvious he'd been scratching at her. That he'd had some kind of episode, out in the boat.

TM: That's why you sent him off, to live with your parents.

DH: I had to be sure he wouldn't hurt Sarah. I had to protect her.

TM: That's understandable.

DH: I didn't want him to be away from us. I didn't want to only see him once a week. I just . . . I had no choice. I took him to the doctors. Got him diagnosed. Got him on medication.

TM: And did things improve?

DH: They seemed to. I don't know if it was the pills or the fact he was apart from Sarah, but he had fewer and fewer episodes. He'd talk about 'them' less. For years he was fine. Until he was about eleven.

TM: Then what happened?

DH: That was when my mother . . . she had a breakdown. It was after Herb died, she never really recovered from that. She got even more religious. We sometimes thought maybe she was . . . well, you know. If Greg is then there's no reason she couldn't be as well. They say it runs in families. And she was always big into church. That's a part of it, I think, the religion. Believing all that stuff, believing in imaginary people, right? Anyway, she got Greg's condition and her own all jumbled. She was trying to help him but she was making it worse, going on about 'them' all the time, taping up all the cracks in the house.

TM: The parcel tape?

DH: That was her, got him doing that. We had

to step in eventually. She was . . . we had to have her put in a home. Greg had to come back to the family.

TM: And how was he?

DH: Good. Well, as good as he ever was. He was still very quiet, but he was fine with Sarah. He rarely had any fits or anything, just the occasional episode. Maybe like once a year or something.

TM: You didn't know it had come back then, recently? That he was having problems again?

DH: No. I mean, there was an incident, a few weeks ago. He was sick in the house, at a dinner party. But I thought that was just one of these stand-alone episodes. I didn't know it meant anything. I didn't know he was going to do anything . . . like this.

[Pause.]

[DH starts crying.]

TM: We can have a break if you want.

DH: If I'd known, I would have done something. I would have.

TM: Do you need a minute?

DH: I'll be OK. I just . . . I'll be OK.

[Pause.]

TM: It's not your fault.

DH: Yes, I think I'd like a minute, actually.

TM: OK.

DH: Just a minute. I'll be fine in a minute.

# III

OK, so I'm just going to try to be honest here. A lot has happened and I want to get it all down and the only way I can think of is just to write it, as best as I can remember. I have to ignore the cold and the tiredness and the pain in my palm and just write.

So here goes.

I opened my window. That's how it started, for me, New Year's Eve. The end-of-year celebrations. I retrieved the key from my *Breakfast at Tiffany's* video-case and opened my fire-escape window. It was hard, after all that time locked up. Stiff. It made this sort of sucking sound, the rubber inlay peeling from the plastic.

I sat out on the roof. The air was icy so I balled into my warm-position. I smoked. I thought I'd better practise for the party. I didn't want to cough all over you like last time. I'd managed to buy some beers, too, from Waitrose, so I practised drinking a few of them. Sarah and Mum were getting ready in their rooms. My father was locked away in his study. And there I was, sitting on the rooftop, sipping a Bud and watching the stars.

After a while I felt tired. I was worried I'd fall asleep, slip and fall down into the garden, so I climbed back inside and lay on my bed.

By the time I woke everyone had left: my parents had gone to the Hamptons', my sister gone off with the Vultures from her year. The room was icy from having left the window open. I had a headache. I huddled under the sheets for an hour, forced down another beer. I tried not to think of the night ahead – the party. I tried to concentrate on what really mattered: you. You had invited me. You'd said you'd see me there. No matter what happened I had to ensure you did.

I packed a few things. Some clothes, deodorant, a toothbrush, stashed in the rucksack with my beers. I took my *Breakfast at Tiffany's* video-case. I figured we'd need money and I now have over £454, built up in Hampton's wage packets – more than enough to get the train down to the coast. More than enough to get the ferry to Finners Island.

I waited till 22:07, then walked to Goose's. I figured this was a good time to arrive. The party would be well underway by then. You'd be there by then. As I reached the corner of Wallaby

Drive I began to make out the chorus of Miss X's 'Screemin Boi'. As I approached number 7 the song had reached the breakdown, where Miss X pants erotically over the steady thud-thud of the bass drum. There were a couple of partygoers, year tens by the looks of it, asleep on the front path – one curled by the flower tubs, the other face down beneath the vomit-splattered bonnet of Goose's parents' Mercedes. The front door was wide open, the hallway beyond it heaving with bodies.

It was even more packed than I'd expected. People were squeezed into every corner, slouched in every doorway, perched on every step of the staircase. They laughed, smoked, swigged various coloured liquids from various cans and bottles. They smelt of beer, cigarettes, cherries and sweat. You were nowhere to be seen. It dawned on me that I was overdressed: the girls were dolled up – tight-fitting dresses, the usual Vulture hair and makeup – but the boys were all wearing T-shirt-and-jean combos. A few had styled their hair with gel but that was the only evidence of any pride in their appearance.

I stepped back out into the front garden. I inhaled a couple of lungfuls of icy night air. The beer-buzz seemed to be wearing off and my hands were trembling, rattling my backpack, clinking the bottles inside. I rested the backpack on the doorstep and dragged off my Christmas jumper. I untucked my shirt and ruffled my hair. One of the year tens raised his head and asked if I had a glass of water. I told him I didn't. I had beer, though.

'That'll do.'

I handed him a bottle. He gave me a thumbs up and hugged it to his chest. He lay his face on the gravel. I didn't want to disturb him with the offer of a bottle-opener so I turned and stepped inside the house again.

I squeezed my way in through the hall crowd. At first the mass body heat was a relief from the cold but it took mere seconds to increase to that uncomfortable neck-sweat stage. I apologised pretty much constantly for the amount of bodily contact I was making but I don't think anyone could hear me. Miss X was still playing, a new song now, the phrase 'Pleaser teaser' or possibly 'Teaser pleaser' repeating over and over and over and over and over leaving the partygoers with no communicatory option but to lean in and scream into one another's ears. All around me were voices but I couldn't make out a single word they were saying. I searched for your face, the red curls of your hair, but the hall was so dark and the crowd was so vast and I couldn't find you.

I pressed on to the kitchen. I figured it might be quieter there, I could cool off, catch my bearings, put my beers in the fridge. Only the kitchen was even livelier than the hallway. The fridge was open, its contents spread across the table and floor. Several foodstuffs were smeared up the walls – ketchup, dog food, something white and gloopy, possibly mayonnaise or fresh yoghurt. Most of the crowd congregated at the entrance to the conservatory, surrounding some fat kid who was standing on the pool table. Ian was over by the sink with Angela, pouring green liquid into two eggcups. They linked arms and downed the contents – Angela coughing, Ian laughing and slapping her back. Miss X was still playing, yet another song now, the chorus: 'Foot fetish / Fetish feet / Give me something good to eat'.

The fat kid on the pool table was Eggy, one of the Oxbridge kids from my class. He was shouting something but it was impossible to distinguish over the music. He lifted an egg high above him, attempting that trick where you squeeze it between your thumb and finger to demonstrate the strength of the shell – only each time Eggy squeezed the egg burst in his hand, spilling yolk down his arm, splattering his shoes and the felt of the pool table. There were stacks of egg boxes piled beside him. People were laughing, shouting things over the music like 'Go on, Eggy!' and 'You can do it, you smelly bastard!' and a variety of other encouragements. Eggy kept trying, egg after egg after egg, angrier and angrier at each pop and splatter.

I pressed on to a section of unsplattered work-surface in the corner, over by the recycling box. I took a beer from my bag and cracked it open. I sipped, thumb-plugging the bottle to keep it from foaming. The beer was warm. It tasted like fizz. It made me thirsty, which is the opposite of what a beverage should do.

There were two partygoers sitting on the work-surface beside me. Hawaiian shirts, three-quarter-length trousers, sandals. One of them was bald but for a single strip of black hair, running from his forehead to the back of his neck. The other was blond, hair down to his shoulders.

Halfway through my beer I began to make out the odd stray shout of their conversation. They were discussing Lucy Marlowe. The near-bald kid was questioning her attractiveness. He thought her new boobs were too big, they looked out of place. He said Lucy was too short to pull them off. The blond kid disagreed, in his opinion there was no such thing as 'too big'. I couldn't help but glance over, following their conversation. The blond kid noticed my glances. Each time he'd catch my eye I'd look away, back over at Eggy and his egg-popping.

Then the blond kid slid from the work-surface, leaning over to scream in my ear.

'Do I know you, man?'

I shook my head. He squinted at me. He leant over again.

'What's your name?'

I leant to his ear and told him.

'What year are you in?'

I told him.

'Hey, you in Lucy Marlowe's class?'

I nodded. He grinned. The near-bald kid screamed 'What?' and the blond kid shouted something into his ear. Then the blond kid told me how lucky I am. He explained how attractive Lucy Marlowe is since her breast enhancement surgery. He asked if I'd got a good look at her post-op breasts. I told him I hadn't. The blond kid advised me to keep an eye out for any breast-glimpse opportunity. He had a friend in the same class as Angela Hargrove and once she'd been running late and got changed for dance practice right in the middle of her Geography class and his friend had seen one of her nipples. I didn't know how to respond to this. More and more party-goers were forcing their way into the kitchen to watch Eggy. He'd given up popping and was now trying to juggle the eggs. Ian was filling a dog bowl with green liquid. The dog was on the conservatory patio, roaring at the army of intruders in its house, barking a diamond of condensation onto the glass. Miss X was still playing, lyrics indecipherable.

You were still nowhere to be seen.

The blond kid asked who I fancied more, Lucy Marlowe or Angela Hargrove. I said I didn't know.

'You've got to know! If you don't know, who does?'

I didn't want to talk about girls any more so I told him I had a girlfriend. I thought that would stop him asking but he just whit-wooed and winked at the near-bald kid and asked even worse questions, which I won't repeat here. I told him that what he was referring to was private, between me and my girl. I don't know what his reaction to this was because by now I was concentrating solely on Eggy. The crowd had bored of his juggling and were hurling stuff at him, other foodstuffs – avocados, rashers of bacon, spoonfuls of the white gloopy substance.

They began to chant: 'E-ggy! E-ggy! E-ggy!'

'Wait, I know you!' the blond kid shouted. 'You're that kid in Ian's class! The psycho!'

The bald kid frowned. The blond kid leant to his ear and shouted something and they both laughed. I sipped my beer. The blond kid leant to my ear.

'I know who you're shaggin'! It's Miss Hayes!'

Ian dropped the dog bowl and began to nibble at Angela's neck. She laughed and tried to push him away. Eggy was retaliating, launching eggs out into the crowd. One splattered across the window, above the dog, and it leapt to bite at it from the other side of the glass. Miss X seemed to be getting louder and louder. The blond kid was saying something about Miss Hayes, about our weekly meetings. The crowd was still chanting.

You were still nowhere to be seen.

I placed my empty beer bottle in the recycling box, smiled once more at the Hawaiian-shirt kids and stepped out into the hallway. I was shaking so much I could feel the bottles in my backpack, clinking together. One of the bottles had dislodged from its cardboard sleeve and was nuzzling my spine. The Hawaiian-shirt kids were grinning. They may have been laughing, I don't know – there was laughter everywhere and it was impossible to single out theirs.

I knew I needed to find you. I needed to say what I had to say and get away from Goose's, before more people noticed me. There were three other doorways across the hall and I squeezed through to each of them in turn. The first was locked. The second led to the dining room, which was in darkness, empty but for a couple perched on the window seat, kissing aggressively.

The third led to the living room. A gang of year tens were cross-legged in the centre of the room, sitting around a Monopoly board. They'd built a small town out of the game's green and red plastic buildings and one of them was flooding the town with beer. The rest were rolling cigarettes using £500 notes. The TV was on, a channel with a topless woman who rolls on the floor while speaking into a telephone, but nobody was watching, everyone was drinking and shouting into one another's ears. Lucy Marlowe and Carly Meadows were over in the corner, stabbing the keys of the Lamberts' piano, roaring with laughter. It was impossible to hear anything over Miss X, still screeching from the stereo:

*L–O–V–E,*
*It is an accessory*

I returned to the dining room. I sat. I figured I'd wait it out. I had to see you eventually. It was impossible to spend the whole night in the house with you and not see you. Fate had thrown us together in the past and it would again. I just had to be patient.

I took my four remaining beers from the plastic Waitrose bag and lined them up on the dining table, along with the cigarettes and box of cooking matches. The kissing couple didn't notice, or if they did then it didn't affect the aggressiveness of their kissing. The party hummed around us, the odd Vulture-screech penetrating the music. At one point there was an almighty crash, followed by mass laughter and applause, which I assume was Eggy slipping from the pool table. Eventually the kissers departed, giggling and handholding. Finally the music died. By the time I'd opened my third beer it was 23:07.

The hallway had cleared when I left the dining room. Its carpet was littered with cans and bottles, reams of toilet roll. The partygoers had raided a box of fireworks and were setting them off in the garden – cheering along with their screeches and pops. I wondered how they'd celebrate the stroke of midnight. They'd already trashed the house, already set off the fireworks. The only possible climax was some sort of explosion, destroy the house completely. Some sort of human sacrifice, perhaps.

I needed the toilet. I stepped over to the stairs. As I passed the living room something gasped.

'Oh my god!'

It was Carly Meadows. She was laid out on the couch, glaring up at me.

'You're that guy from class,' she said.

I nodded. The living room had also pretty much emptied. There was Monopoly money everywhere. A different woman was topless on the TV, sucking a telephone like it was an ice-lolly.

'Lucy, look,' Carly said. 'That guy from English is here.'

Lucy Marlowe sat up from behind the couch. She was chewing gum, clutching a half-drunk bottle of Navy Rum. Her top had slipped down so much that one of her nipples was sticking out. She looked me up and down.

'Fuckin' hell,' she said.

I nodded. I sipped my beer, coughing as I swallowed. I tried not to look at the nipple.

'That was amazin' when you ran out of class the other day,' Carly Meadows said. 'Wasn't that amazin' when he ran out of class the other day, Lucy?'

'It was amazin'.'

'Amazin'.'

I thanked them, still nodding, still sipping my beer. Carly and Lucy glared up at me and I sipped until my bottle was empty. Then I picked at the label. The woman on the TV turned and raised her backside to the camera. She reached back and wobbled her bum cheeks.

I asked the girls if they'd seen Ian anywhere. Or Angela. Or even Goose.

They laughed.

'What the fuck do you want with Angela?' Carly Meadows said.

I asked if they'd seen you at all. They laughed again.

'Alith? Have we theen Alith?'

'Who the fuck'th Alith?'

I rubbed my tongue against the roof of my mouth. Sometimes this helps my lisp. A rocket struck the window, ricocheting into the crowd. The partygoers swarmed in circles, laughing, screaming. The dog bounded between them, howling.

I asked the girls to excuse me. They laughed again.

'Excuthe me!'

'Excuthe!'

I stepped back through the hall. Lucy and Carly carried on talking. One of them used the world 'psycho' but I ignored it and carried on up the stairs. They were slick with sick and spilt beer and various partygoers were curled in various positions, sleeping in one another's arms. At the top of the stairs were a guy and girl, huddled, aggressive-kissing. The guy was sucking the girl's neck, pressing her face into the wall with one hand, thumb-rubbing her nipple with the other. The girl murmured. She clutched a bottle of Lambrini, tipping it too far, hissing a waterfall down the top three stairs.

The girl's eyes opened.

It was Sarah.

She squealed and pushed the guy from her neck. It was the blond Hawaiian-shirt kid from the kitchen. He smirked. He wiped his mouth. Sarah frowned at me. It was that same frown she used to give the St Peter's kids when they called her 'Flake' in the playground, like she was angry at my very soul.

Sarah excused herself, standing, fixing her top. She dragged me across the landing to the bathroom. The blond kid shouted, 'Hey, she's mine!' but Sarah shushed him and slammed and locked the door.

The bathroom was vast and granite-tiled, adorned with candles, seashells, scented hand soaps. It made me think of Mum. The sink was brimming with water, wadded with toilet paper and some sort of green leafy foodstuff – spinach, maybe, or rocket salad. Sarah dragged me over to the shower. The curtain was pulled right across. It was patterned with little grey ducks.

'Why are you here?'

I told Sarah that Goose was in my year. I came because of the party. It was New Year's.

She continued to frown. 'Who invited you?'

I couldn't think of any names off the top of my head so I just said, 'Ian Connor.'

She snorted. 'As if.'

The shower curtain danced slightly in the breeze. The ducks swayed back and forth. Behind it lay a blurred pink figure. Sarah started to speak again but I had no idea what she was saying – I was too busy trying to work out if the pink figure was in fact a living, breathing, possibly naked person, listening in on our conversation. Sarah stopped talking. She turned her frown to the shower curtain. She turned to me. She tore the curtain back.

There was a woman, slumped in the foot of the shower, skin pink and glistening, mouth lipstick-red and open in an O. She was wearing a shower cap, which was pointless as she was made entirely of plastic and therefore already waterproof. The words 'Flat-Chested Slut' were painted across her inflated breasts in Tipp-Ex.

Sarah sighed and grabbed the woman and slung her across the room. She bounced off the door before settling, head wedged beneath the sink. Sarah dragged me into the shower and pulled the curtain across.

'Look,' she whispered, 'you're not going to fit in here. It's just not going to happen. Plus Tony said a gang of Pitt kids are coming to trash the place any minute and let's face it, if anyone's getting a beating, it's you.'

I told Sarah that I had to find somebody.

'Who?'

I couldn't say.

'Whatever. Just hurry up and get out of here. If anyone asks, we're not related, OK?'

I nodded. I thanked Sarah for the warning. She said, 'Whatever,' again and stepped out from the shower. After a quick mirror-check she left, slamming the door behind her.

I stepped over to the toilet. I placed my beer on the basin and took a pee. It was the longest pee of my life. Halfway through I noticed the plastic woman, still slumped on the floor, watching me, her mouth still shocked into an O.

By the time I stepped out onto the landing again, Sarah and the blond kid had gone. Out in the garden someone was screaming, possibly a victim of a ricocheted firework. The dog was barking. There were three doors along the landing, all of which were shut. At the far end was another stairway, leading up to some sort of attic room. I could make out giggling. A lingering chipotle-smoke smell.

I climbed the stairs. The giggling was accompanied by a squeaking. At the top of the stairs was another door, slightly ajar. I could make out Ian, or half of him at least, cross-legged at the foot of a wardrobe, holding his face. His shirt was torn, chin resting on his bare white chest, fringe curled over his knuckles. He was rocking back and forth and at first I thought the squeaking was coming from him, perhaps from his back pressing against the wardrobe behind him. But as I crept closer to the door-crack it was clear the squeaking was coming from the other side of the room, along with Goose's laughter and a faint repetitive slapping.

I pressed the door open. A TV glared from the wall, broadcasting a blizzard of static. Goose's bed was over by the window. There was a girl on it. At first I thought it might be you but I quickly recognised Angela. Her head bobbed, hang-mouthed, off the side, chin in the air, hair swaying into a puddle of vomit on the carpet. Goose stood beside her, giggling, tipping a bottle of beer onto her chest. It fizzed over her face, trickling through her hair into the ever-expanding vomit-puddle. Beer bubbles glistened on her forehead and eyelashes. The near-bald Hawaiian-shirt kid was there, hunched halfway down the bed, teeth gritted, gripping the mattress. He was jerking back and forth. His Hawaiian shirt was open, flapping about him. His eyes were closed, tight – his forehead locked into a frown.

Every few seconds Angela's head turned from side to side, as if by turning her head she could avoid the sticky torrent of beer, but Goose was relentless in his pouring. When the bottle was empty he reached for another from a box beside the bed, cracking the lid with his teeth. I wasn't sure if he'd noticed me – if any of them had. It didn't seem to matter. Occasionally Angela would let out a sound – a grunt, or a short sharp intake of breath – and the Hawaiian-shirt kid would repeat the sound, imitate it. I'm not sure if he was aware he was doing this. The static light washed over them all. It danced chaotically, especially on Angela. Shadows flickered over her, like **Them**, hundreds of **Them**, swarming on her cold white skin.

As I retreated to the attic stairs Ian looked up from his lap. He took a second to focus on me but when he did he gave me a thumbs up. Then he shook his head, let it slide back into his hands.

I sat in the bathroom for a while. I don't know how long. First I was sick in the sink and then I just sat on the side of the bath, watching my vomit chunks float amongst the leafy green stuff. I thought over the situation. If you weren't up there with Goose, then you weren't at the party. If you weren't at the party then you must be at home. You must have a reason for staying at home and that reason was more than likely your father.

I knew then, what I had to do. Things were going to be more complicated than I'd thought. I wasn't able to just meet you at the party, that was too easy. I was going to have to go out to the Pitt and get you.

A banging came from downstairs. I thought it was the party-goers. I assumed they'd decided to set off their fireworks indoors. The big New Year's climax.

When I reached the foot of the stairs I realised it was the Pitt kids – a gang of them had arrived with baseball bats and were in the process of destroying the kitchen. The partygoers were still out in the garden. They'd built a bonfire from the last of the fireworks (the least entertaining ones – fountains, roman candles, Catherine wheels) and were sitting in a circle watching the screaming flames, crackling and flashing in various colours.

There were four Pitt kids in total. One of them was wearing a blue hoodie, not unlike your brother's. I couldn't be sure it was him because of the scarf covering his mouth, and he wouldn't stay still long enough for me to assess the blueness of his eyes. He brought his bat down on the kitchen sink, the porcelain splitting clean down the middle. Two others were smashing the crockery. Another was dragging out the drawers, emptying them out onto the floor.

I knew that if I was going to face your father I couldn't go empty-handed. I considered the Pitt kids' bats. They were threatening enough but there was no way I could do any real damage, if it came to it. Not against your father. I doubt I could even reach his head.

Then one of the Pitt kids emptied the knife drawer and a selection of knives clattered across the tiles.

I crossed the kitchen to the knives. The Pitt kids stopped their smashing and stared at me, bats loose in their hands.

They glared from under their hoods. I chose a knife, a large carving knife, like the ones at the butcher's. I could feel the Pitt kids' eyes on me as I examined it. Then I crossed the room again, to the door, and left.

The Pitt's always been firework crazy. I remember those New Years with Nan and Herb, how they'd always make a big deal about getting fireworks. They wanted to make it special because at Christmas and birthdays we went to Skipdale – this was the only night my parents brought Sarah down to the Pitt. It was the only night I remember Herb leaving his chair. I used to believe Herb spent all year plugged into the wall, charging, waiting to launch into New Year's Eve – into the drinking of Guinness and roasting of chestnuts and piling of rockets on the kitchen table, which I would inspect thoroughly. I'd pick the order in which the fireworks were to be launched, which would depend on the size of the rockets and the tradition of saving the biggest, most orbit-likely till last. Every year Herb would tell me we'd get at least one of the bastards into space.

Herb did the dangerous stuff. The garden was concrete so he couldn't stab the tubes into soil the way the instructions said. Instead he'd arrange the rockets in their own individual plant pots. The garden was only twenty foot long, so the hundred-foot safety distance was out of the question, but for this one night of the year Herb would take a 'Whatever happens, happens' attitude (perhaps due to the Guinness) and would light as many rockets as he could, only hobbling to the relative safety of the kitchen doorway when the first few were screaming into the air. It seems odd but when I think back to New Years, to Herb skipping about with his safety lighter and Sarah balanced on Mum's knee scratching at her toes and all the fireworks in their plant pots with all their screaming light and banging, my favourite part is still thinking about Nan, sitting in silence at the back of the kitchen, Mr Saunders curled on her knee. Thinking about Nan's furry face as it followed each rocket up into the sky. It was as if after all those years she still wasn't sure how it was done.

Tonight was no different. Rockets screeched from every garden, thundering and flowering through the murk of the sky, bathing the streets in light: red, green, golden yellow. The streets were misted in smoke. It was like a war zone. I crossed at the Rat and Dog. A crowd of drinkers had spilt from its doorway and were standing in a circle, linking arms and singing. Music hummed from the pub – chatter, laughter, shattering glass. I pulled my hood up and kept my head down. I hurried to the estates.

The knife was still tucked into my belt, cold against my hip. I couldn't help but imagine it, pressing it into your father's stomach, the resistance at first, before his belly gave way to it. It was a large belly and I'd need to give it some force. I'd need to be quick, if it came to it.

I stopped at the end of your road. I leant against the wall and heaved. Nothing came up. I couldn't help but feel it, again and again, the knife popping your father's stomach. I remembered Artie Sampson's Father Christmas, doubled over on the pavement. That's how your father would fall, sinking slowly till his face pressed into the ground. I clutched the handle of the knife and thought of you, your eye all swollen and black.

Your house was in darkness. Your father's car was missing. I rang the bell. I couldn't hear the ring so I tried knocking instead. I knocked again. Nothing. I knelt to the letterbox and pressed it open but it was too dark to see anything. It was only then I realised how much I was trembling. How much I was gritting my teeth.

I stood and knocked again, repeatedly.

A voice called out, 'Are you the police?'

I stepped back, hiding the knife under the hem of my jumper. I scanned the front of the house but I couldn't see where the voice was coming from.

'You're not the police.'

There was an old woman, squinting down at me from next-door's bedroom window. She was wearing a fluffy red dressing gown, a large pair of glasses dangling from a cord round her neck.

'He's not in,' she said. 'Did all his roaring then left. As always.'

I asked if she knew where you were.

'There'll be hell to pay when the police get here.'

I knocked again. I waited a couple more minutes, the old lady still squinting down at me. Then I walked round to the park.

The back of the house was as quiet as the front. Your TV lay on the floor in the middle of the lounge, projecting its light up the far wall. The rest of the house was in darkness.

I crawled in through the hedge. A whining came from the shed, high-pitched like Scraps, only interspersed with short sharp sobs. I knelt to the missing-plank gap. There you were, a moonlit silhouette in the corner, Scraps across your lap. You hugged his head over your shoulder, nuzzling his chest. You rubbed the side of his face, dragging the skin back to reveal the white of his eye.

I stood, brushing the mud from my palms and my knees. I dragged my hood down and fixed my hair the best I could, though there was no reflective surface to check my appearance. I took the knife from my belt and stashed it in my backpack. I stepped round to the front of the shed. The grass was frozen and crunched beneath my feet. As I stepped up to the door the whining stopped.

I knocked.

'What?' you said.

I couldn't think of anything to say so I just knocked again.

'What the fuck do you want?'

'I . . .'

The floorboards creaked. You sniffed.

'Well if you're going to come in, then come in.'

I opened the door.

And then came the shot. I must have registered you somehow, in that split-second, standing there in the shed doorway, because I can still picture your face as it was at that moment – stern, frowning, unsunglassed. I can still see the hate in your eyes. I must have seen the gun, too, because I raised my arm the instant the trigger cracked, hand spread as if commanding you to stop. When the pain hit I found myself outside again, stumbling from the steps to the lawn.

I landed on my back. My jaw locked. Each breath hissed through my teeth. I was holding the hand above me by its wrist, limp and clawed and burning, a hot-sharp sting that spread from my palm to the tips of my fingers. Next thing you were kneeling beside me. You were telling me how sorry you were. You were still holding the nail gun but as soon as you realised you tossed it into the hedge. You reached for the hand but I clutched it to my chest.

'It's fine,' I hissed. 'It's nothing.' My lisp sounded even worse through clenched teeth.

Then you saw the blood.

'Shit.'

You clutched your hair. You rubbed your palms into your eyes. You shook your head. You were wearing that pink dressing gown, beneath it a white dress, patterned with blue flowers.

I wanted to reassure you but the pain was clouding my thoughts. All I seemed to be able to do was lie there, gritting my teeth, so hard my gums ached.

'Wait there,' you said.

You disappeared into the shed again. The toolbox rattled. My hand was shaking and I struggled to hold it still. My stomach was churning. I breathed slowly. Within seconds you were back at my side, clutching a pair of pliers.

'Come on.'

You reached under my armpits and hoisted me to my feet, took hold of my un-pierced hand and led me over to the house. You were shaking as much as I was but your crying seemed to have stopped, replaced by a frown of deep concentration.

The kitchen was in darkness. I waited at the doorway while you switched on the light – a bare bulb hanging from the ceiling. It was small for a kitchen, like Nan's used to be – more of a utility room, only with a cooker and a stack of dirty plates on the side.

There was a single stool over in the corner and you told me to sit. You scrambled about, emptying every drawer and cabinet

– utensils, shopping bags, half-empty cereal boxes. I nursed my hand on my lap like a bird with an injured wing. It was only in the light of the single bare bulb that I noticed the bloodstain, spread across the hem of your dress. I looked down at my hand again. It made me light-headed. I should have known, really, that it wasn't my blood on your dress, because it had already blackened to that sticky stage.

You ran out through the hall, up the stairs, shouting for me to wait where I was. I don't know where you thought I was going to go. My hand was still trembling, coat-sleeve sticky with blood, all the way down to my elbow. I cupped my right hand beneath my left, to catch the drips.

You arrived at the doorway again. You placed a pair of tights and a bottle of whiskey on the sideboard. Then you knelt and reached for my hand.

I pulled away.

'Show me.'

I shook my head. 'It's fine.'

'It's not fine.'

'It is.'

You sighed. 'We need to get it out before the tetanus kicks in.'

'I don't think that's how it works.'

You looked me in the eye.

'Show me.'

I uncurled my hand as much as I could. You took my wrist and held it to the light. My palm was cupping a pool of blood. You turned it, examining it, not seeming to mind when the blood spilled onto the floor tiles. I retched. Not because of the pain (although that in itself was pretty intense) but because of the sight of it – the nail – jutting from the back of my hand like some sort of small metallic fang. I couldn't believe what a good shot it had been, right through that cigarette burn on my palm, the scab that was finally healing.

'Here.' You handed me the whiskey bottle. I thought you just wanted me to hold it but then you said, 'Drink, it'll help.' I tried to open the bottle with my teeth but it was tightly screwed. You apologised, resting my hand on the side while you twisted the top off for me.

I took a swig. I retched again.

You told me to look away. I tried to concentrate on the light bulb. It was rocking slightly in the breeze. I could already feel the whiskey, warming its way up through me.

I couldn't help but glance up as you placed the teeth of the pliers on the nail head.

'On three, OK?'

I nodded.

'One . . .'

I gritted my teeth.

'Two . . .'

You yanked. My arm jerked. The pain burnt right up to my elbow. I screamed out and stumbled from the stool to the far side of the room. I crouched in the doorway, biting into the collar of my coat.

I held my hand to the light. The nail was still there.

'You said on three,' I said. I was sweating and shaking and my lisp sounded worse than ever.

'It's wedged right in there,' you said. 'We'll have to go again.'

I told you I thought we were maybe better off calling an ambulance. You shook your head. You said it was never a good idea to get the authorities involved in situations like this. Besides, by the time they got here my arm would be riddled with the tetanus.

I perched on the stool again.

'On two or on three this time?' I asked.

'On three.'

But that was another lie. This time you didn't count at all. As soon you'd gripped the nail you tugged, so hard that, when the nail did break free, you stumbled right across the kitchen into the sideboard, tipping the pile of plates onto the floor. The pain was like nothing I'd ever felt. It was like you'd ripped out one of my bones. I managed not to cry out this time but I still stumbled forwards and dropped my rucksack. My *Breakfast at Tiffany's* video-case clattered across the kitchen floor the same moment the plates did, my journal and wage packets and various keys and trinkets scattering amongst the shattered ceramic.

You examined the nail in the light.

'We got it!'

I bent to gather the contents of my video-case. I tried to piece together the pages of my journal but I was getting blood all over everything. You knelt, trying to help.

'What is this stuff?'

'Don't read it,' I said. 'It's private.'

It was only after I'd spoken that I realised how hostile I'd sounded. You lifted the video-case and starting stuffing the pages inside. You glanced at the title on the spine.

'It's just a box,' I said. 'It's where I keep things.'

'What things?'

'Just things.'

You picked up the cigarette butt. The one I saved from outside your house.

'Is this one of your things?'

I nodded. You weren't paying attention, you were too busy studying it. I added a 'Yes' and you looked up and placed it in the box. Then you reached for the pliers from the sideboard. You held out the nail.

'You want this? For your box?'

You didn't wait for an answer. You dislodged the nail and wrapped it in kitchen roll, placing it in the video-case with everything else.

'Here, keep it,' you said. 'From now on you can always look at it and remember the time that crazy bitch fucked up your hand.'

The box clicked shut. You smiled.

'How does it feel?'

'The hand?'

'The hand.'

'Like the mother of all bee stings.'

You stood and passed me the video-case. I slipped it back into my bag.

'Now we just need to sterilise it.'

I sat on the stool again. You reached into the cupboard for a couple of mugs and poured us both a shot of whiskey. You poured the rest of the bottle over my hand, washing all the blood away. It stung like crazy but by now my hand had been stinging so consistently it was almost expected. I could pretty much remove my mind from the pain. What really bothered me was the smell.

You stretched out the tights and bound my palm. You apologised for your lack of bandages, assuring me the tights were clean. I said it didn't matter. After a few minutes you looked up, eyes fixed on mine.

'Sorry I shot you,' you said. 'I didn't know you were you.'

I nodded. 'It was a mistake. People make mistakes.'

You took a pin from your pocket, fixing the tights in place.

'You weren't at the party,' I said. 'I just came to check you were OK.'

You stared down at your lap, the black stain on your dress. You glanced out at the shed.

'I'm not.'

We crossed the garden to the shed. You stopped at the steps and sat, rubbing your eyes. I stood beside you, waiting. You told me it wasn't pretty and I said it was OK. I raised my hand and told you that, after what we'd just been through, I was ready for anything.

You smiled. You stood again. You stepped up to the shed door.

Under the spotlight of your torch we examined the mess. Various tools had fallen from their nails on the wall. The toolkit lay side-on, its contents spread across the floorboards. Scraps was laid out in his corner, mouth hanging open, tongue limp on the shed floor. There was a black patch across his face I tried not to fixate on. Several black boot marks patterned his ribs.

You switched off the torch then and all we could make out was our breath, curling before us in the moonlight.

'We should bury him,' I said.

You nodded. 'The park. He liked the park.'

I slid off my coat and wrapped it over Scraps. The blood had hardened. It was sticky in the cold air and peeling him from the boards was more difficult than I expected. His legs had stiffened, bobbing as I lifted. He ached my hand a little but the pain eased when I shifted his weight into the crook of my arm. I caught a glimpse of the right side of his skull, buried in the hood of my coat: face caved, fur black and bloody. His right eye was missing, or maybe just so far buried into its socket it was no longer visible. You unhooked a shovel from the wall and led us, out through the hedge gap and across the field.

By then the fireworks had finished and the Pitt was quiet again. I couldn't hear any traffic out on the carriageway. The only sound was our feet, crunching the grass.

You stopped over by the climbing frame.

'Here.'

I laid Scraps down. You sat on one of the swings, beside him, rocking back and forth slightly, reaching down to stroke the un-caved side of his face. I lifted the shovel. It was cold, the metal sticking to my fingers. I hacked it into the ground, gasping at the sting in my palm.

'Sorry,' you said. 'Of course. Here. Let me.'

You took the shovel and told me to sit. I took the other swing. I wanted to reach down and stroke Scraps like you had but I just played with the fur on the hood of the parka instead.

You placed the blade of the shovel onto the grass and stamped. Nothing. The ground wouldn't give. You stamped again. Nothing.

'It's frozen.'

You stamped one more time and the shovel cracked, the blade dislodging from its handle.

'Fuck.'

You laughed and looked up to the sky. The fog of the fireworks was clearing. The stars glittered above us.

'I have a better idea.'

You tossed the shovel and lifted Scraps, nursing him over your shoulder like a baby. You led us back across the field, back through the hedge and over to the shed. You laid Scraps in his corner. I waited at the doorway with the torch as you knelt beside him, whispering to him. Then you started rummaging through the shelves at the back. You lifted out a half-empty bottle of whiskey and placed it on the floor beside you. You lifted out another, two more, not stopping till there were half a dozen, lined up across the shed floor, each with varying amounts of alcohol inside. You placed one bottle – about a third full – in your dressing-gown pocket. The others you opened, one by one, emptying them over Scraps, my coat, the floor of the shed, washing the blood through the cracks between the boards.

You stepped down. You took the last bottle of whiskey from your pocket and splattered half across the steps. You asked me for a match. I offered you the box and you snatched them from me, lighting them and dropping them one by one onto the steps. I waited over by the patio furniture. Eventually the whiskey caught, a blue tide of flames spreading, then engulfing the shed.

I tore two plastic patio chairs from the overgrown grass. We sat. We watched the fire. We listened to it crackle. You put on your sunglasses, the flames dancing in their lenses. The heat baked our faces. After a while there was a crash and a billowing of sparks as the roof fell in. We moved our chairs back a little. A column of smoke towered up into the sky.

'Do you have any cigarettes?'

I offered you the packet. You took one and stepped over to the fire, holding the tip to the flames. Then you sat again and we smoked, passing the cigarette back and forth. I could smell Scraps. He smelt like any other burning meat. I was sure you could smell him too, but neither of us mentioned it. You took out the half-bottle of whiskey and we drank, a taste hotter than the fire. By the end I'd learnt not to grimace as I sipped.

Then the sirens started. I asked what you wanted to do.

'Can we go somewhere?' you said. 'I don't think I want to be here any more.'

I nodded. 'I know somewhere we can go.'

By the time we left the house a crowd had gathered. They let out a collective gasp when they saw us, as if they were shocked anything could have survived the fire. Somewhere the sirens still whirred. The old lady from next door shuffled over, still in her dressing gown.

'Are you OK, dear?' she said. 'Are you OK?'

'Fine,' you said.

You tried to hurry past but the old lady grabbed you, hugging you to her chest.

'Don't you worry, love, they're on their way.'

You wriggled free and pushed on through the crowd. The old lady cried out your name but you just wiped your eyes and screamed that she should fuck off and mind her own business. The crowd glared.

I kept my head down and followed. You didn't stop till you reached the corner. You glanced in both directions, then leant against the wall, hood up, head slumped.

'I don't even know where we're going.'

I led us the rest of the way. You were wrapped in your coat, the one with the red fur trim. My parka had burnt up with Scraps so you'd lent me your father's leather jacket, which was enormous on me, the sleeves hanging to knee-level. It was the smallest you'd been able to find. You held on to the cuff, head down, occasionally sniffing.

Then the snow started. You were shaking and I wanted to hug you to me, to keep us both warm, but I didn't. The sirens were getting louder. At one point you shoved me, stumbling from the pavement, into the street. There was a set of three grids, veiled by the thin layer of snow.

'Sorry,' I said. 'Didn't see it.'

You nodded and took my sleeve again.

We didn't stop again till we reached the Rat and Dog. You wanted to scavenge for booze. The pub was shut, the crowds having returned home, but you found a half-drunk bottle of wine under one of the tables out front and we carried on walking, you taking the occasional swig.

As we crossed the dual carriageway the fire engine came roaring past us, lights flashing, sirens screaming. By the time we reached the church its sirens had ceased and the only sound was our feet, creaking on the snow.

I asked if you'd ever been inside the church.

'Once, maybe.'

'I used to go there when I was little,' I said. 'My nan used to take me.'

'What does that mean?'

You nodded to the church sign.

It said:

## GOD WELCOMES ALL
## INTO THE KINGDOM OF HEAVEN

'I guess it's to try get people inside. All different sorts of people. Rather than just old ladies.'

'You reckon it's ever worked?'

I shrugged.

You downed what was left of the wine and tossed the empty bottle at the sign. It shattered, dislodging some of the letters.

Now it said:

## GOD WE OMES ALL
## INTO THE KI G OM OF HEAVEN

'Why'd you do that?' I said.

You shrugged.

I crossed the lawn and picked up the letters and slotted them back into place. I kicked the broken glass into the flower bed. You sat on the wall and watched. Then you took my sleeve and we carried on, across the street to Kirk Lane.

It's always a shock to see Nan's house again. It's amazing how much damage we did just by leaving, just by not being there. The front windows are long since smashed (presumably by Pitt kids) and boarded (presumably by my father), the front garden a mass of overgrown brambles and grass. I doubt it's still on the market. The 'For Sale' sign's still there but it's slipped down the side of the hedge now, just the F and the O visible through the leaves.

I remember when we first moved out Mum wanted to lower the price and get rid, but my father said she couldn't just give away her childhood home like that. My father had this theory that one day the government were going to bulldoze the Pitt and they'd give us a good price for the place. A year or so later (when the government still hadn't bulldozed the Pitt) my father organised a few viewings, though nothing ever came of them. Since then they've stopped discussing it. My father still comes down here sometimes, though, with his secretaries.

'This it?' you said.

I nodded. You looked it up and down, frowning, as if you didn't believe someone could live there. I explained that I didn't have keys, that the only way in was round the back. Were you OK to wait?

You glanced up the street. Everything was still and silent now that we'd stopped walking. I thought I could make out the sigh of each snowflake, landing on the shoulders of your father's jacket.

You nodded.

I hurried through the alley to the back wall. Climbing over was tricky, due to the usual broken-glass-scattered-across-the-top-of-the-wall-like-rows-of-glittering-shark-teeth Pitt trespassing deterrent. The bricks were slick with ice and the hole in my hand was screaming with pain and at one point I slipped and caught my elbow on the glass and tore your father's jacket.

The garden is still a graveyard of Nan's old plant tubs and there was a fairly large one (more like a trough, really) running along the back wall, packed with soil, which helped break my fall. I stumbled over to the kitchen window and climbed up, only then realising I'd left a shoe behind in the plant tub. There were more important things to think of, though. You were still out there, out front, alone. I had to get inside and let you in.

There's a trick to the window. Jiggle the handle and the lock falls right out. It was stiff and stuck to the frame with grime but I forced it open as wide as I could and wriggled through, tumbling head first into the kitchen. The tiles were furred with a layer of dust. I tried not to think of how many potential webs were about. I reached for the light switch and was relieved to find the lights still worked, the electricity was still on. It was a shock to see it again, the kitchen. It didn't look the same somehow. It was all there – the table and chairs, the old gas cooker, the fridge complete with photographs of Sarah and me, held in place by various colourful magnetic letters – but something wasn't right about it, something wasn't the same. It was like a replica, like a display in some museum. I didn't linger for long. I hurried out through the hallway to the front door. I knew I had to find you. I knew I had to get you inside.

The street was empty. All was still but for the snow – thick now, falling fast. I figured you had run home. To a friend's, maybe. Angela's. Ian's. Goose's. I figured you'd sobered in the cold and thought better of me.

Then I noticed your hair, spilt across the pavement at the end of the path.

I waded through the grass to the front gate. You were laid out, shivering, flecked with snow. I dragged the gate open. I knelt to you.

'Alice.' I shook your shoulder. 'Alice.'

You turned away from me.

'Let's go inside,' I said.

'I'm tired.'

'Me too. Let's go inside.'

I helped you to your feet, brushing the snow from the fur of your coat. By now you must've forgotten about the hole in my hand because you held it tight, clutching for balance. You didn't let go till we'd crossed the lawn, till we were safely inside the house.

You sat on the stairs while I bolted the door.

'This is where you live?'

I thought about explaining but I couldn't think of how to explain, so I just nodded.

'It's even colder than out there.'

I bent down to the cupboard under the stairs. 'I'll switch on the boiler. It'll warm up soon.'

You picked at the sleeve of your coat. 'I want to sleep. Where can I sleep?'

'I'll show you.'

I led you upstairs. I weighed up the options. Nan's room was safest, but I thought all the parcel tape might freak you out, so I took you over to my old room instead. The window was adequately boarded so I figured it'd be warm enough, plus there'd be less light to disturb you in the morning. You bobbed down onto the mattress. There was still that old bedding on it, the *Peanuts* bedding, with Snoopy and Charlie Brown and all the rest. 'Happiness is being part of the gang' it says. You stared down at your lap.

After a minute or two you appeared to be asleep. I turned to leave.

'Wait,' you said.

I stopped in the doorway.

'Stay.'

I shut the door. I sat beside you on the bed. I don't know how long we sat there. You continued to stare at your lap. You stroked your coat cuff. You kept opening your mouth as if to speak, then closing it again and shaking your head. The pipes clunked around us. They made sounds like bowling balls, rolling through the walls.

'It's the heating,' I said. 'It's temperamental.'

You nodded. You motioned to my hand. Blood had soaked through the tights, leaking onto the quilt between us. My fingers were sticky with it. I wiped them on my trousers.

My new Christmas trousers, stained with blood. I felt sick.

'You need a new bandage.'

'It's OK,' I said. Then, after a few seconds, 'I cut my elbow, too.' I showed you the tear in your father's jacket. 'Sorry.'

You didn't look up. You were staring at something.

'You lost a shoe,' you said.

I glanced at my sock, caked in mud. I told you I'd lost it in a flower tub. You snorted a laugh. Then you squealed. I glanced around – at first I thought it was the pipes. Then you did it again, a short sharp squeal. You giggled, looking up at me, hand over your mouth. You pointed to your throat. You did it again, shoulders jerking.

Hiccups.

I laughed too. With each squeal our laughter grew, which only made the hiccupping worse. Tears spilt from under your glasses, lining your cheeks. I asked if you wanted a glass of water. You shook your head and coughed the word 'Cigarette' and I took the packet from my pocket and gave it to you. You lit up. You hiccupped the first drag, spilling its smoke into the air around us.

The second you breathed down, held in your chest.

You sighed.

'Sorry,' you said, the smoke escaping with your words. 'I'm not a regular drinker.'

'Me neither.'

You offered me the cigarette. I took a drag and passed it back and you placed it between your lips. You coughed a couple of times but you didn't hiccup again.

After a while, you sighed. 'It was my dad.'

'I know.'

'He's not a bad man. Not really.'

I didn't reply.

'He just loses it sometimes. Takes it out on others. Scraps . . .'

'That's why you wanted to shoot him?'

'Yes. I still am going to shoot him. Next time I see him. And not in the hand.' You shook your head. 'That's if I ever see him again. Which I won't. I'm not going back there. Not now Scraps is gone.'

'I know somewhere we can go.'

'We?'

I looked down at my feet. My one shoe. You took another drag.

'We,' you said, as if answering your own question.

You rested your head on my shoulder. Your hands lay palm-up on your lap. Your hair smelt of smoke.

'You went to the party, right?'

'Right.'

'How was it?'

'Busy.'

'You see Goose? Was he sad? Was he missing me?'

Before I could answer you snorted, a sort of laugh I couldn't equate to anything.

'No,' I said. 'I didn't see him.'

We didn't speak for a while. I don't know how long. I could feel the warmth of your body next to mine. The weight of your head on my shoulder.

'I forgot to say,' you said. 'Happy New Year.'

'Happy New Year.'

Soon after that you began to snore. I shifted so I could see you – mouth hanging open, cigarette smouldering. I peeled the butt from your bottom lip and stubbed it out on the headboard.

I stood, laying you out on the mattress.

'Goodnight,' I said.

I slid the quilt out from under you. You shuddered in your sleep. I was in the process of tucking you in when you sat up, your face inches from mine.

You glanced round the room.

'It's OK,' I said. 'You're here.'

You lifted your glasses, propping them in your hair like a headband. Your eyes were wide, pupils dilated into two black coins. Your eyelashes had begun to grow back, just bristles at the moment. Half-formed wishes in the making.

You examined my face, from my scruffy bowl of hair to the

tip of my chin. Then you shut your eyes and leant forward, all the way forward, until your cold lips were pressed against mine. You smiled, sighing through your nose, your breath hot against my chin. I didn't dare move. I didn't dare breathe. I just crouched there, watching.

Your eyes opened again.

'Happy New Year.'

Your head tipped forward, your eyes focusing on my shirt collar. A frown dipped your brow. I glanced down, thinking there was maybe a stain or something.

Then you heaved. Your sick splattered my chest, warm and whiskey-stinking. It ran down the front of my Christmas jumper. You heaved again, all down the front of your dress this time. Your sunglasses slipped back over your eyes. You retched twice more but nothing came.

Then you slumped back, asleep.

For a minute I just crouched there, counting each vomit-drip as it dotted the duvet. You lay still, mouth open, chin glistening. Your lap was puddled, a pale red-wine liquid the consistency of spit. The odd fleck of unidentifiable foodstuff.

'Alice,' I said.

I shook your shoulder. Everything smelt of whiskey.

'Alice? You OK?'

Nothing.

'Alice.'

I stepped through to the bathroom. The door was stiff and at first I thought it was locked but then I remembered the bathroom door was always stiff, that you have to sort of barge it with your hip to get it open. The bathroom's still the same – same towels, same toilet-roll holder, even Nan's facecloth, still curled at the side of the sink. I wasn't really paying attention to all this at the time, though – I was thinking about the vomit, dripping from the hem of my jumper, dotting the dusty tiles. I examined myself in the mirror. My hair was sticking up in ways I'd never thought possible, far surpassing my usual scruffy bowl. Two large curls corkscrewed from my fringe like horns. I was still feeling the buzz of the whiskey and I ended up standing there for I don't know how long, staring at my own reflection.

I dragged off your father's jacket, draped it over the toilet seat. I peeled off my jumper, my shirt, slid off my one remaining shoe, my socks, trousers, boxers. I stepped into the bathtub. It was layered with dust, gritty and dry between my toes. I held the showerhead to my chest, the pipes clunking and shuddering as water glugged out, cold and brown at first, then steaming, hot and clear. It scalded my chest, my stomach, my legs. It burnt like crazy but I didn't add any cold. I just stood and watched it, pooling at my feet, blackened with grit and dust, gurgling down the plughole.

Once I was clean I stepped through to the bedroom again and fetched some fresh clothes from my bag. I hadn't thought I'd need them so soon. You were still on the bed, head tipped to the side. A string of spit hung from your mouth.

I leant over you, shook your shoulder.

'Alice?'

Nothing.

I told you you could sleep soon, but wouldn't you rather get out of those sick-splattered clothes?

Nothing.

I slid my arms beneath you, one under your neck, the other under your legs. I hoisted. A pain shot through my hand. You were much heavier than Scraps had been. You struggled in your sleep and I told you there-there, told you it was OK. Halfway to the bedroom door I had to stop and crouch, your weight on my knee while I re-gathered my strength. I stood again, heaving you over my shoulder into a fireman's lift, before stoop-stumbling out across the landing.

I lay you on the bathroom floor. You shivered in your sleep. I rinsed and plugged the bathtub and turned on the hot tap. The water rose. Steam fogged us, misting the mirror, gathering at the ceiling.

I took off your coat. I had to guide your arms out then drag it from under you. There didn't appear to be any vomit on it except for a few strands of drool, dried across the collar. I cupped some water from the bathtub and scrubbed them away. Next I peeled off your dress and tights, which were saturated, clinging to your legs with webs of spit. Finally I removed your sunglasses. I carried your clothes through to my old room, everything whiskey-stinking together in the corner, and shut the door behind me.

You looked so cold, lying there in your underwear on the bathroom floor, so I sat beside you, back against the tub and held you, icy in my arms. I pressed my face into your hair, breathed in the smell of whiskey and smoke, trying my best to ignore the tang of bile. The bath rumbled behind us. The pipes clunked in the walls. Once the water had reached the three-quarter mark I stood and lifted you. It was hard because I didn't have your clothes to cling to, just your skin, so cold and goose-pimpled. You struggled at first, flinging your arms in your sleep. I nearly dropped you. You soon settled once I'd lowered you into the water. I cradled your head above the surface. I was shocked at first to see blood, spreading from the back of your neck, clouding the water, but then I remembered the hole in my palm and passed your head to my right hand, holding my left in the air to try decrease the blood flow. Once the bath had filled I reached over and turned off the taps and just knelt there, holding you.

I tried not to look at you – your body, I mean. I kept my eyes fixed on your face. For a few minutes the tap dripped, rippling the water. Then the dripping stopped and the water was still and what was left was a near-perfect silence. I thought maybe I should break the silence, talk to you, only I didn't know what to say. My knees ached against the floor tiles. How long are you supposed to bathe someone? I checked my watch but the screen was blank. I rubbed it with my thumb, the ink of the digits blurring beneath. I must have submerged it. I guess it wasn't waterproof.

I decided to wash your hair. I know girls can be particular about exactly when and where they wet their hair but the ends were crunched with dried vomit and I thought it best I rinse them. I dipped your head back – your red curls danced below the surface. Their redness mixed with the tinge of my blood, tinting the water pink. I spread my fingers across your scalp, massaging every notch and socket of your skull. I thought of the times Mum'd wash my hair, the feel of foreign hands on my head. There wasn't any shampoo but I figured that didn't matter too much, so long as I got the sick out.

Somewhere outside a firework screeched. I lifted you from the water, picking the loose strands of hair that clung to your forehead. You looked so beautiful, your face pale and clean, glittering with beads of bathwater. I wanted to kiss you but we'd already had one failed kiss and our next had to be romantic, an embrace on a station platform, hand-holding at sunset on Finners Island beach. I thought of Finners Island again and couldn't help but smile. I hadn't had a chance to tell you where we were going yet, but there'd be time for that later. Plenty of time for that later.

You murmured in your sleep. Another firework crackled outside. It flowered at the window, giving the room a green glow. I turned to watch it descend. It was then I caught a glimpse of you, the rest of you, your body, blurred beneath the water. I'd shifted slightly when I turned and the movement was still passing through you, your legs bobbing, your breasts rising then sinking. Your feet were crossed. Your hands lay motionless on your belly. Your bra was plain black but your knickers were grey with a sort of pink frill. Something was swelling inside me, some pressure, rising from my stomach to my forehead and I turned away, glanced up at the ceiling, and that's when I noticed one of **Them**, wriggling out through the slats in the air vent.

I kept my head down. I concentrated on you. Your sleeping face. I figured that, if I ignored it, then maybe it could be like I hadn't seen it. We could carry on our bath in peace. Only it doesn't work like that. Once I knew one of **Them** was there I couldn't help but glance above me. Couldn't help but notice it, edging along the wall towards us. Just as it reached the window another firework burst outside, red this time, spreading its gangly shadow across the white-tiled wall. The water rippled out around you. You were shivering. No, not you, *I* was shivering. I was shivering and you were just lying there, sleeping, shaking in my arms.

I should have lifted you out then, should have carried you through to the safety and solitude of Nan's parcel-taped bedroom, only I was determined we weren't going to be disturbed by **Them**. I wasn't going to let **Them** do it again. They're Metaphorical Phantoms, all I had to do was block **Them** out of my mind and there was nothing they could do to harm us. I kept telling myself this. I may have said it aloud as well, I don't know – everything from then on seems blurred – my head was still throbbing from the whiskey.

Then a scratching started over at the sink and I turned in time to see another, crawling out from behind the mirror. This one was enormous, about the size of your hand – which I was holding now, clutching in my bloodied fist – and it too approached the bathtub, only quicker than the first, not so slow and steady but in these short scurrying bursts. Two more followed from behind the toilet cistern. I noticed another, over by the extractor fan. Another, up on the rings of the shower curtain. I breathed steadily. I closed my eyes. I told myself I had nothing to fear, they were Metaphorical Phantoms. They were Metaphorical Phantoms. They were Metaphorical Phantoms. Then one of the tiles slipped, bouncing from the bathtub and shattering across the floor and a swarm of **Them** scrambled through the hole, spreading up the bathroom wall.

By this point the fitting had started. I was shaking violently, my arms slapping the surface of the water. You were shaking with me, your head rocking over the crook of my arm. I clutched you tight to my chest, trying to hold you still, your eyelids flickering, beads of bathwater quivering on your forehead, but I couldn't seem to hold you, couldn't seem to stop you from shaking with me. Blood ran down my chin, dripped onto your cheek and I realised I'd bitten into my tongue. The water was splashing right over the side of the bath, splattering on the dusty floor.

They started to hiss. The usual stuff, calling me a psycho and a pervert, etc. I tried to concentrate on something else, some pure, happy thought – Finners Island, that day with Nan, that time with the eagle. I started to tell you about it, about Finners Island, about how we could live so happily there, the two of us – whispering to you, my face pressed against your hot wet scalp, but with my tongue bitten up I was lisping more than ever and I found it hard even to understand myself. Your hair was getting in my mouth, matted with blood from my tongue. I retched. I glanced up one last time. By now there must have been hundreds of **Them**, a great black tide of **Them**, spreading out across the ceiling. Steam collected around **Them**, their bodies glistening like a sea of fat black olives. I remember laughing. I remember wondering how they could keep a grip on the bathroom ceiling when everything was so damp and then, right on cue, one slipped and thudded to the floor, wriggling on its back. A couple plopped down into the water. Others began to descend on webs.

I shut my eyes. Pressed my forehead to yours. I told myself they weren't there, they weren't real, but the truth is they were. I could feel **Them**. On my neck, my arms, crawling down the back of my shirt. I could hear **Them**, their mass hiss growing, surrounding us. I could see **Them**. Even with my eyes shut I could see **Them**. Wriggling from their cracks in the ceiling, from the collar of Goose's fleece, from the dark corners of your shed, the Lair. More and more of **Them**, every second. I saw **Them** on your father as he sucked at his whiskey bottle, on the Vultures as they danced around the stage in their leotards, on Mum and my father and Ursula and Ken as they sat scooping forkful after forkful of burnt salmon into their fat grinning mouths. I saw **Them** on Miss Hayes, creeping out over her face as she read at the front of class, all those pointless words that don't mean a thing. I saw **Them** in the meat at Hampton's counter, wriggling between the folds of flesh. Infested. I saw **Them** pouring from Mum's Italian leather couch, its stitches splitting, its white folds parting like some great sagging mouth, vomiting a sea of **Them** out across the living-room carpet. I saw **Them** on Angela Hargrove as she lay unconscious on Goose's bed, head bobbing to the thrusts of the near-bald Hawaiian-shirt kid. I saw **Them** spilling from the belly of your fat fuck of a father as I forced the knife into him again and again and again and the tide of **Them** just kept on coming, on and on. Metaphorical Phantoms. I saw Sarah, not as she is now, but when she was little, when she'd scratch and scratch at **Them**, just like I was scratching at you now, trying my best to claw **Them** from your skin, but there were just so many, too many. It was like the time in the boat all over again, the other time on Finners Island, the time I try not to think about, with all that splashing and shaking, your head dipping back below the surface just like Sarah's, mouth open as if screaming, only silent, bubbles rising through the water. Metaphorical Phantoms. My jaw locked, my shaking churning the bathwater.

Metaphorical Phantoms.

Clutching you to my chest, as tight as possible, everything getting dark until there's only the warm metal taste of blood.

Metaphorical Phantoms.

Metaphorical Phantoms.

Metaphorical Phantoms.

The robin's back. I haven't told you about him yet, have I? The robin? He appeared first thing this morning, woke me up. I was on the lounge carpet. I don't know what time this was because my watch is still blurred from the water, but I sat up as soon I heard him cheeping. He was perched on those boards across the lounge window, head poking through the gap. By the time I stood he'd gone again but he's been back about five or six times since. Each time he does the same thing – pokes his head through, cheeps at me, then disappears. It's been going on for about two hours now. I don't know what he wants. I just can't work it out.

It's strange, being back at 1 Kirk Lane. I know I said so last night, but here in the daylight it's even worse. Right now I'm sitting in the lounge and the longer I sit here the more unfamiliar everything gets. There's something missing, that's the only way I can describe it. And I know Nan's missing, I know that's the obvious answer, but it's more than that. The colours are wrong – everything's too dark, the boarded windows murking everything in this veil of gloom. There's a strange smell. The damp's got to the wallpaper, giving the various floral designs this warped, wrinkled effect. Everything's so much smaller. I found a bag of half-knitted jumpers, Nan's final batch, tucked down the side of the armchair – how did I ever fit into those jumpers? And those plates, those cat plates that line the stairway wall, the ones Nan sent off for each week from *Love Cat Magazine*, each decorated with a different-coloured cat, they used to seem enormous, the cats' heads as big as mine, but now they're no more than saucers.

What really gets me, though, is the silence. All I can hear is my pen, scratching the paper. The steady rasp of my breathing. In and out. In and out. It's far quieter than I ever remember. I've been trying to put my finger on why all morning and it wasn't until just before, when I went up to check on you, that I finally realised. It's the grandfather clock in the hall. It's stopped, forever reading five to twelve. Forever losing its steady tick.

I'm sitting in Herb's armchair. It's the first time I've ever sat here. We'd never use the armchair, Nan and I – we'd share the couch, hunched together with our necks straining so we could see the TV. That's how we sat every night, watching those old movies. It seemed wrong, once Herb was gone, for one of us to switch to the armchair, just for the sake of comfort. The house is freezing again. The heating must have given out. I hope you're OK up there. I wrapped you as snug as I could, using Nan's old sheets, as well as my Snoopy duvet. 'Happiness is being part of the gang'. I put you in Nan's room. I thought it'd be safer, what with all the parcel tape.

Nan and I spent vast amounts of time and resources securing this house, barricading **Them** out. We went to such extremes that Mum feared we'd seal the place completely, that it'd become some sort of airtight tomb and the two of us would suffocate in the night. Mum banned us from parcel-taping downstairs so Nan and I concentrated our efforts on her bedroom, taping the walls and windows and Herb's old wardrobe, transforming it into a pretty-much-impenetrable parcel-taped nest. For the last few months she was taping pretty much constantly, buying the entire stock down at the post office each time she went to pick up her pension, stockpiling. All she ever talked about was the Great Influx. That and the Devil. I think Nan knew what my parents were planning. Somewhere deep in the jumbled logic of her brain she knew I was moving back to Skipdale. She knew about Golden Pines. She was sealing off her bedroom from her own versions of **Them**.

The snow's started up again. I went out before, to the shed, to get more boards. The shed, the plant tubs, the back wall, they're all iced in whiteness. I doubt we could leave today even if you were up to it. The buses are probably all cancelled. I doubt we could even get through the front door, with the snow.

My tongue-hole feels wider than usual. I must have chewed it pretty badly up in the bathroom. My hand keeps bleeding too. I've still got your tights wrapped around it. I should find a new bandage. I keep meaning to. I keep finding bloodied prints everywhere and wondering whose they are and realising they're mine. I just can't seem to focus on anything.

I've boarded the back windows. I figured if we're going to stay a while I'd better secure the place. We need to at least try and keep **Them** out. It's hard, hammering the boards with my hand messed up. I have to hold each board in place with my shoulder or my elbow and the boards keep slipping and to be honest I could really do with your nail gun. I boarded the gap in the lounge window too. Sorry, Mr Robin. Whatever it was you wanted, I hope you find it somewhere else.

I checked Nan's wardrobe and there're still rolls and rolls of parcel tape up there. The stockpile. I've counted it out: twenty-seven rolls. It should hopefully be enough. It'll have to be enough.

I've just been up to check on you. You look better now, in Nan's room, all wrapped up. I hated seeing you like that, in the bathtub. You were so silent, so still. The water had settled over you and your hair had settled in the water and you looked frozen. You looked as if you were frozen in glass. There was no sign of **Them**, of course, by then. No chipped plaster or tiles missing from the walls. They crawl back to their holes once the fitting's over and then everything's back to normal. I can still feel that chill as I reached into the water. The cold sting. The splashing and trickling as I lifted you. You were stiff and your stiffness made you hard to carry but I carried you anyway, across the hallway to Nan's room, the only safe room left in the house. I lay you on Nan's bed. I wrapped you up. I wanted to keep you warm but also to cover you, to cover those scratches, the marks I must have made when I was fitting. I kissed you once on the forehead and sat there for a while, beside you, on the bed. I felt as if I wanted to say something but I didn't know what, so that's when I came downstairs.

I just retrieved my *Breakfast at Tiffany's* video-case. I emptied it, laid out our money, the feather, the button-eye of Mr Snow. I laid out all the entries of my diary. There's so much writing, all those words, even more than I thought. Poor Miss Hayes, she never even got to see it.

I took the journal upstairs, read you a few extracts. Only short ones. I just wanted to break the silence – I can't stand it. I read the parts about you and the parts about Nan and the parts about Finners Island. Then I got distracted – I told you all about Finners Island, about the birds and the church and the beach. I told you about the opportunities for an artist there, the beauty of the landscape. I told you that maybe we could get another dog, call it Scraps II or something. Then I realised how insensitive that was and apologised and assured you we could never replace Scraps, we'd have to think of a new name, or get a different animal altogether. Maybe the animals that already live on Finners Island could be our pets instead – all the different birds, the exotic ones and the regular ones. The ducks. They could all belong to us.

Then I told you about the eagle. I've never told anyone about that. I promised Nan I wouldn't.

After that I tried to sleep. The throb in my hand wouldn't let me. Maybe you were right, maybe I left it too long and the tetanus set in. Maybe it's working its way up my arm to my brain. Sorry to bring that up again. I don't blame you. It just hurts, you know? Maybe I need a doctor or something.

I haven't taken my medication today. I forgot my pills, can you believe that? I brought my clothes and my toothbrush and my money and deodorant, but somehow forgot my pills. I hate to think what Mum'd have to say about that.

It's kind of gloomy here, in Nan's nest. It got bad near the end, with Nan. It got to the point where I was the only person she'd let enter her parcel-taped bedroom. I'd bring her meals and medicine and more and more rolls of tape, picking up what I could on the way home from school. The two of us would watch our movies. She'd even let me sleep in here, sometimes. She always called me 'Fly'. Even when she'd forgotten everyone else, when she was calling Mum 'Ellie' and my father 'Herb' and Sarah 'Mr Saunders', she'd still smile when she saw me, she'd still say, 'Hi, Fly – fancy a movie?'

The sun's just about risen over Crossgrove Park, the snow glittering in its glow. I peeled some of the parcel tape from the window so we could see. Not a single person's passed in the last two hours, by car or foot, the snow remaining clean, untouched. It's impossible to make out your house from this side of the park, or your garden, or even what's left of the shed, but each time I press my face up to the window I can detect that singed scent in the air. A hint of barbecue-char from the fire we made.

Your hair's dry now. It seems to have faded since last night. Perhaps I shouldn't have washed it. You probably have some special kind of shampoo, to keep the colour in. It's strange, I'm so used to watching you on the bus, your head rocking against the window and it's amazing how peaceful you look, laid out on Nan's bed. How calm. It makes me feel calm just looking at you.

I'm going to try and sleep again. That's all I really want, to lie beside you and sleep. That's all that's really left to do.

## TRANSCRIPT

Extract of interview between Detective Sergeant Terrence Mansell (TM) and Gregory Hall's father, Dr Howard Hall (HH).

TM: Thanks for coming in.

HH: That's OK.

TM: I realise this is a difficult time.

HH: I just want to get it over with.

TM: Understandable.

HH: Whatever this is. What is this, a follow-up?

TM: I just want to clarify a few things. That's all we're doing today.

HH: Right.

TM: About that night. January third.

HH: OK.

TM: About Greg.

HH: Right.

TM: How is Greg?

HH: They're looking after him.

TM: He hasn't said anything?

HH: Not yet.

TM: And Deborah?

HH: She's . . . it's hit her hard. I don't
think it helps, seeing him like this. She's
been through rough patches before, but she's
struggling to get through this time.

TM: Right.

HH: The whole thing's just . . . it's a mess.
You know?

TM: It's a terrible situation.

HH: It's a mess.

TM: For all of you.

HH: Yes, but especially for her. I mean,
I haven't always been the best father. I
haven't always been there. But her . . .

TM: Shall we get this over with, then?

HH: I guess.

TM: Then you can get back to her. To them.

HH: What is it you want to know?

TM: Well, as I've said, I'd like to start
with that night, January third.

HH: OK.

TM: Why don't you talk me through what
happened.

HH: I did make a statement at the time.

TM: I've read the statement. I know what's in
the statement. I'd just like to hear it
first-hand, if that's OK.

HH: I guess.

TM: I just want to go through, step by step.
See if there's any stone . . . you know
. . . unturned.

HH: Right.

TM: So, January third. What happened?

HH: Well, we went to the house.

TM: We?

HH: Yeah, the two of us. Miss Hewitt and I.

TM: And Miss Hewitt is?

HH: My secretary.

TM: And the reason for your visit to the
house?

HH: Is that important?

TM: I don't know, is it?

HH: Not really, it was just I was showing her
around. She was thinking of buying the
place.

TM: Buying it?

HH: Yeah.

TM: OK . . .

HH: Why?

TM: It's not exactly a show home.

HH: She wanted somewhere with potential, she said. Somewhere to renovate.

TM: So you took her for a viewing?

HH: That's right.

TM: At a time when your son, Greg, was missing. Had been missing for three days.

HH: No. I mean, we didn't know he'd gone missing. Not for sure. Deborah was freaking out, obviously, but I thought he was probably staying at a friend's or something.

TM: A friend's?

HH: Yeah. I mean, I know it was unusual, for him to stay away like that, for a couple of nights. But it was the school holidays. He'd been to a party. He'd been drinking, according to Sarah. And then there was the snow. Snow brings everything to a halt. I was sure he was staying with someone. I was sure he'd show up.

TM: You weren't worried?

HH: Not like Debbie, no. And may I remind you

that's exactly what your people said too, when she called them. 'He'll be at a friend's.'

TM: Right.

HH: Plus we didn't know about her then. About the girl, I mean. Her father hadn't reported it.

TM: No.

HH: Anyway, look, this isn't important, OK? Jo wanted to see the house and so I took her. So we were there. I mean, that's what's important right? That we were there? That we found him?

TM: What time was this?

HH: Half-nine, maybe?

TM: And I'm guessing you expected the house to be empty?

HH: Well, obviously. It has been for years.

TM: You hadn't considered the possibility Greg might go there?

HH: It makes sense now. Why he'd go there. It was his home, once. I hadn't considered it at the time, otherwise I'd have gone and got him. I obviously wasn't expecting . . . that.

TM: And so when did you realise the house wasn't empty?

HH: Well, I knew something was wrong when the door wouldn't open. I mean, my keys worked, the door unlocked, I just couldn't get it open. I tried kicking it. Barging it.

TM: He'd sealed it.

HH: Right. So then I went round the back. I still didn't know it was Gregory at that point. I didn't know what it was. I thought maybe the cold had warped the frame or something. So I got this shovel from the shed. I figured I could pry it open. The door, that is. That's when I noticed the extra boards, at the back of the house.

TM: Extra boards?

HH: I'd put some up over the windows years back, the ones that were broken. But there were more now, even on the unbroken ones. That's when I started to panic. I cut my hand climbing back over, see? Just there? There's all this glass on the back wall Deb's mum put there, probably to stop trespassers, but I'd forgotten all about it, hadn't realised until it was too late. Anyway, I managed to climb back over and went back round the front and wedged the shovel under the door and pried it. That's when I knew something was really wrong. Because that's when I could . . . well . . . smell it.

TM: What was Miss Hewitt doing at this point?

HH: Freaking out.

TM: She was suspicious?

HH: She wanted to wait for the police.

TM: So this was after the 999 call?

HH: Yeah. She rang straight away. While I was still in the shed.

TM: She no longer wanted to buy the house I take it?

HH: She wanted to get back in the car. She wanted to lock the doors and wait for the police.

TM: But you didn't?

HH: No. I probably should have. I mean, I still wasn't sure it was Gregory in there. But I knew I had to find out what was going on. I ended up hacking the door to pieces with that shovel. The smell was terrible, he'd sealed that place up pretty good it was all . . . festering . . . you know? And I could see him, over in the corner, head down. I could see him and I thought . . . well, I

307

don't know what I was thinking really. I mean, he wasn't moving. I saw he wasn't moving. And then the adrenaline took over.

TM: And you got inside?

HH: Eventually. It seemed to take forever, but I tore my way inside. There was all that tape . . .

TM: The parcel tape.

HH: Right. He'd sealed the place up pretty tight.

TM: And what kind of state was Greg in?

HH: I don't think he knew I was there.

TM: He was unresponsive?

HH: I don't think he knew what was going on. He seemed to just be staring into space. His face was just blank. There was, like, zero expression. The least expression I've ever seen on the face of a living human. Bear in mind that I'm a plastic surgeon.

TM: I've seen the website.

HH: Yes, well . . .

TM: 'Breast Man.'

HH: Right. But as I said, he was just sat there, glaring at the ceiling. And he was wearing this massive leather jacket. And his

hand was all bloody. And he was holding
something, a video-case with all this stuff
in, leaflets and papers and stuff, spread out
over his lap. Oh, and money, there was a wad
of money. And a cigarette butt. There was
this cigarette butt in his other hand, the
non-bloody one. I know it's a strange thing
to notice, but it struck me as odd at the
time because Gregory's never been the kind to
smoke. Not like me, I love a smoke. I could
do with a smoke right now, actually . . .

TM: So then what?

HH: Well that's when Jo arrived at the
doorway. She took one look and ran out,
screaming. I was annoyed at the time because
I thought that was the last thing he
needed, some screaming bimbo. Though to be
honest I don't think he even noticed.

TM: So you took Greg outside?

HH: Well, first I tried to talk to him. I
slapped his face a little and got nothing.
But yeah, I knew I had to get him out of
there. Get him warmed up. Get him away from
that smell. So I carried him out to the
car. He felt like ice. I sat him in the

passenger seat and put the heaters on. I
had this bottle of water. I remember trying
to get him to drink and it just running
down his chin, all down the front of him.

TM: And where was Miss Hewitt at this point?

HH: Sat on the kerb. She wouldn't come
anywhere near us.

TM: Did she know Greg was your son?

HH: Probably not, actually. I presumed she
would have at the time, but thinking back
. . . She's pretty dense, to be honest.

TM: Right.

HH: I'd love a cigarette right now.

TM: We can take a break soon.

HH: I'm guessing it's against the rules,
smoking? In here, I mean?

TM: Yes.

HH: So I'm not allowed to smoke in here?

TM: Unfortunately not, no.

HH: Right. It's fine.

TM: So you waited in the car until the
officers arrived?

HH: Yes. Except for Jo. She stayed out on the
kerb.

TM: You didn't venture upstairs?

HH: No.

TM: Neither you nor Miss Hewitt?

HH: No. Neither of us saw upstairs.

TM: Right.

HH: And if you're about to show me pictures I don't want to see it.

TM: I wasn't.

HH: I know all about her. The girl. I know all about it.

TM: OK.

HH: I mean, anything you want to show me, it can't be worse than what's in my head, believe me. I mean, really we should be made to see, Debs and I. We're to blame, really.

TM: No one's to blame here.

HH: Of course someone's to blame. Someone's always to blame. That's the whole point, right? That's why I'm here, that's why you're involved. And the truth is it has to be us. We're the parents.

TM: I'm not blaming anyone. I'd like to be clear on that. I'm just trying to get the facts straight.

HH: The facts?

TM: That's all I want.

HH: This isn't the first time this has happened. Did you know that? Were you aware of that fact?

TM: I've spoken with your wife. I know about Sarah, if that's what you mean.

HH: His sister. His own sister. Our own daughter. I mean, we should have known it'd happen again. It was obviously going to happen again. And what did we do? We just sent him away. We just ignored it.

TM: Dr Hall?

HH: And I know we got him on diagnosed. And I know we got him medicated. But we weren't there for him. He needed us and where were we?

TM: Dr Hall.

HH: At the fucking Hamptons' that's where. I don't know. I don't even know. I . . .

[HH takes a cigarette from his pocket and lights it.]

TM: Take a minute if you want.

HH: No, you're right. I'm sorry. I . . .

TM: It's OK.

HH: Sorry, I'm just venting here. It's just

. . . I have no one . . . I mean, Debs is ill, I can't talk about this stuff with her, and Sarah . . . she's too young to lay this on. I have no one. I'm a fifty-three year old man with no one in his life to have an adult conversation with. Not about this, anyway.

TM: Are you OK?

HH: There's nothing we can do. We just need to be there for him now. I know that now. I know that.

TM: I'm sure he'd appreciate your support.

HH: And when I think back to that day, holding him my arms, trying to get him to drink from that bottle of water. Telling him it was all going to be OK. And there was nothing, you know? Nothing there. Just that blank expression. That was the scariest day of my life.

TM: I can imagine.

HH: Do you have kids, Detective?

TM: I do.

HH: Then you know.

TM: We can take a break if you want.

HH: You know.

IV

I know I haven't written in a while. I'm sorry for that. And I'm sorry about my handwriting – I can't seem to stop shaking, I think it's this new medication. I hope you don't mind but I've decided this is the last time I'll write to you. It was Dr Howard's idea. She said that, since I didn't get to go to the funeral, this would be a good way of saying goodbye.

It was my father who found us, back at the house. I don't remember any of that. Or them bringing me here. Those first few days are a complete blank, the weeks that followed sketchy at best. Being here dawned on me gradually, more like a slow realisation that I wasn't dreaming. When I did dream it was about you, Finners Island, Scraps. At the time I wasn't sure which parts were real, which parts were dreams or nightmares. And then there was **Them**. It was a hard time.

Things are getting better. I'm into more of a routine now, especially with my sleeping. My hand's finally healed. Apparently it was badly infected when they found us but now all that's left is a scar, a numb white spot in the centre of my palm. It's not too far from that little grey fleck Andrew Wilt's pencil left. Sometimes at night I press the scar, hard, until it starts to ache. I don't know why. I just like to feel it.

Mum hasn't visited much. She's seeing Dr Filburn again and he's advised against regular visits. Even when she does come, she never says much. She always starts crying halfway through and has to leave the room. She's sure to return, right at the end, to tell me not to worry. I'm not the cause of the tears, she says. They've been building up for years. This whole thing's just opened the floodgates.

Dad and Sarah visit more regularly, usually every other day. It's getting warmer now and yesterday we sat out and ate together on the grass. Dad brought tuna sandwiches (he knows I don't like the food here) and Sarah lent me one of her earphones so I could tap my head along to her thud-thud music. It was actually quite relaxing, in a weird way, even though the music is horrific. Sarah's eczema's back. I've noticed the odd patch of flaked skin, on her neck and the backs of her hands. She only scratches when she thinks nobody's looking. It's probably stress – the doctor said it could come back in times of stress. This has been a time of much stress.

Dr Howard is nice. She reminds me of how Miss Hayes used to be. She lets us just sit in silence. She's just there to talk to, she says, if I ever need somebody to talk to, though the truth is I haven't spoken since New Year's. I can't seem to get any words out. The more I try, the harder it is. Dr Howard told me to stop trying so hard and just relax. The words will come when they're ready, she says.

A lot of people went to your funeral. That's what Sarah said. She didn't go, of course, but her classes were nearly empty that day and Miss Hayes let the rest of them go early as a mark of respect. I haven't seen or heard from your father. I know he's no longer at the butcher's. The rumours are that he hacked off three of his fingers, drunk on the job, but I don't know how true that is. Sarah said she heard it from one of the girls in her year, but it was hard to verify because not many of the girls in her year are talking to her. My father couldn't verify it either because he hasn't spoken to Ken Hampton in over a month. Sarah said they've had to close the clinic for the time being. Dad's never mentioned this. He only talks about the weather or lunch. He doesn't like to talk about serious stuff.

I know you won't read this, by the way. I know now that I'm not really writing to you, that I was never really writing to you. That you never got to read any of what I wrote. I know now that there were in fact two yous – the real you, who I shared a few chance encounters with, and the you I wrote to, the you I found myself talking to, in my head. Right now I don't know which you I'm writing to. Both, I guess. And myself. Ultimately I know I'm writing to myself.

Spring's just about here. Every morning I wake to the sound of the birds. They're so loud, I forgot just how loud they are. They're the perfect alarm clock. Without them I'm not sure I'd ever wake up. I've been pulling out my eyelashes. It's a new habit. Dr Howard advises against it. She says it's a problem, but not such a problem, considering my other problems. This morning I discovered a couple of fresh ones, just starting to show. I managed to pluck them. I went out to the gardens at lunch with them cradled in my palm. I shut my eyes and blew them away. I can't tell you what I wished because then it might not come true. But there was a good breeze today. I'm sure they'll go far.

## DATE UNKNOWN

I remember it was sunny when we left the hotel but by the time we reached the forest the rain had come. It fell in waves, like the sea had taken to the sky. It hissed through the leaves above us, rattling the hoods of our raincoats.

Nan said she knew a short cut, a secret path down to the lily pond. We loved feeding the ducks. It was our favourite part of the day. Sarah, my parents, they weren't bothered, they'd given their sandwich crusts to us and we'd headed off straight after lunch. Nan kept saying we had to go west, pointing: *this way's west* and *that way's west*, but I doubt if she knew which way west actually was. It seemed to me we were going in circles.

After a while Nan began to panic. 'How can you get lost on an island this small?' she said. 'This is the sixth time I've been here.'

Eventually we found a cliff edge but there was no secret path. Nan was exhausted and needed to sit for a while so we took shelter under an overgrown blackberry bush. We watched the rain, fizzing like static on the surface of the sea. Nan said not to eat the blackberries, just in case they were poisonous.

After a few minutes the rain died. After another few minutes the sun came out, so hot we began to steam. Nan said it was a true British holiday, all weathers at once. That's when I first noticed it, perched there in the branches above us. I nudged Nan and pointed. I couldn't stop staring at it.

'Look away,' Nan whispered. 'Else it'll claw your eyes out.'

Nan and I huddled there, staring at our shoes while it perched above us, scanning the horizon. I asked Nan what it was doing here and she said there were several theories. One was that it escaped from a zoo. I asked if there was any chance it had flown here by choice but Nan said she doubted it could have made it all the way from America.

As its shadow passed over us we couldn't help but look, couldn't help but watch it cross the sky. It soared low over the sea, disappearing behind the trees that lined the far side of the cove.

'We don't tell anyone about this,' Nan said. 'It's our secret. It's just for me and you.'

We waited, just in case it circled back. It didn't. Then we waited a while longer, just sitting there in silence.

Nan stood. She sighed and smiled. She said, 'We'd best get back, Fly, else your parents'll think we've drowned in the rain.'

I nodded and stood too and we both headed off through the forest. We still didn't know which direction we were supposed to be heading in, but for some reason it didn't seem to matter any more.

# Acknowledgements

Thanks to everyone on my MA, especially Robyn Donaldson, Mike Holloway, Paul Abbot, Denise Bundred and Christof Häberle. To my inspiring teachers Alicia Stubbersfield and Jim Friel. To 'The Dicks', Josh Mansell, Matty Herring and Liam Sillett. To Mike Morris and everyone at Writing on the Wall. To Niall Griffiths and Julia Bell for making me feel like a writer. To Luke Brown for the encouragement and Karolina Sutton, Norah Perkins and Kate Howard for making all my childhood dreams come true.

To my friends, my family, Nat and my cats.

And to anyone that reads it, cheers.

# A Q&A with
# JAMES RICE

**Where do you find inspiration for your books?**

Over-thinking, really. My first novel came from dwelling on school, thinking a lot about that period of my life, finding inspiration in that. I had plenty of material. My second novel came from a walk I went on with a friend, having a lot of time there to think and plan ideas. I sometimes worry I'll run out of ideas but then I read a news article or hear an anecdote and suddenly my mind's running away with it.

**Can you tell us a little about your average writing day?**

Usually I'll spend about three hours being distracted; tidying up or looking on Facebook or watching TV shows or eating. Anything that requires virtually no brain activity. Then I'll notice how much non-writing time has passed and the guilt will seep in and I'll force myself to open the laptop. The stupid thing is that as soon as I start writing I realise how amazing the process is and how much I enjoy it and I regret not getting up at 6 a.m. and jumping straight into it. I think it's natural to avoid writing though – it takes a lot of serious concentration and your brain's going to do what it can to avoid it. I only ever get serious writing done when there's an even harder brain-engaging task looming, e.g. a tax return or a job application.

## When you are writing, do you use any famous people or people you know as inspiration?

I pick things from real life, but none of my characters are completely lifted from reality. I couldn't deal with that; I don't have the guts. I'm a victim of my own subconscious though, because there were things in *Alice* I thought I'd invented that turned out to be true, much to my family's horror. (No, I don't want to be specific here, haha.)

## What is your writing process? Do you plan first or dive in? How many drafts do you do?

I hate first drafts so I tend to dive in and try and get something down – anything I can work with. I much prefer editing and elaborating than the blank page. I usually plan stuff out in my head but don't often write my plans down. I probably forget half my plans. I don't know if this is a bad thing or not. If it's forgettable then I guess I shouldn't be writing it.

## What was your journey to being a published author?

I started writing as a child and all I ever wanted to be was a writer, so I studied Creative Writing at university. When I finished I still couldn't write that well and didn't have much to my name, other than a few short stories, and I wasn't quite ready to decide what to do with my life so I applied for a part-time MA. I got a job at a bookshop and spent the next three years reading as much as I could and writing as much as I could and figuring out what to do with my debut novel. My break came when I entered a competition called 'Pulp Idol', part of Liverpool's Writing on the Wall festival. I won the competition, which got an editor interested in me, which led to me getting an agent, who ended up getting me the deal at Hodder. I still don't really believe any of this has happened, by the way. One day I'll wake up and the past three years will have all been a dream and I'll be a failure at life, like I'm supposed to be.

**What do you think is the biggest myth about being a novelist?**

That it will solve your existential crisis, i.e. 'Oh my God, what am I doing with my life?'

**What advice can you give to our readers who want to write a novel of their own?**

Start today, not tomorrow. Put the hours in. Time = good writing. In spite of the world around you try and believe in yourself – you can be a writer, it's not impossible, other people do it. I did it. Why not you?

**What are you working on at the moment?**

My second novel, a story of two friends walking in Wales. I'm enjoying writing it so far, but it's still hard to work out how good it is. When I'm writing it I think it's quite good but then when I'm asked to explain what it's about I always crumble. This is how it usually is with me though.

**Can you share your top five writing tips?**

1. Write a lot, edit a lot, and don't be afraid to throw stuff away.

2. Put your writing away for a while and come back to it. Hindsight is your best friend.

3. Hold on to why you started a piece of writing. Hold on to the part of the story that's you.

4. Don't be dissuaded by how long it takes to write anything good. Anything worth reading took a long time to write.

5. Enjoy it. (Or try.)

# READING GROUP
# QUESTIONS

1. The social disparity between Skipdale and The Pitt sets
the scene for the novel. Why do you think this is important?

2. What motivates Greg to tell his story?

3. How does the inclusion of the police transcript add
to the narrative? Does it alter your opinion of Greg's
reliability as a narrator?

4. Did this novel contribute to your understanding of phobias?

5. What role does the notion of obsession play in the novel?

6. Greg's parents are fixated on projecting a perfect image.
How does this contrast to the reality of their situation?

7. Can we see Greg's obsession with classic Hollywood films
influencing his own outlook on life and on romance in particular?

8. 'Miss Hayes has a new theory. She thinks I'm not really scared of **Them**. She thinks they're just something to blame my anxiety on. She thinks I hide my real fears behind Metaphorical Phantoms.'

What do you think of Miss Hayes' theory? Are there other characters in the novel besides Greg and Miss Hayes with their own 'Metaphorical Phantoms'?

9. Do you feel sympathy for Greg's mother?

10. What is the significance of Finners Island?

11. This novel deals with some difficult social issues and the world that Greg inhabits is almost dystopian. Is there room for happiness in a world like this?

12. How far do you think the author has used Greg's social alienation to expose intricate truths about our modern lives?

13. Sarah accuses her mother of being repressed. What part does repression play in the novel as a whole and how does it manifest?

14. Greg's father claims that 'someone is always to blame'. Do you think this is the case in this situation?